THE INNOCENTS

Also by David Putnam

The Vanquished
The Squandered
The Replacements
The Disposables

THE INNOCENTS

A BRUNO JOHNSON NOVEL

THE EARLY YEARS: BOOK ONE

DAVID PUTNAM

OCEANVIEW PUBLISHING
LONGBOAT KEY, FLORIDA

This book is a work of fiction. Names, characters, businesses, organizations, places, and incidents either are the products of the author's imagination or are used fictitiously. Any resemblance to actual events, businesses, locales, or persons living or dead, is entirely coincidental.

ISBN 978-1-60809-257-4

Published in the United States of America by Oceanview Publishing
Longboat Key, Florida
www.oceanviewpub.com

10 9 8 7 6 5 4 3 2 1

PRINTED IN THE UNITED STATES OF AMERICA

“Sometimes bad people help you do good things.”

THE INNOCENTS

CHAPTER ONE

East Compton 1988

Millicent hesitated, cocked her head to the side.

I turned the water off in the shower and listened. "*Shh!* I think I heard it, too."

"Was it the door?"

The noise came again, a knock. Millie had been right: she'd heard it first. I'd been a little distracted.

"I better see who that is."

"Ah, Bruno, can't you let it go for now? I mean, really? I still need the conditioner or my hair is going to frizz." She put her hand up on my chest. "You wouldn't want a girl's hair to frizz, would you, big guy? A real gentleman wouldn't."

I didn't want to leave the beautiful, wet redhead wanting. Her lovely skin was littered with freckles; her green eyes flashed with anger over the interruption. She whirled around, her back to me. "Damn you, Bruno Johnson, hurry, then."

I gave her a hug and kissed her on the neck. She turned and kissed me back.

I started to step out. She shoved me aside and went first. "What kind of gentleman are you to leave a lady hanging like this? Now I can see where your priorities are and where I fit in." She grabbed a towel and turned her back to me.

I really couldn't afford to make her angry. As the captain's secretary, she had the absolute ability to influence him, whisper in his ear about a deputy who left a woman in the shower before the conditioner was applied. She faced the mirror and raised her arms to dry her hair with the towel. Her breasts bounced and jiggled. She watched my eyes in the mirror, knowing exactly what she did to me. I moved up behind and put my arms around her. "Just let me get the door. I'll be right back and I promise I'll make it up to you."

Then I yelled to the person at the door, "Coming!"

She turned in my arms and kissed me on the mouth. I groaned.

I pulled away then leaned forward and whispered in her ear. "I've just been assigned to a new team. This is the first day. It could be something important. I really need to answer the door, or believe me, I—"

She giggled. "I believe you, sweetie. Hurry and answer it, then get that cute little black ass back in here before I cool down."

"I'm goin'. I'm goin'. You keep your engine runnin'. I'll be right back." I grabbed the second towel off the rack and hurried into the short hall, angry now at the intruder ruining a near-perfect morning. I tracked water as I wrapped the towel around my waist, my skin still slick from the exertion of the water sports. My feet thumped on the wood floor of my micro-small studio apartment that sat over the Anytime Dry Cleaners on Atlantic Avenue in East Compton.

I kept the curtains closed for privacy, which made the living room dark as pitch.

I jerked open the door. The bright sunlight blinded me. I brought my arm up to block the glare. My eyes gradually adjusted. A woman stood on the small landing at the top of the wooden stairs. She held something in her arms. At first I didn't recognize her. Maybe my subconscious didn't want to recognize her. No, that wasn't it. When I knew her, she'd always been smiling, always had a smile for me. She didn't smile now. She said nothing and tried to hand me the bundle she held in her arms.

My mouth sagged open. I stepped back from her. "Sonja? What are you—?"

She followed me into the small living room.

The baby in her arms squirmed and gurgled. Sonja looked half-crazed, haggard, her hair a mess, dark circles under her eyes, her skin pasty. "Here, Bruno, take her. She's yours. I can't handle her anymore." Her voice held an urgency that scared me.

I staggered back. "Mine? That's my child?" The room spun as I fought the dizziness from this new information, the sudden shock of it.

Millie came out of the bathroom in a rush, tracking more water, not concerned enough about her nakedness, the towel held loosely to her chest and not covering everything. "You have a girlfriend? You have a baby?"

Sonja looked at Millie and said, "I see you didn't waste any time."

"Sonja, you can't be serious. That's my child?" She tried to hand her to me again. I still couldn't acknowledge my paternity or accept her offering. I took another half-step back.

Millie stooped and grabbed her dress off the floor, where we'd stripped it off her the night before. She turned her back and slipped it on over her head. The material clung to her wet skin. She grabbed up her black lace bra and panties, shoved them in her purse, and picked up her shoes. "You're a real asshole, Bruno Johnson." She moved around Sonja on her way to the door. She didn't slow when she said, "I'm sorry. Really, I didn't know. Good luck."

With Millie gone, the room still felt overcrowded by one.

I backed up and sat on the couch. "I didn't know you were pregnant. You never said anything about it. Why didn't you tell me?"

She came over and stood next to me. Tears rolled down her cheeks. "You're going to find you don't know a lot of things, big guy." She gently placed the child in my lap. "She's all yours."

The warm bundle smelled of baby powder and squirmed as if trying to escape her cotton cocoon. "Sonja, I can't. Let's talk about this, okay? Please?"

Sonja turned her back, her hands going to her face. Her body gently shook as she sobbed. "I can't, Bruno. I can't take her anymore. It's too much. She cries all the time. She never sleeps. I haven't slept in two weeks, not since she was born. I'm going out of my mind. I'm afraid of what I'll do—"

She headed for the door.

"Sonja, wait."

She froze, but didn't turn around.

"Bruno, I killed a man. You were there. You warned me. You told me to be careful. I hit him too hard with that blackjack and I killed him. I don't deserve a beautiful little girl like her. I'm having a hard enough time living with myself. There just isn't any room for her in my screwed-up brain. Not right now."

She started for the door again.

"How can I reach you?"

"You can't."

Sonja passed through the door onto the landing. A thousand words clogged my tongue, and I could only push out the less significant ones: "What's her name? What's the child's name?"

Sonja's voice came in through the door as she descended the stairs. "I didn't give her a name. The County Hall of Records has her as Baby Girl Johnson. Go ahead and give her a name, Bruno. She's all yours now."

And Sonja was gone.

CHAPTER TWO

I STOOD ON the landing, outside in the brightness of the early morning with a towel wrapped around my waist, dripping water and holding . . . and holding a baby girl.

My baby girl.

The thin blue cotton blanket covered most of her pink little face, her forehead, eyes, and nose. Only her mouth peeked out.

My entire world had turned on its ear just that quick. It had only taken seconds. It had only taken a simple little knock at the door.

What the hell just happened? What was I going to do? I had one hour to get to work, my first day on a new team. One hour. Every detective in the Sheriff's Department wanted one of the four slots on this team, and I'd been lucky enough to be chosen.

I didn't know how to care for a child let alone an infant barely two weeks old. I couldn't move, though I knew I should get inside. I just stood there unable to twitch. I never felt so conflicted, so confused, and at the same time smothered in guilt and shame.

Dad.

Dad would know what to do. I hurried inside and tripped on the doorsill. I stumbled and almost fell. I juggled Baby Girl Johnson, who didn't know how close she came to a tumble on the floor. My heart jumped into my throat at the thought of hurting her. I needed to be more careful. Far more careful.

I turned around and found I'd tripped on the strap to a diaper bag Sonja had left on the landing. I pulled it into the apartment and closed the door.

I went to the phone on the wall and stuck the receiver between my shoulder and ear as I held the baby in my other arm and dialed.

"Good morning. This is the Johnson residence. Xander Johnson speaking."

"Dad. Dad, its me."

"Bruno? What's the matter, Son? What's happened?"

"I'm in trouble, Dad, and I . . . I don't know what to do." I didn't want to tell him. The guilt and shame rose up and choked my words. Dad didn't deserve this. He'd raised my brother, Noble, and me to live with honor and to always do the right thing. Having a child like this in no way fit into his principles of life. What a God-awful mess.

"Take it easy, Son. It can't be that bad. Calm down and tell me what's happened."

As always, his controlled demeanor had a calming effect. But I still couldn't tell him, couldn't say the words. Those four simple words: *Dad, I'm a father.*

Reality struck. I'm a father. I'm . . . I'm a father. My knees shook.

In a half-whisper, I said into the phone, "Dad, can I come over?"

"Of course you can, Son. But why can't you tell me over the phone? What's happened?"

"I can't, I just—"

Little Baby Girl Johnson chose that moment to make herself known. She cried out.

On the other end of the phone my dad said, "Oh, my Lord."

A lump rose in my throat and tears burned my eyes. The coward in me took over. I gently hung up the phone. I held on to it in the cradle and whispered, "I'm sorry, Dad."

My baby squirmed in my arms and continued to fuss, reminding me that no matter how I felt, the world continued to spin. I hurried into the bedroom and laid her gently on the bed as if she were made of fragile porcelain. Would she stay there? Would she roll off and fall on the floor if I didn't watch her every second? I picked up two pillows and put one on each side of her. There, that was better.

I dressed in denim pants, a blue long-sleeve shirt, and black combat boots. I put on a wide belt and laced in a pancake holster on my hip. I picked up the .38 off the dresser, the blue steel cold in my hand. I looked from the gun to the innocent child on the bed. The contrast made me freeze and reevaluate the world I'd chosen. A father for less than ten minutes and everything had changed, even the way I looked at my career.

I strapped my backup gun to my ankle as more wild thoughts roared through my brain. What did babies eat? I didn't have any food she could eat, did I? I had some oatmeal, maybe. What kind of diapers did I need to buy? What kind of bed? I set my foot back on the floor and realized that once she got older and began to crawl, I wouldn't be able to wear an ankle holster. She'd have access to it. Wait, how ludicrous was that? And I'd need a gun safe to keep both my guns secure.

I put my flat badge wallet in my back pocket. With a child to care for, would I be able to continue working as a deputy? Working as a detective on a violent crimes team with irregular hours and no home life? If something happened to me, what would happen to the child? Should I go in this morning and ask for a hardship transfer to court services, a job with regular working hours? A nasty little go-nowhere job working inside all day with chained-up prisoners?

My God, what a horrible mess.

No, no, I had to stop thinking of this as a mess, not with a child involved. What would Dad call it?

A blessing.

Yes, that's exactly what he'd call this unexpected package left at my doorstep.

I gently scooped up my baby and froze. For the first time, the blanket had fallen entirely away from her face. I sat down on the bed, absolutely flabbergasted. Baby Girl Johnson was the most beautiful baby in the world, maybe even in the entire universe. The way she looked at me with those huge eyes, I would do anything for her.

Anything.

CHAPTER THREE

I CARRIED MY child down the steps to the dry cleaners' parking lot, which was now filled with early, go-to-work folks who stopped in to get their clothes before their coffee and donut next door at The Big O donut shop. I didn't normally hold on to the stairs handrail, but I did this day, with the diaper bag hanging off my shoulder.

The wonderful aroma of fried dough and cinnamon wafted on the air. My stomach growled. I hadn't eaten since yesterday noon. Millie hadn't wanted dinner; she'd only wanted to come back to my place for "dessert" and a little "slap and tickle." Last night, life had been so simple, full of adventure. Now, even the thought of "a little dessert" would have to change.

I unlocked the door to my Ford Ranger pickup and got in. I went to set Baby Girl Johnson on the bench seat next to me and froze. What the hell? I couldn't leave her unsecured on the seat. I put on my seat belt and started the truck, a four-speed stick. No way would it be safe to drive with a child in one arm and shifting and steering with the other. What choice did I have? Dad only lived a few miles away. I'd take side streets and, at the first opportunity, get a child's car seat.

I drove slow in and out of two different neighborhoods, crossed Compton Avenue into Fruit Town and on up into the Corner Pocket in the county area of Los Angeles where I'd grown up. My mind remained numb to all the serious ramifications this small child's presence implied—hundreds of them. I just needed to get to Dad. He'd know what to do.

I pulled up and stopped in front of our house on Nord Avenue. In all my daydreams as a kid, with my ideas of what life had in store, never did I think about being a father. That was just too much responsibility and far too difficult a job. I only wanted to play cops and robbers, chase the bad guys and make the neighborhood a safer place to live. Had all that just changed?

Dad came out of the small house and stood on the wooden porch. He wore his blue-gray postal carrier pants and a sleeveless white t-shirt. He wrung his hands and stared, his eyes full of concern. All I had thought about for the last fifteen minutes was getting to Dad's. Now I fought the urge to just drive off and keep driving for hundreds of miles rather than face him.

I took a deep breath and got out. I walked slowly up to the porch with my child in my arms.

Dad shifted his gaze to the blanketed bundle and came down the three steps. He held out his hands and said, "Ah, Bruno."

I didn't realize I'd been holding my breath and let it out when he didn't scold me. Of course, he wouldn't scold me. What was I thinking? This was my dad.

Dad took her from my arms, cooed to her, and gently moved her up and down. He looked so damn natural at it. He looked up and smiled hugely at me. My knees went weak. I moved around him and sat on the stoop.

"What's her name?"

Of all the things I thought he'd say—Who's the mother? How could you let this happen? And the worst one: I raised you better than this—he'd simply accepted the situation for what it was and asked her name.

Still not entirely able to talk just yet, I merely shrugged.

"What? This child doesn't have a name?"

"Not yet, Dad." My voice came out a croak. "When a child is born and the parents don't have a name ready, what goes on the temporary birth certificate . . . well, for right now she's called Baby Girl Johnson."

He'd gone back to cooing to the baby and again looked up at me. "Baby Girl Johnson? It does have kind of a ring to it, doesn't it, Son?"

"Yeah, I guess it kinda does."

He spoke to the baby. "Don't be silly, we'll think of a proper name for you soon enough, little girl. Come on, Son, let's take her inside."

"Dad, what am I going to do?"

"What are you talking about? You're going to raise your daughter." He walked up the steps and went into the house.

The simplest answer was always the best, I guess. Only this answer couldn't make it past my mental defenses.

I came in right behind him. Dad sat in the rocking chair, rocking the baby. Somehow the scene looked so incongruous: Dad caring for a child of mine in the house I grew up in.

I resigned myself to my fate and went to the phone to call in sick. I picked up the receiver.

Dad said, "What are you doing?"

"Calling in sick."

"You will not. I never called in sick a day in my life. I thought I taught you better than that."

"What are you talking about? How can I go to work?"

Someone knocked at the door. My stomach sank. I'd probably get that same feeling for the rest of my life anytime someone knocked.

"Hang the phone up and get the door. It's Mrs. Espinoza. I called her and asked her to come over. She's looking for a job and jumped at this one."

"Mrs. Espinoza? A job? What job?"

"Son, you have to go to work, and you can't take the baby with you. Get the door."

All of a sudden I realized everything just might work out.

CHAPTER FOUR

Lennox Sheriff's Station

I sat at a desk, one of five in a small office, my mind reaching far out into the future trying to rectify what it'd be like to have a daughter in high school.

Lieutenant Robby Wicks entered the small squad room, moving fast. He stood at the front of the room and looked over his team: four newly minted detectives chosen for this new idea, The Los Angeles County Sheriff's Violent Crimes Team. Organized to target the most violent criminals preying upon the victims of Los Angeles County. The team only answered to a Deputy Chief and was allowed to pick its own targets. In my wildest dreams, I never thought I'd be chosen for such a position, especially with only two years' patrol under my belt. The other three deputies in the room, who had at least five times the experience, gave up choice deputy positions to be there. We'd been handpicked by Lieutenant Wicks.

I sat up in my chair and tried hard to shake off my thoughts of Baby Girl Johnson. I needed to focus or risk losing this job.

Wicks stood with one thumb hooked in the front of his belt, his other hand—his gun hand—hung loose at his side, always there, always ready to draw his custom .45 Colt Commander. I'd only known him a short time, only really met him twice, but the stories of his exploits stood out as legends, old stories that grew bolder and wilder with each passing year. He wore his brown hair combed back, dry without grease. His mustache didn't meet department dress and grooming standards; the tips went almost down to the edge of his chin. The gunfighter mustache. The .45 was also an unauthorized weapon. No supervisor who came in contact with him said a thing about these gross violations. Wicks carried too much juice with the higher-up brass. No one bucked Wicks.

He said nothing and looked at each of us in turn, then reached over and flipped the cover to a large pad on an easel, exposing a blown-up booking photo of an African American crook. No one needed to read the name written in black felt tip underneath. This guy had made every newscast on all the networks for the last forty-eight hours. Damien Frakes Jr., a Holly Street Crip, a parolee at large.

Detective Johnny Gibbs, who'd transferred in from Metro and sat to my right, said, "Now we're talkin.' I thought we might be going after this smoke."

Wicks stared at Johnny and said nothing. Johnny looked around and saw me next to him. He reached over, placed his hand on my shoulder, and said, "No offense, bro. You know I didn't mean anything by it, right?"

I didn't like his hand on my shoulder nor his comment but didn't want to cause a scene. I took up Wicks' method, said nothing, and looked back to our boss.

Wicks' left hand slapped the easel. "All right, here it is, and I'm going to give it to you guys straight. This is the most violent asshole out there right now. He held up that jewelry store in Torrance and shot dead the owner and two patrons. A Redondo Beach copper inadvertently got onto him on a routine traffic stop. Frakes stepped out of his G-ride and shot up the patrol car, wounding the officer. This is the guy we should be going after. This is the guy I planned to go after. But it's just not going to work out that way and I'm sorry."

The other three detectives groaned.

He gave us the news as if it were some kind of death notification, and that's the way we took it.

Wicks continued. "Listen, it's not your fault. It's mine, and I promise you I'm going to fix this."

If anyone could fix it, Robby Wicks could.

He said, "I was promised absolute autonomy with this team. They promised me that I could pick our own targets, and what happens the first day? We get redirected."

He let that soak in. Then, "As a supervisor, as your leader, I am not supposed to show this side of me. I am supposed to accept this new target with quiet dignity and do as I'm told. I'm supposed to sell this new target to you guys as the real deal.

"I won't do it. I want to be totally honest with you at all times and I hope you'll do the same with me. I want us to work as a cohesive team. I also want you to know exactly where I stand so when it's time to take care of business, you're not worrying about what the boss is going to say. I want you to act. I want you to think on your feet. I want you to pull that trigger."

He hesitated to let that sink in. This wasn't the kind of speech I'd expected. I didn't know what I'd expected.

Wicks said, "And most of all . . . most of all, this is going to be a shotgun team. That means I want—" He looked to the open office door. He quickly crossed the few steps over and closed it.

I squirmed in my seat and wasn't sure I wanted to hear what came next. Secrets in law enforcement usually didn't bode well for the ones tasked with keeping them.

Wicks came back and stood right next to our small cluster of four desks; his heavy aftershave moved with him. He again looked at all of us. "Each of you was chosen for one reason and one reason only. You like to hunt men and you're not afraid to pull the trigger. A shotgun team means just that. We are going to run and gun. We are going to drop the hammer on anyone who does not immediately and unequivocally give up. Anyone who wants to resist, anyone who throws down on us, I don't care if all they've got in their hand is a comb, we are going to gun them. You understand?"

He made it sound so glamorous, so righteous; I wanted to feel proud to be a part of this new idea and didn't know why I didn't. Maybe I would have if I hadn't been a father worried about much more important things.

Wicks said, "This is a violent-crimes team that chases confirmed criminals. Animals who have murdered in cold blood the folks we were sworn to protect and didn't. We are here to right that wrong. So, if any of you have any reservations at all, if you don't have the guts for this, now's the time to leave." He pointed to the door.

He waited a moment, as if expecting half of us to get up and slink out with our tails between our legs.

That last part about keeping the community safe got my attention. I was in for accomplishing that task.

Johnny Gibbs said, "I'm not going anywhere. This is exactly where I want to be."

The other two, like me, only nodded, choosing to keep silent until we had a better grasp of this man before we opened our mouths and made fools of ourselves as Gibbs tended to do.

Unlike the others, I didn't belong in that room. I'd never shot anyone.

But Wicks was right. I had hunted a man, and Wicks had been there when I caught him. Only I wasn't proud of the way I did it. And that's probably why Wicks chose me for his team.

Almost a year ago now, I'd investigated the death of a young girl. The memory of it swooped back in and snatched at my breath. I was the father of a baby girl, which made the memory all the more frightening.

CHAPTER FIVE

LAST YEAR I was assigned a code three to a traffic accident, car vs. pedestrian. I beat the paramedics and other patrol cars to the scene. A little girl by the name of Jenny was down in the street, knocked right out of the crosswalk, knocked right out of her shiny black patent leather shoes.

The night was hot. Groups of people clustered on the sidewalk, quiet, pointing, as if I wouldn't see Jenny.

At first I thought Jenny was some little girl's doll tossed haphazardly from a passing car.

No first aid or medical attention was going to help her.

Half her face was mashed and disfigured; the other half was perfect, angelic in the scant aura of the streetlight.

There was very little blood.

Mercifully, she died on impact.

Her blue gingham dress masked the horror underneath.

Sweaty Marty said later that he came up and spoke to me but I was "zoned out" and that "I had the blood spore with my nose to the ground."

From the debris field—the bits of headlight glass and aluminum trim knocked off the car on impact—I knew the car was old and large. Then I noticed the asshole had hit poor Jenny hard enough that her little body had ruptured the radiator. I started following the water trail in the street, a trail that would be gone in minutes, evaporated into the hot summer night. The swath started out large and wide and narrowed when the murderer picked up speed, as the coward fled.

I ran.

The water narrowed further and then turned to sporadic blotches.

Then to droplets.

At an intersection, I lost it entirely. He'd caught the green, only I didn't know which way he went. I ran in a big arc. Cars skidded to a stop to avoid the tall, black, uniformed deputy who'd lost his head and was running in a circle in the middle of a busy intersection.

My flashlight dimmed as it started to fail.

I thought I picked up the trail headed north, which meant a left turn. I got down on one knee and still wasn't sure. I got down on my hands, in a prone position, and sniffed. I got up and ran in a full sprint, fighting the heat that now helped the suspect to escape, drying up the evidence.

The footrace worked.

At the next intersection, the murderer caught the red and left behind a puddle. He continued on through, went two blocks, and turned on Spring Street. He'd been close to home, a mile and a half away, when he ran Jenny down.

The water turned rusty and led up a concrete drive to a garage door closed and padlocked. I took a minute to catch my breath and tried to shove back the lion that wanted to get even, to make things right.

In the academy, they called it "your professional face." No matter what happened, you had to put aside your personal feelings and be professional.

I went up to the door, sweat stinging my eyes, my uniform wet under the arms. I wiped my eyes clear on my shirtsleeve and left a sweat smudge.

I knocked.

The door immediately opened. The room on the inside was dark, the screen door between us. I couldn't see him and didn't know if this man—who, without conscience had run down a defenseless little girl in the crosswalk—had a weapon.

His rich and deep-timbre voice said, "Can I help you, Officer?"

"Yes, I would like you to come out here and open your garage door."

Silence, then: "*Heh, heh*. I don't think so, Officer. You don't have a search warrant."

I carefully, with as little movement as possible, reached up and tried the screen door.

Locked.

He started to close the inside door.

"Wait."

"Yes? Is there something else, Uncle Tom? Something you want to do for whitey, the people you serve?" He didn't try to mask the anger and hate in his tone. He was safe and he knew it; swaddled, nice and comfortable, in the shroud of the law.

The next second, I sniffed it.

Alcohol.

A drunk driver.

The scent of metabolized alcohol set something off inside me, snapping the last straw. The professional face came off.

I roared.

I shoved both hands in through the screen and took hold of a large black man wearing a white Stetson cowboy hat. I pulled him through the screen door and out onto the ground. I put the boot to him.

Robby Wicks, a sergeant at the time, had followed me in his patrol car. He pulled me off. He had to slug me in the stomach to bring me out of my blind rage.

But that wasn't how he'd saved my bacon.

As a supervisor, he had witnessed a crime I'd perpetrated when I took the cowboy into custody with excessive force. Wicks was obligated to stop me then turn me in for felony prosecution.

No, the way he'd really saved me came after he got everything calmed down with med aid responding for the suspect. He told me I'd done a hell of a job tracking the car, that he'd never seen anything like it, the tenacity, the perseverance. Then he helped with the story, the way it would be written, the way the courts would accept it, and, at the same time, save my career and let me get at least some token of justice for Jenny.

A year later, Robby was transferred to run the newly formed violent crimes task force and specifically asked for me to be on his team.

* * *

Back in the squad room, Gibbs said, "If we're not going to chase Frakes, then what is our first assignment?"

Wicks looked at Gibbs, and for a moment, said nothing.

Gibbs wasn't going to last.

Wicks said, "Our assignment, gentlemen, is a special handle. A request from the Taj Mahal to recapture one that got away. A small-time hood, a paperhanger who escaped from Chino Prison."

I couldn't help it, the words slipped out of my mouth: "Ah, shit, not a paperhanger, a no-nothing forgery convict."

CHAPTER SIX

LIEUTENANT WICKS IGNORED my comment. "That's right, an escaped prisoner from CIM, California Institute for Men. The state prison in Chino. But you see, I have something else I have to do. Something real important. I have to get a haircut."

By that he meant he wouldn't be the diligent, kowtowing lieutenant and do what they asked of him. He'd let his team handle this little problem that didn't require a lieutenant, especially one of Wicks' stature. Not being in on the takedown would send a message to the brass.

He must have read the disgust in my expression. He came over and stood in front of my desk. "I promise you, it will not always be like this. I'm taking a meeting with the chief to iron out this little glitch. In my absence, Bruno, you'll be running the team on this operation."

My mouth sagged open. "You can't mean that."

"Weren't you listening? We're a team. When out in the field, we're all equals. Every one of you will have your chance to be case agent and call the shots. This first go-'round is yours, Bruno. Don't screw it up." He waved his finger at the others. "And I expect all of you to listen to Bruno the same as if his words were mine. He calls the play. Everyone got it?"

We all nodded.

"Good, that's it until three o'clock this afternoon. Go to the range and shoot and then clean your guns. We'll be going to the range a lot, so get used to it."

The four of us stood.

"Bruno, hang back a minute, would you?"

The other three hesitated and then continued on out of the small office.

The door clicked shut. I stood by my desk. Wicks took a step closer, within a foot, and right up into my personal space. His eyes didn't leave mine, as if he were searching my soul for some sort of hidden truth. He reached into his suit coat and pulled out a folded piece of paper. "This is the guy, Pedro Armendez. He was in Chino for PC 470, forgery. He has priors for grand theft auto and one strong-arm robbery ten years ago. He's a heroin hype hanging paper to support his habit."

I fought the urge to take a step back. I took the paper and unfolded it. Armendez looked like your typical hype, with dirty hair and a gaunt face pocked with acne scars and dark rings under his eyes. He looked scared at the time of the booking photo and probably didn't do well in a correctional environment.

Wicks said, "He was in the low mod at Chino and went over the fence yesterday afternoon."

I nodded.

Wicks said, "Questions?"

"Why me? Why'd you put me out front like that with these guys? I don't have half the experience they do. They have investigative experience where I've only worked the street. They're not going to like it."

He moved in closer yet, right up in my face. His breath was peppermint fresh. "I don't give one shit what they like." He poked me in the chest. "You want the job or not? Just say the word, my friend, and you're out."

"You already know the answer to that."

With this job, I had the opportunity to really effect change in the violent neighborhood where I grew up. Not to mention how proud Dad had looked when I told him of my appointment to the team. That moment was now tarnished with a child out of wedlock—even though Dad didn't say anything or let his expression reveal his true feelings, I knew.

"Good. This afternoon at three, meet SIU, parole's special investigations unit, in the parking lot of Industry Station. They know where this punk's girlfriend lives. Set up surveillance on her and keep on her twenty-four/seven until this guy pops. I expect updates at least every eight hours—if it even goes that long. I don't think it will. You page me, you understand?"

"Yes, sir."

"Page the team, let them know about the meet. Do your homework on this guy and work up a package on him. I know you can do this."

"I understand."

Wicks nodded and hesitated as if thinking something over. "What kind of gun are you carrying?"

"The department issue, a .38 Smith and Wesson model 15 Combat Masterpiece."

"Ammo?"

"Regulation, hundred-and-fifteen-grain semi-jacketed, plus P hollow points."

"Backup?"

I stepped back and picked my foot up, put my boot on the desk. I pulled up my pant leg to show the ankle holster. "A model 60 Chief, five shot."

Did he do this to the others or just me because of my lack of experience?

He shook his head. "That's a rookie move. The whole idea in having a backup is in case you have to fight over your primary weapon. And if you're in a fight for your life, you can't afford to pick up your foot to get to your gun. That's your entire foundation for balance. You'll lose for sure. And we never lose. Especially not on my team."

I didn't like being called a rookie, even though I believed him to be correct. "Then tell me."

"What I said before, I meant it. This is a shotgun team. We are going to get into violent confrontations, and you're going to have to get ready for it." He pointed at my ankle holster. "Not only with the proper equipment"—he poked my forehead with his finger—"but up here as well. I'm worried about you, Bruno. Are you sure you're ready for this?"

"I'm ready." I took another step back out of range of his finger.

"Get your mind right. Go over scenarios in your head. What if this guy pulls a gun? What if he runs? What if he tries to run you over with his car? Continually ask yourself the 'what-ifs' so your mind is ready when it does go down. You understand?"

"Yes, sir."

"Cut that shit out. When we're alone, you call me Robby." He reached under his coat to the small of his back and came out with a large blue-steel automatic, a Smith and Wesson model 59 9mm. "Here, carry this. Get a shoulder holster for it. Keep it out of sight under a big shirt or jacket. This is your backup from now on. It's got a fifteen-round mag." He pushed the release button on the side and popped out the magazine. "It has two safeties, one on the side, here." He pointed to a little lever. "And unlike other autoloaders, once the mag is out, this weapon will not fire the round still in the chamber. That's the second safety feature. Take it to the range and get real familiar with it. Shoot the hell out of it."

I took the gun, the steel warm from his body heat.

He read my expression. "What?"

I said, "This is a ten-thirty weapon. It's not approved by the department to carry."

"Of course it's not; that's why it's a backup only."

"It's still not approved, even as a backup."

He smiled. "Kid, your dedication to the policy manual is refreshing. Listen, if you go through all your rounds in your duty weapon and that little belly gun, then that means you're in deep shit, and some bullshit policy isn't going to save your ass. You pull that 9mm and kill 'em all. You'll be alive and they won't. It's better to be judged by twelve than carried by six. Now put your foot back up here."

I did.

He pulled my model 60 Chief from my ankle holster and stuck it in my waistband. "Keep it here, the stock hooked in your belt just barely peeking up like that. No one will know what it is, and you'll be able to get to it when you need to. And if you ever have to pull that nine when I'm not with you, you call me right after the last shell casing hits the ground. I'll take care of everything. I'll cover for you. You got it?"

"Yes, sir."

"Now, about this afternoon, you understand what's expected of you?"

"Yes, sir."

"Listen to those other guys; they have a lot of experience. But make your own choices."

"I know. I will."

"And, when you catch up to this guy Armendez?"

I knew what he wanted me to say and couldn't. "We use whatever force necessary to effect the arrest."

Wicks didn't smile; he grinned with no teeth showing. "You're a smart guy, Bruno, or you wouldn't be here." He hesitated. "An escapee from state prison can be shot if he runs from you. That's the law. So, you do what your heart tells you. But if that son of a bitch runs, I want you to do your job." He brought his finger up ready to poke. I stepped back out of range as he stepped toward me.

"You don't have to worry about me," I said. "I will always do my job."

CHAPTER SEVEN

DETECTIVE GIBBS SAT in the passenger seat of my Ford Ranger, one foot up on my dash as he sipped from a Big Gulp cola and munched on a bag of salted peanuts. We parked down the street from Armendez's girlfriend's house in Ontario, a city in San Bernardino County and one that adjoins Chino, where Armendez escaped.

"This is my personal vehicle," I said.

Gibbs turned to look at me and grinned. "Very good, Deputy, brilliant deduction. Another couple of weeks working with me and you'll be a real detective."

I didn't like him, and he didn't like me. "Please take your foot off my dash."

He tilted his head back and tossed some peanuts into his open maw, then took a glug of cola. He spoke around the mash in his mouth. "Get a life, ya twit."

I let it slide off. No way could I risk a problem on the first day in operation, the first day with me running the team. I suspected Wicks made me case agent for this very reason, to test the cohesiveness of the team, to see if we could all get along without killing each other. No doubt, if Gibbs had not sounded off this morning in the office, one of the others would be running things instead of me.

We'd met up with two SIU agents in the parking lot of Industry Station. I split up the other two deputies on our team and put each with a parole agent to make our communications interagency compatible. I knew Gibbs would be a problem. I wanted the problem close to me to keep a handle on him. I already regretted it.

The SIU guys looked experienced and handled themselves well, at least in the parking lot and on the radio. We had three teams of two to take down a low-grade, nonviolent paperhanger. Overkill for sure.

I could only hope the girlfriend moved soon, before I pulled Gibbs out of my truck and put the boot to him.

Darkness took a long time to catch up to us, to help cover our surveillance. Gibbs sat with one shoulder on the door, the other on the seat, his head back, his Dodgers ball cap down over his eyes. "Let me know if anything moves."

Yes, by all means, go to sleep so I don't have to listen to your childish tripe anymore.

He must've read my mind and fired one more jibe from under his tilted cap. "Good thing it finally got dark; no one in this hood's gonna believe a white guy and a smoke just sittin' in a pickup doin' nothin.'"

Jack Hendricks in Zebra Two came on the radio. "We have movement. Looks like the primary just came out of her apartment. Stand by."

Gibbs didn't move. "Perfect. Just when I was about to grab a coupla z's."

"Zebra Two, it's confirmed the primary's moving. She's in a maroon Toyota Celica, driving east from the location. Anyone have her?"

I picked up the large handheld radio. "We'll take the eye."

The Celica drove by us. I started up, pulled a U-turn with my headlights off. After a block, I turned them on. I followed her south to Holt Boulevard and turned west. I shoved the radio over to Gibbs. "Hey, call it out. I'm driving."

He didn't move, the ball cap still down over his eyes. I keyed the radio and gave the other two units our direction of travel.

After several miles, Zebra Two, in an old beat-up blue VW bug, came up beside us. The SIU agent in the passenger seat put the radio to his mouth; his words came across in my radio. "You've been on her too long, we'll take the eye. Go ahead and fall back."

Jack Hendricks gave me a two-fingered salute and smiled. I gave it back to him. He pointed at Gibbs. I just shrugged, as if saying, "What can I do?" I eased off the accelerator and dropped back. The VW bug had a headlight out and wouldn't be able to stay with the Celica too long if it started making a lot of turns. As long as it stayed in a straight line, the driver shouldn't tumble to the tail.

The surveillance left Ontario and went through Montclair and into Pomona, the first city at the east end of Los Angeles County. I switched the radio to channel nine and spoke to the dispatcher. "Zebra One to control, can you please ten-twenty-one Pomona Police Department and tell them we are in their city on a surveillance, and give them the description of our vehicles?"

"Ten-four, Zebra One."

I caught a stale red signal and stopped. I switched back to the tactical frequency in time to hear Zebra Two say, "Zebra Three, do you have the primary?"

Zebra Three said, "Negative."

I looked both ways, waited for a break in the opposing traffic, and busted the red light. A car skidded and almost broadsided us. Gibbs came alive, put both hands on the dash. "Hey, hey, what the hell you doin'? You trying to get us killed? Take it easy, man."

I shoved the radio at him, grabbed the stick shift, and went through the gears, weaving in and out of traffic. "Ask Zebra Two where they lost her."

Gibbs keyed the mike. "Zebra Two, what was the primary's last DOT?"

"Westbound Holt at Lewis. She might have turned somewhere while in a cluster of cars and we missed it."

I said, "Tell Zebra Two to haul ass westbound on Holt in case she got ahead of us. Tell Zebra Three to take the northwest quadrant of Lewis and Holt and start a widening grid search. We'll take the northeast quadrant."

Gibbs looked at me for a second and then relayed the information.

We'd been on her for less than fifteen minutes and we already lost her. A simple little task and we'd blown it. I started to envision how the conversation with Wicks would go when I paged him, his anger, his disappointment. He'd never again trust me to run another op. If he didn't bounce me back to patrol.

Zebra Two came up on the radio. "I got the primary walking south on Lewis toward Holt."

Gibbs asked, "Where's her car?"

Zebra Two said, "Not her, the primary. We have the primary, Armendez, walking south on Lewis toward Holt."

I had turned into the residential neighborhood in the northeast quadrant to start the grid search. I pulled a fast U-turn and headed back to Holt just as Zebra Two started screaming in the radio.

CHAPTER EIGHT

"ZEBRA ONE, THE suspect is running. Foot pursuit. Southbound Lewis at Holt."

I came up on the intersection of Lewis and Holt, the six-cylinder engine of my Ford Ranger wound wide open. In front of us, Armendez ran south and turned west on Holt. Hendricks was still at least a full block behind, running on the sidewalk. I blew through the intersection against the red and braked hard to keep a Bimbo bread truck from slamming into us. I shoved the gearshift into first, popped the clutch, and smoked the back tires. I gained on Armendez, who ran too fast for a skinny-assed heroin hype.

In the seat next to me, Gibbs had his gun in hand. He stuck his head out the window, the wind blowing in his hair, the look of a predator in his eyes.

I quickly caught up to Armendez and cut the wheel, aiming to hit him on the sidewalk. The front tires of my Ford blew out when we hit the curb, or I would have hit Armendez and ended it right there.

He kept going, running hard.

Gibbs got out first and ran after him. I caught up to Gibbs, running full out. Gibbs brought his gun up and took aim at Armendez's back, his arm bouncing too much for a decent shot. I shoved him.

He stumbled but immediately righted his balance. I pulled ahead. I yelled, "Don't shoot him! We can catch him!"

Behind us, I heard Hendricks and the SIU agent as they rounded the corner to westbound Holt, too far behind to do us any good. The SIU agent yelled, "Shoot him! Shoot him! Don't let him get away!"

Gibbs caught up, running beside me and huffing. "Don't you . . . ever . . . put your . . . hands . . . on me again."

I'd had enough of Gibbs and poured on the speed. He wouldn't fall back and did the same, staying with me, only two steps behind. The distance between us and Armendez shortened. He slowed to step off the curb to a side-street intersection.

He made it to the other side as I leaped.

Gibbs slipped off the curb, turned his ankle, and went down. I tackled Armendez high. We went down in a jumble on the sidewalk. Armendez, desperate to escape, kicked and clawed and tried to bite.

I was angry with myself for being unable to gun Armendez like Robby Wicks wanted, shoot him down like a dog in cold blood. Armendez continued to squirm and kick and try to get away. I couldn't get control of his hands. And the hands were what killed you. I pulled back my gun and pistol-whipped him in the head. I pulled back to hit him again and felt a wetness on my face and a coppery taste on my lips. I hit him one more time. He went limp.

I stood up, breathing hard, just as a Pomona black-and-white slid to a stop in the street right in front of us, its overhead red-and-blue lights turning. The two uniformed police officers jumped out, guns drawn and aiming right at me, a black guy with a gun assaulting a Hispanic who lay on the sidewalk unconscious.

I didn't understand why they didn't shoot.

I thrust my hands in the air and yelled, "Sheriff's Department. Sheriff's Department. Don't shoot."

Even in the summer heat, I'd put on a white cotton bomber jacket to cover the shoulder-holstered 9mm Wicks had given me, the one he'd ordered me to carry. When I put my hands high in the air, the jacket rode up and exposed the gold Sheriff's star clipped to my belt. The Pomona police officers must've seen it. They lowered their weapons and put both spotlights on us, the light blinding in the dark night. I raised my arm as a shield.

Gibbs got up off the ground, brushing off his pants, and came over, favoring his injured foot. "Shit, that was close. These bastards almost gunned us."

He said it as if he'd been a part of the takedown and had been in real jeopardy.

The two Pomona cops came around their car doors just as another unit pulled up and got out. All four walked over to us. In the brightness, I could only see their shadows. One of them said, "Jesus, H. What the hell did you shoot him with?"

"What?" I asked. "No, no, we didn't shoot him." For the first time, I looked down at Armendez lying at my feet. Blood soaked his shirt and the top of his pants. It covered the sidewalk underneath him in a dark reflective pool. I looked closer, stunned. Blood pumped from a gash that gaped open on his neck. I looked down at my jacket, which was splattered with blood, and quickly wiped my mouth on my jacket sleeve and spit several times.

One of the cops said, "If you didn't shoot him, what the hell happened to him?"

I looked at Gibbs. He shrugged, clueless.

I said, "I guess he must've cut his own throat."

One of the cops said, "Oh, no. Shit no." They all ran for their cars, got in, slammed their doors, and took off. They wanted no part of a caper that stank of cover-up like this one.

Gibbs laughed. "Cut his own throat? Really? Come on, man, I'm your partner, and I don't believe that one. Come on, you can tell me. Where's your knife? It's cool, really. This mope's an escaped prisoner from state prison. You were fighting with him and . . ." He suddenly lost his smile. "Hey, wait a minute, you did this with a knife just to get on the good side of the lieutenant, didn't you?"

"Are you outta your mind? I don't have a knife and I didn't cut this man."

Off in the distance a siren headed our way from the west, parting traffic.

Paramedics.

I bent over and put my hand on Armendez's neck to stem the flow, his blood hot and wet on my fingers. The throb under my hand immediately started to ebb.

Hendricks and the SIU agent caught up, huffing and puffing. They both stood close, bent at the waist, hands on their knees, eyes wide. Hendricks said, "Holy shit."

The SIU agent said, "Good . . . job . . . guys."

I said, "No, it's not."

The ambulance skidded up. Two paramedics jumped out and pulled rescue boxes from the side of their truck. They ran over, set the boxes down, and donned blue latex gloves. One of them got on his knees and said, "Okay, let go. I got him."

I stood and said to my team, "Bring the cars over here. Tape off this area as a crime scene. Get your flashlights, walk back the way we came, and look for the knife. He must've tossed it somewhere back there."

They all stood staring at me. I yelled, "Move!"

They took off running.

I needed to find a phone and fast. I had to page Wicks.

Jeez, what a mess.

I started to do what he'd told me to do, go over in my head the "what-ifs." Only in this case it was the "what-if" explanations that even I didn't believe. The words echoed in my brain as I practiced saying them to Lieutenant Wicks. "I think this guy cut his own throat."

No matter how I wrote it, this caper came out as an "Ah, shit."

CHAPTER NINE

SEVEN AND A half hours later, homicide released me, sent me on my way with my badge and gun still in my possession.

A small miracle.

I walked out of the Industry Station's detective bureau, into the lobby and then on out into bright morning sun, exhaustion hanging off me like a warm, wet blanket. The light burned my eyes and I squinted.

Under similar circumstances—had I been assigned to investigate the Pedro Armendez incident—that's what they called it, an *incident*—I probably would've booked my sorry ass for murder. The Pedro Armendez incident was considered an "in custody death," the true cause of which was yet to be determined.

In those seven hours of interrogation, homicide continually asked if anyone had identified themselves during the foot pursuit. I told them I hadn't and didn't remember if anyone else had either. A screwup of monumental proportions. Nobody yelled, "Stop, Sheriff's Department." I only recalled the SIU agent yelling, "Shoot him! Shoot him!"

The night before, paramedics tried to save Mr. Armendez and failed. I notified dispatch by radio, as I stood over the corpse and while the medics gathered up their gear and left. Dispatch, in turn, notified homicide and paged Lieutenant Wicks several times to no avail.

Homicide grilled me again and again, trying to break down my outrageous story. During those seven hours, I sat alone in an interview room just like a crook and assumed they did the same to Gibbs.

Armendez's blood dried on my jacket and pants to splotches of dark brown. I'd cleaned most of the blood off my hands and face with a bottle of saline at the scene.

No one believed Armendez slit his own throat. Why would they? When they asked me why I thought that he did what he did, I postulated that he saw us gaining on him and didn't want to go back to prison. He didn't want to go back so badly, he took his own life with his own knife. That's what I wanted to believe.

Only no one found the knife at the scene. And the investigators made no excuses for the impropriety of the situation; they searched me from head to toe looking for the blade.

At the curb in front of the station, Detective Jack Hendricks stood leaning against my Ford Ranger. When I'd gone to the station the night before with the shooting team to be interviewed, I left my truck at the crime scene with the blown tires. He tossed me the keys. "You owe me for the two front tires. The rims, too—they were bent."

I caught the keys. He'd changed the tires for me. "Thanks, I'll write you a check." I didn't know Jack Hendricks other than meeting him yesterday at Lennox Station when Wicks gave us his violent-crimes team philosophy speech. Just the sight of him and his smile went a long way to make me feel better about what happened. He moved to his Pontiac Firebird parked behind my truck. "Hey, that was a helluva lot of fun last night. Great caper. Good job."

Even if I had not been the one to tackle Armendez, or taste his blood or stand over him while he expired, I didn't think I would've ever called what happened "a great caper" or a "good job." Jack just wanted to support me and I appreciated it.

I said, "You seen Wicks?"

"Nope, dispatch said he never answered his pages. Hey, man, I gotta run. I'll catch ya later."

I nodded. Jack got in his Firebird, started up, and took off.

I wanted to get home and drop into bed, sleep straight through to tomorrow. Only I couldn't get Armendez's expression out of my mind, the image of him lying on the sidewalk on his back, in his own blood, his eyelids only open to slits revealing a bit of the whites and a sliver of his pupils. His mouth slack and gaping open.

And worse, the coppery taste of his blood.

I got in my truck, started up, and was unconsciously drawn back to the crime scene. I needed to see it in the daylight to burn a new image in my memory over the one I no longer wanted.

I played the truck radio loud to try and stay awake. Twenty minutes later, Holt and Lewis looked totally different in the light of day. The ominous darkness no longer added to the ugliness of sudden death. I drove past it going eastbound, made a U-turn at Lewis, drove back, and parked a few feet from the large brown stain on the sidewalk. The yellow Sheriff's crime-scene tape lay on the ground and fluttered in the light breeze. Torn paper packages, blood-soaked gauze, and other items used in the fierce battle to save Armendez's life still remained in a clutter. Lots of cars zipped by, people going to work unaware that not hours before, someone's life had ended in that spot.

I turned the truck off, leaned forward, and rested my head on the steering wheel, my eyes closed, disgusted with myself. Somehow, in all the chaos, I'd forgotten about my daughter. How could that happen? I'd left that huge responsibility to my father, and that wasn't fair. I hadn't even called him. What he must think of me. I needed to get home.

A loud rapping on the passenger window startled me. Lieutenant Wicks stood on the sidewalk, slightly bent over, peering in. Fatigue showed in his face, in his tanned skin and eyes, though his hair was combed perfectly and his brown suit coat looked fresh enough. He rapped again. In his hand he held a burning Tiparillo cigar, the small kind with the plastic mouthpiece. I didn't know he smoked.

Anger welled up inside me. This man, my supervisor, should've responded to all the pages. He should've been there last night to back his team. I got out, slammed my truck's door, and walked around to the sidewalk. I knew I should cool off before confronting him, but fatigue overcame good sense. He said nothing, smiled hugely, and offered me the box of Tiparillos from his shirt pocket.

"No thank you."

Still with the smile. "Take one."

"I don't smoke."

"Take one."

The anger started to subside. I took a cigar, unwrapped it, and stuck the plastic mouthpiece in my lips. He took out his Zippo with the Marine Corps emblem and lit it. We leaned against my truck and puffed. I tried not to inhale and suppressed several coughing bouts as the smoke burned my nose and throat.

I couldn't look at the crime scene and stared at the flowering ice plant on the other side of the sidewalk. The nicotine lit me up. It made my blood rush and my heart beat faster. The fatigue melted away.

The stupid thing was, Wicks had said nothing about what happened the night before and yet I somehow knew he approved.

Still, I had the urge to defend my actions. I said, "He cut his own throat."

Wicks took his cigar from his mouth and blew on the tip. Some ash fell away as the cherry tip glowed hot. "Come over here."

I followed him to his county car, a maroon Chevy Malibu, parked behind my truck. He reached into a brown paper bag sitting on the hood and brought out a tall can of cheap beer, Pabst Blue Ribbon. He popped the tab and handed it to me. I hesitated. "You're kidding me, right? We're right out in public here. Everyone can see."

"Take it, that's an order."

I took it, the can cold and wet in my hand. He pulled another out of the bag, popped the top, and tilted it back, his throat working a long slug of beer. I did the same and once I started, couldn't stop. I tossed back the entire can and choked a little on the last part of the foam. It tasted better than anything I'd ever drunk, and since I hadn't eaten anything for the last twenty hours, the sixteen ounces of carbonated liquid stretched my empty stomach and the alcohol immediately went to work.

A Pomona police car drove by and slowed. The officer saw us with the beers in our hands, drinking in public, an ABC—Alcohol Beverage Control—violation. He pulled out of the flow of traffic and came right at us.

CHAPTER TEN

WICKS RAISED HIS can and toasted his beer to the cop car and took another long drink. The cop pulled to the curb behind Wicks' county unit. He picked up his mike and started to call it in. Wicks took a step away from the hood of his car, kept drinking, and pulled his coat back to reveal his Los Angeles County Sheriff's star and his gun on his hip. Only this time, for some reason, he didn't have his favored .45 Colt Combat Commander. Instead he carried the department issue .38 in his holster.

The cop shook his head with disgust, put the mike down, and pulled back into the passing traffic.

Wicks burped, tossed his empty into the ice plant on the other side of the sidewalk, and pulled another out of the bag. He offered it to me. I took it and popped the tab. The alcohol from the first beer had already hit me pretty hard. I rarely imbibed. I drank more slowly from the second can. I still had a long drive home.

While I did, Wicks said, "Damn fine job last night."

I jerked the can down and looked at him. "I didn't cut his throat."

"I know you didn't."

"You do? How?"

He took another long pull on his Pabst, his eyes not leaving mine. He set the can on the hood of his county car. He reached into his suit-coat pocket and pulled out a folded piece of paper. "I tracked down the girlfriend."

"Armendez's girlfriend?"

"That's right."

"You did? When did you do that?"

The responsibility of Armendez's death played heavy on my mind, much more than I thought. I wanted to snatch the paper from Wicks' hand. I needed relief from the guilt, some explanation, no matter how minor, as to why a man died under my hand.

I casually reached for the folded paper. "What did she say?"

He pulled the paper out of reach and smiled. "She said Armendez called her, said that some men were after him. He said that he wouldn't go back to prison. Said no matter what, he wouldn't go back."

I shook my head. "Ah, shit."

"What?"

"You said he thought some people were after him."

"That's right."

"I don't think we identified ourselves last night. He might've thought we were those people, whoever they were, that were chasing him."

Wicks let me take the paper from him. I opened it, a supplemental report form, handwritten and signed by Wicks. One paragraph stating what he'd just said along with Armendez's girlfriend's information.

He smiled, took a pull off his beer, and then said, "That was a mistake, but nothing to lose any sleep over. You might get a couple days on the bricks for it, no big deal. You'll know better next time, won't you?"

"I don't care about any discipline. What I do care about is whether Pedro Armendez would still be alive if he knew we were cops and not 'these people who were out to get him.'"

Wicks brought out his finger again and poked me in the chest. "Don't go second-guessing yourself on this one. It came out in the good, so let it go."

"Don't poke me in the chest again or we're gonna have a problem."

He leaned back a little and smiled. "Really? You really just said that?"

"I did."

I crumpled the beer can, shoved it down in the bag, and headed for my truck. He said at my back, "Hey, my wife, Barbara, and I are having some folks over for a barbecue this Sunday, day after tomorrow, to celebrate the team's first kill. I want you to come. We're going to grill some shark steaks. Bring whoever you like."

I stopped and took a couple of steps back toward him. "Celebrate? Are you kidding? A man died. That's nothing to celebrate."

He pointed at me. "You need to get over yourself or you're not going to make it." He pointed to the dried blood on the sidewalk. "That puke sealed his own fate when he went over that low mod fence at CIM. You did what you were supposed to do. You did it by the numbers, and I'm proud to have you on the team. But if you can't cut it, you let me know, and I'll get you reassigned."

"That's fine by me."

He looked shocked. We stared at each other for a moment. He said, "If that's what you want, fine. But you better think about it first. Cool off a little before you make a decision like this. I'll give you until tonight at six. We have an op going down at Lynwood Station. If you're there, we'll forget we had this conversation. If you're not, I'll put in your transfer back to patrol."

"Like I said, that's fine by me. Don't wait on me tonight. I won't be there."

We stood there a moment longer. I pulled his 9mm from the shoulder holster, took the few steps back, and tried to hand it to him.

"No, keep it until tonight. I know you'll cool off and see the error of your ways."

I didn't want to argue, stuck it back in my holster, turned, and headed to my truck.

"Bruno?"

I stopped but didn't turn. I didn't want any more to do with him. "What?"

"Come here, I wanna show you something."

I hesitated and thought about not doing what he asked, thought about just getting in my truck and driving away. I turned around. He'd walked over to the ice plant close to where he'd tossed his first empty beer can. I didn't move. He pointed at something in the ice plant. "Look."

I walked over and peered into the ground cover. Something very small glinted in the early morning sunlight. I got down on one knee for a closer look. I pulled away some of the ice plant and saw it: a bloodied X-Acto knife blade without the knife handle. No wonder the crime-scene techs didn't find it. They'd been looking for a knife, not a small X-Acto blade.

I looked at Wicks. He smiled.

Wicks had come on his own time to look for the weapon Armendez had used on himself. He came to try and help clear his team member.

Me.

CHAPTER ELEVEN

I TURNED THE music up to stay awake on the long drive home and fought to keep my eyelids from drooping shut.

Wicks called the crime-scene techs to officially recover the X-Acto knife blade. He told me not to wait around, to go home and get some sleep, that he wanted me fresh for the op tonight, a robbery surveillance. I didn't have the nerve to tell him again that I wouldn't be there. He'd figure it out when I didn't show.

I jumped on the Pomona Freeway headed west, mingling among the last of the folks going into LA to work. All that had happened in the last twenty-four hours played in a kaleidoscope of scenes in my mind. The part with Pedro Armendez came out more like some horror flick in stark Technicolor. All it lacked was the ominous organ music.

I couldn't turn it off. I also couldn't resolve Wicks in the whole scheme of things. I really wanted to dislike him and couldn't. He remained an enigma I couldn't read, not even a little.

The news came on as I continued to fight the nod. I woke up a little from the adrenaline push. Would they describe the *incident* in Pomona? Would they say Pedro Armendez's name? Would they say my name in an accusatory manner? Air what happened to the entire world?

Angelinos can rest easy tonight. A brutal robbery and murder suspect is officially off the streets. Damien Frakes Jr., a Holly Street Crip gang member and a parolee at large, was shot and killed last night in the back alley of 123rd Street off of Central Avenue, in South Central Los Angeles. Damien Frakes Jr. was wanted in connection with the triple murder at Franco's Jewelry store in Torrance and for the shooting and wounding of a Redondo Beach patrol officer.

A lieutenant from the newly formed Los Angeles County Sheriff's Department's Violent Crime Team tracked Frakes to the back alley. The name of the lieutenant was withheld pending the shooting team's investigation. A witness at the scene said that when the lieutenant confronted Frakes, they were no more than ten feet apart. The lieutenant yelled, "Drop your gun, Sheriff's Department." They both fired their guns at the same time. Frakes was hit in the chest multiple times and was declared dead at the scene. The lieutenant sustained a grazing wound to his left arm, was treated and released.

To recap—

I shut the radio off and drove in stunned silence. Wicks had said nothing of what happened to him the night before—just hours before, really. He had casually offered me a cigar and a beer and invited me over to his house to barbecue shark steaks on Sunday, the same as if nothing at all had happened. Cool and calm.

Cool with a gunshot to the arm.

He didn't go get his haircut, which I'd recognized at the time as nothing more than rhetoric. But still, I didn't think he'd go after Frakes, not alone.

What he did do though, and it wasn't fair at all, was wind up his little toy soldiers and send us off on a bullshit assignment. He then went after the hard target on his own. He went toe to toe in a real gunfight with Frakes.

Son of a bitch.

I'd just stood out there on Holt Boulevard pissing and whining like some kind of baby. And he let me do it. I got mad at him all over again.

That's why he wasn't carrying his Colt .45 Combat Commander; the shooting investigators had taken it for routine ballistics comparison.

I still couldn't get around the fact that he said nothing about the shooting. He didn't brag or offer it as an excuse or reason why he had not responded to the pages.

Afterward, he didn't go home to rest, to be consoled by his wife, Barbara. No, instead he drove all the way to the east side of the county to find a bloodied X-Acto knife blade to pull his detective's cookies out of the fire.

How in the hell could I quit his team now?

Something niggled at the tip of my brain. Something didn't quite jibe with what happened, either last night or that morning, and I couldn't identify the problem. Fatigue wouldn't allow the answer to bubble up. I'd have to think about it tomorrow after I'd had time to sleep.

Thirty minutes later, I came to, sitting in my truck in front of Dad's house, the house I grew up in, the house where my baby girl now resided. I had no recollection of the drive home and could only believe my truck, like a faithful horse, knew the way and took care of its master.

Dad had already left for work as a postal carrier for the USPS. His work ethic came under the same umbrella as his principles in life: he never missed a day for any reason. Once, he even went to work with pneumonia and a hundred-and-two fever. He ran himself down to the quick. Noble and I thought he might kill himself over his misplaced sense of honor. I didn't think that would've bothered Dad at all. Death in the name of honor held a noble calling. Working the street, I found that dead was dead no matter how you cut it.

I staggered into the house and plopped facedown on the couch. I didn't move until hours later when Dad nudged me awake.

Drool wet one side of my face. Pedro Armendez and the people chasing him populated my dreams, the taste of his blood, the look of his hooded eyes. I rubbed my face and sat up blinking.

Dad, dressed in his blue-gray postal pants and his white shoulder-strap t-shirt, sat down next to me holding Baby Girl Johnson. My daughter. His grandchild. She made cute little noises. He held a bottle in his nudging hand. He said, "You awake yet?"

"Just gimme a minute, and I will be."

Fatigue had burrowed deep into my bones, took up residence, and fought the eviction. I shook myself awake. I wanted to hold my daughter.

"You smell like booze, Son. Have you been drinking? I'm going to be mad if you went out carousing when you have a child at home waitin' on you. You have too much responsibility now to—"

"It's not like that, Dad. I had a beer with my boss. He kind of forced it on me. But, I know, I'm an adult, and I didn't have to take it. I wanted it. I needed it. I came straight home as soon as I could. It was a helluva night, Dad, one of those that . . . well, I hope I don't have any more like it."

"I'm sittin' right here, why don't you tell me all about it." He gently moved the baby up and down to keep her happy. I thought babies that young cried a lot more.

I shook my head. Right after the thing with Armendez happened, all I wanted to do was get home and spill my guts to my dad, a need I had to fulfill. As he sat next to me ready to receive my confession, I couldn't say the words. The words seemed dirty and laden with so much guilt I couldn't drag them out to make him a part of such an awful tableau. Especially not in front of my baby girl. "Not now, Dad, okay?"

I reached out to take my daughter from him.

He pulled her away. "Not with all that blood on you. You can hold her after you get cleaned up."

Of course, he was right. I wasn't thinking. I looked down at my ruined clothes; the sight of them reaffirmed what happened the night before. My stomach churned. I needed something to eat.

He must've read the heavy emotion in my expression and patted my leg. "I understand; you can tell me when you're ready. Why don't you tell me about this beautiful child? You didn't have the time yesterday. Where's her mother? Where did you meet her? What's going on?"

Another topic I didn't want to discuss, but I'd pulled him into it and he deserved the explanation. "I screwed up, Dad. Plain and simple, I screwed up."

"Don't be too hard on yourself, Son. I know you. You didn't set out to do something wrong. You'll feel better if you talk it out."

I turned my head and looked at him for the first time since I woke. "You know, I don't know if I've ever said it before, but I did all right in the dad department."

He smiled.

I sat back and closed my eyes and started talking. I didn't want to see his reaction to the truth.

CHAPTER TWELVE

"I MET SONJA at work. She came to Lynwood Station as a trainee. I trained her to work the street—to survive on the street." The words sounded inappropriate even to me.

"Dad, she has the whitest skin, with these wonderful freckles. And her eyes, she has these green eyes that are so beautiful and at the same time mischievous. I was smitten right off. Don't get me wrong, I did try to resist. I knew the dangers of having a liaison with someone I worked with on the street. But I couldn't help it. We fell in love. She loved me as much as I loved her, even more."

Least I thought she did.

The entire situation was wrong from the beginning. Not just the trainer and trainee part, but much worse, the white and black issue. I waited for him to comment on it. When he didn't, I continued.

"But then I started making mistakes on the street. I was distracted, and if you do that while working patrol, the street is an unforgiving mistress. She'll reach up and drag you down. She'll eat you whole. So I made the decision to transfer out of the station. I can't tell you how much it hurt to think I wouldn't be working with her anymore, that I'd only be seeing her at the end of our shifts. That is, if our shifts didn't conflict altogether.

"That last night she was angry at my decision. She said she should be the one to transfer, that I would ruin my career. I told her it needed to be me and it needed to be right away because if the brass at the station found out, both of our careers would be ruined."

I hesitated, afraid to tell the rest of it.

Dad said, "It doesn't sound like you did anything wrong."

I nodded. "Dad, I should've told you all of this back seven, eight months ago when it happened. That was a mistake and I'm sorry."

"You're twenty-five years old, a grown man, and you need to go your own way. I understand why you didn't say anything."

A lump rose in my throat. I wished he'd get angry and not be so understanding. I continued. "The night I told her that I was putting in for a transfer, we were working swing, two to ten on patrol, and she was really upset. She refused to talk about it until after shift. Looking back on it now, I realize that she had to be pregnant. She carried that extra information as an added burden. She had to be afraid of how I'd react, how being pregnant really complicated matters even more."

I leaned over and put my head in my hands. A half-black child, what a horrible predicament I left her with.

"And then I go and tell her I was transferring to get away from her. She must've thought I was some sort of monster."

I sat next to Dad, marveling at my own stupidity.

I needed to get it all out. "That night . . . that shift that night was one of the worst I'd ever encountered."

Dad lowered his tone. "That was the night those gang members firebombed the Abrams' house, wasn't it?"

I'd told Dad that part when it happened, only he had the sequence wrong. "That's right, but first we went to a domestic with this huge guy, his name was Douglas Howard. I'd dealt with him before on similar calls for service. He'd battered his wife again, broke her arm and socked her up pretty good. He was coked up and didn't want to go to jail. We had to fight him."

Dad said, "Mmm."

He'd heard about how Douglas died. News in the ghetto spreads faster and was more reliable than the flu on a wet winter day.

The part I didn't tell him was that I thought I could talk Douglas down and told Sonja as much. She didn't listen to me, flanked him, and inadvertently started the fight with her needless tactical move. She'd forced Douglas into a fight.

"Sonja used a blackjack on him. She . . . hit him too hard. Douglas died later at the hospital from a depressed skull fracture. Right after that we were also in that crazy officer-involved shooting and . . . anyway, at the end of shift she just sort of disappeared. The watch commander told me she turned in her badge and gun and resigned. I looked all over for her, Dad. I did. I loved her like nothing else in this world. I guess I still love her now, maybe more than ever, and she won't have anything to do with me. She won't even tell me where she's living. I swear I didn't know she was pregnant."

"And she just showed up at your doorstep yesterday?"

"That's right. She dropped the baby off and wouldn't listen to reason. She just left."

He nodded. "Sometimes women go through this kind of episode right after they have a child. The natural chemicals in their bodies are all mixed up. She'll calm down. She'll come back and talk it out with you."

"You think so?"

"I do."

An uncomfortable silence sat between us like an unwanted guest with serious body odor.

Dad reached over to the end table and picked up a folded paper. "Found this in the diaper bag. It's the county paper for the birth certificate. You have two more weeks to give this child a name. Have you given it any thought?"

"Ah, jeez, Dad, I really haven't. What do you think?"

"She's your daughter. You need to give her a name."

"It's been crazy the last couple of days. Let me think on it, okay?"

"Of course, take your time. We can just call her Baby Girl Johnson. It's kind of a cute little name."

Dad never did sarcasm unless he wanted to make his point or wanted to move me closer to his way of thinking. No way could my daughter keep the name Baby Girl Johnson.

"Don't be ridiculous. Give me until Sunday, okay? Please?"

"I don't want to name her because if you don't like it, you'll always hold it against me."

"I'd never do that. Give me some ideas. That'll help me decide what I like and don't like."

"Nope, not going to do it. Now, when do you have to work next?"

"I have to take a shower and get ready right now."

I wanted to go, and at the same time I wanted to stay. After a few hours' sleep and with a clear head I felt I owed Lieutenant Wicks for what he did, the way he went the extra mile to make the incident with Pedro Armendez justified. He'd cleared my name.

Baby Girl Johnson started to fuss. Dad held her gently to his shoulder and patted her back. A simple action that reminded me I knew absolutely nothing about raising a child.

Dad said, "Sure, we can watch this sweet little girl until her mother snaps out of it. Though, with your job and mine, we'll have to hire Mrs. Espinoza full-time to take care of her."

"Thanks, Dad, you don't know what a relief this is. Thanks for supporting me."

"You going to tell me why you have all that dried blood on you? You'll feel better once you air out what happened. I won't judge you, Son."

"If it's okay with you, maybe another time."

"I understand. Why don't you go on and get ready for work?"

CHAPTER THIRTEEN

I SAT AT the long table amongst all the other detectives waiting for the briefing to begin. The noise rose as everyone talked and joked and laughed.

I wore Levi's, a button-down long-sleeve shirt, and heavy work boots. Even though I loved working the street in a patrol car, I took pride in the fact I now wore the plain clothes of a detective. The sheriff's star hung on a chain around my neck.

I'd returned to the work assignment I'd just left, Lynwood Station, the downstairs briefing room. I felt comfortable in the place where I'd spent the last . . . almost three years. I had not yet cleaned out my locker. I figured I'd wait until the training sergeant called to say my replacement had arrived at the station. Lynwood would always be home to me, my first patrol assignment, the first place I truly fell in love.

And now the place where I'd conceived my daughter.

Wicks was conspicuous in his absence.

I knew most everyone around the table, the station detectives and my new team. I sat next to Jack Hendricks and wrote him a check for the tires and rims damaged on my truck the night before. I handed it to him. He handed me an X-Acto knife new in the package. "Here, I heard you lost yours."

Everyone at the briefing table busted up laughing. My face glowed warm.

Johnny Gibbs came into the briefing room and handed an operation plan to each detective. When he came to me, instead of handing over the stapled papers, he dropped the packet on the table in front of me. He leaned down and whispered in my ear, "Tonight, it's my turn. I'm running the team for this op. Check out where I have you positioned."

He moved on. Hendricks, beside me, leaned over and said, "Wicks is on five days' mandatory leave. You know anything about that? He never said anything about it yesterday. I'm beginning to wonder if he's ever going to join us. It's really crazy. The team's just starting out and he's not here for the second op. You think he's in the grease over something?"

Had Hendricks not seen the news? Had he seen the news and not put it together?

Now wasn't the time to get into it. I'd tell him what I knew after the briefing.

Two more detectives came in whom I didn't recognize, one shorter Hispanic, the other a tall, rawboned white guy with jet-black hair and a white tuft in the front. The abrupt shift in colors kind of made him look like a skunk. He had deep acne scars in his cheeks. His piercing blue-gray eyes took in everyone in the room like those of a predator.

Each of them wore his sheriff's star from a chain around his neck. They looked like narcs, with their hair shaggier than the rest of us and by the way they moved. You could always tell a narc, no matter what environment they tried to blend into. Some did it naturally, some looked stupid at the attempt. These two just looked dangerous.

I pulled my gaze off them and thumbed through the op plan looking for my assignment and found it. Gibbs put me in X-Ray One, in uniform and in a marked patrol unit. I'd be working with a guy named C. Thibodeaux. I looked around the room. I didn't know Thibodeaux. Out of everyone involved, we were the only two working in uniform. I didn't want it to bother me, but it did. I'd left uniforms just a few days ago and now I was back.

Jackson Kohl, the station detective sergeant, came into the briefing room at a fast walk and went to the head of the briefing table. "Good evening, gentlemen. Let's get started; we're running a little late. As you know, this is a robbery surveillance. We have been tasked with abating the armed robberies occurring on Imperial Highway in our geographical policing area. Please turn to the back page of your briefing material."

Everyone followed his direction.

"The pin map, here, depicts the locations of these robberies, the vast majority of which have occurred at the gas station at Mona Boulevard."

I knew all about these armed robberies. I'd taken the reports on a few of them while working a black-and-white.

Sergeant Kohl caught my eye and said, "Hey, Bruno, good to have you back."

I nodded, my face again burning hot for being singled out.

Kohl smiled and addressed the group again. "Guys, tonight we're using issued handguns and shotguns; knives are not authorized."

The group at the table chuckled at my expense. I didn't look around and instead just smiled, playing along.

Kohl let the group calm down then started again. "Patrons getting gas at this station have been hit fifty-six times in the last three months. It's turning into an embarrassment and we—"

A switchblade thumped into the wood table; the blade stuck inches from my hand. The room went quiet. The tall narc pulled his left arm back from the throw. He said nothing and only smiled.

Kohl said, "Not funny, Thibodeaux. See me after briefing."

Thibodeaux didn't take his eyes off me and leaned over, his hand extended, expecting me to pull the knife free and hand it to him. Only I'd had enough and needed to send a message. I pulled the knife loose, pushed the release, and closed the blade. I stuck it in my pocket with everyone watching. They looked at me then back at Thibodeaux.

When nothing more happened, Kohl went back to the briefing. "The suspects are three unknown black males who live in the Imperial Courts housing projects, half a block to the west. They wait by a hole in the back fence of the gas station, scoping out the victims pulling in to gas up. When they like what they see, they put on their ski masks and take their guns out from under some bushes.

"They have lookouts who whistle when any cop car comes down Imperial from either direction. We can probably take them down on a gun charge, but they won't be in the can long for a misdemeanor. We're going to wait and take them down in progress. Questions?"

I raised my hand and didn't wait for him to call on me. "Isn't waiting for a robbery to go down going to put the victim in jeopardy?"

Kohl paused for a moment. "That's why we're not going to move in until the robbery is over. Everyone hear that? Do not move in until the suspects try to leave the scene and the victim is out of the picture. Okay, turn to the second-to-the-last page."

Papers fluttered in the silent room.

"The gas station is on the north side of Imperial, three businesses over from Mona Boulevard. When they do the robbery, they run north, pop through the hole in the fence, and run west in the alley. As soon as they cross Mona, they're in the projects, and it'll be impossible to root them out. So, here's the plan. We'll have two station detectives, Jenkins and Phillips, in a van parked in the dirt field just above the alley directly north of the gas station." He nodded to Jenkins and Phillips. "You guys be sure you wait for all three to come through the fence before you exit the van, you understand?"

Jenkins said, "Nice."

He said it because he and his partner had the takedown position, and if there was going to be any shooting, they'd be in the thick of it.

"Ricky Blue?" Kohl said to the Hispanic narc, who'd yet to say a thing. "You and Sims will be in a plain-wrapped car down Imperial. When it goes down, you haul ass up into the parking lot of the gas station and block their escape to the south and at the same time contain the victim. Bruno, you and Thibodeaux will be parked in a marked unit on Mona, south of Imperial. When I call out the 211 in progress, you're to come north on Mona, cross Imperial, and pull into the alley to block their escape to the west. We'll have them trapped between you and Jenkins and Phillips.

"Remember, all of you, this isn't the best situation, and if it goes to guns, watch your crossfire. In fact, let's designate shooters right now. If they don't give up, Jenkins and Phillips, you're the designated hitters. Bruno and Thibodeaux, you stand down, stay behind your car doors for cover. Everybody good?"

Everyone nodded. "Okay, I'm going to be up on the roof of the building across the street with a high-speed 35mm camera, so everyone watch your ass. You understand what I'm sayin' here? Okay, good. I'll be calling the play from the roof." He looked at his watch. "Let's be suited up and ready to roll from here in thirty minutes."

I got up and headed to the locker room to change into my uniform. Thibodeaux came up to me and said, "Hey, it's not funny anymore. Gimme my knife."

"It wasn't funny to begin with." I turned to head for the locker room just as the narc named Ricky Blue said in a low tone to Phillips, "I'm swappin' with you. Tell your boss. Make it right."

I looked back in time to hear a stunned Phillips say, "Bullshit."

Blue said nothing and stared Phillips down with hard brown eyes.

Phillips kicked the wall. "Son of a bitch. All right."

Who did Ricky Blue think he was, changing the sergeant's game plan like that?

CHAPTER FOURTEEN

FORTY MINUTES LATER, with the sun dropping below the horizon, casting the world in fading oranges and yellows, I sat in the passenger side of the black-and-white with Thibodeaux behind the wheel, on Mona just south of Imperial Highway. He'd not said a word and continued to fume about his confiscated illegal switchblade.

The leather straps for the new shoulder holster bound up under my arms and made the simple task of sitting in the car uncomfortable. Only time would make carrying the illegal weapon easier. The department-approved green windbreaker I wore with "Sheriff" emblazoned in large yellow letters on the back covered it up.

Thibodeaux kept his hands on the steering wheel, looking out the windshield. The tanned and smooth skin on his arms sported an anchor tattoo, the kind I'd seen on people who'd been in the Navy or Marines. He also had a crude black cross on the back of the middle finger of his right hand, the ink faded with time. He looked to be about forty years old and carried a quiet air of confidence.

We needed to depend on each other, especially during a robbery surveillance. I took his switchblade out of my pocket and handed it to him, the weapon a violation of policy, on or off duty, and a misdemeanor if prosecuted criminally under PC 653k. He took it, pulled his pant leg up, and stuck it in his boot.

"You're welcome."

He again stared out the windshield. "I didn't say thank you. You took my knife."

"You threw—"

Sergeant Kohl came up on the tactical frequency. "Heads up, everyone, we have a possible. Three suspects are in play by the fence, and they're scoping a white female in the center gas island, gassing a baby-blue Volvo. Stand by."

His words made my heart race. I grabbed onto the upright shotgun in the rack with my left hand and the spotlight handle with my right. Thibodeaux started the car, put it in drive, and kept his foot on the brake.

"They're picking up their guns."

Two or three tense minutes ticked by, our nerves on edge.

"Okay, ten-twenty-two, stand down, the victim drove away and they put the guns back."

Thibodeaux shoved the gearshift into park and turned off the car. I tried to relax. The two detectives parked in the van, Blue and Jenkins, must have had a clear view of that back fence and of the three suspects with their illicit activities. Blue and Jenkins had to be climbing the walls in this tense game of go-don't-go.

Dusk settled in all at once as the yellows and oranges disappeared and the low light crept toward darkness. Without daylight, the ghetto turned that much more dangerous. Now even the shadows could kill you.

"So, you're working narcotics?"

Thibodeaux looked over. "That's right. They just started a new street team and dropped one of those single-wide mobile home trailers out back behind the Lynwood Station for us to use."

"And you work with Ricky Blue?"

He didn't answer right away. He smiled. "You don't work with ol' Blue, you only try and keep up."

"Sure, I know the type, gung ho and ready for anything, always pushin' the edge."

"You don't know Blue or you wouldn't be talkin' like that. He doesn't appreciate folks talkin' smack. Fair warning."

"What do you mean?"

"That's okay, never mind. This is a one-off. We won't be working together after this, so it doesn't matter."

I shrugged. "All right. That's probably true. Where'd you do your patrol time?"

"Firestone."

"A Stony Boy, huh?"

He smiled and looked at me. "That's right."

He liked the reference to the time-honored nickname. He asked, "Where'd you do your time?"

"Right here in Lynwood. And I saw them put the trailer in back. They had to take down a section of the chain-link fence and then put it back up again. The brass told us the trailer was for OSS, Operation Safe Streets, the gang unit."

"That's right, the trailer's sectioned off. Half is for dope and the other side's for OSS."

"That makes a lot of sense; dope and gangs go hand in hand."

Kohl came up on the radio. "Units stand by, we have another candidate, a red Toyota Supra, white male victim wearing a gray pinstriped suit and tie. He's at the gas island closest to the street, south side of the lot."

Thibodeaux started the car, put it in gear, and kept his foot on the brake.

"Standby units, the suspects are going for their guns . . . ah . . . ah, ten-twenty-two, they changed their minds."

Thibodeaux turned the car off. "Son of a bitch, this is really gettin' under my skin. We gonna have to do this shit all night?"

"I know what you mean," I said. "My stomach's headed for an ulcer." I let go a little acid burp I'd been holding in.

"That sergeant's finally going to cry wolf for real, and no one's gonna believe him."

We sat quietly, our nerves resting on a jagged edge as darkness finished slamming down around us, bringing with it a stronger dose of paranoia.

After a while I asked, "What's a narco street team doing working a robbery surveillance?"

"I hear ya, brother. Believe me, I do. I had no say in it. Ol' Blue, he caught wind of this gig and just decided to throw in with it. I think he needs the overtime to pay for his tricked-out powerboat on the Colorado River. He's also got a second home out at Havasu that's a money hole."

I didn't think overtime was the reason. Blue was probably an adrenaline junkie, needed a fix, and three gangsters armed with handguns, pullin' robberies, fit the bill perfectly.

"You hear him a little while ago?" I asked. "When he just, all on his own, bumped Phillips from his position in that van in the alley on the north side of the op?"

"Blue's like a little tornado, like a Tasmanian devil. You can't contain him. Blue, he does exactly whatever the hell Blue wants to do. If that spot's the most dangerous, that's where Blue wants to be."

"Huh."

Blue sounded a lot like Wicks. I stuck my hand out. "My name's Bruno."

He took it and shook. "Mine's Claude. My friends call me Dirt."

"Claude, where were you before you came to Lynwood narco?"

"Here and there, you know. After working Firestone, I moved around. Most recently though, me and Blue, we worked SPY."

"Oh, I hear that's a great job."

"It was all right, I guess, but we like it better here at the Wood where we actually get a chance to feed our handcuffs."

He didn't really sound convinced, and now merely espoused the party line.

He looked at me and said, "We're working a case right now on a heavyweight dude. We've got some good inside info from a proven CI in the joint. This guy out here, he's runnin' a huge coke operation, sells to all of South Central. His name's Lucas Knight. You heard of him?"

Everyone referred to Sheriff's Prison Intelligence, or SPI, as SPY. They didn't work cases; they just gathered intelligence on prison gangs and passed it on to whatever law enforcement agency was affected by the information. SPI was one of the most elite jobs in the department, and no one would ever leave it voluntarily for a street-level narco job. For some reason, Thibodeaux and Blue got pulled from SPI and dumped in an out-of-the-way corner of the county. Out of sight, out of mind. And Thibodeaux wanted to make it sound like it was their choice to make the move and that they hadn't been ejected from the assignment.

None of my business.

It also sounded like wherever ol' Blue went, Thibodeaux followed along like a little puppy.

"Of course I've heard of Knight, but he's too far up the food chain to be touched by anyone at our level. He's so far removed from the dope, no one's been able to link him to any crime—none of the murders or any of the big money."

"Just give ol' Blue a little time to put a case together. He'll bring that old boy down, you wait and see. He'll get it done. You wanna put some money on it?"

Kohl came up on the radio. "All units stand by, the suspects are moving quickly to the fence to get their guns and masks. It looks like the victim is going to be a Hispanic male adult in the center island driving a one-ton flatbed truck. Stand by. Stand by."

Thibodeaux started the car, put it in gear, and this time eased his foot off the brake so the car crept along the street with the headlights off. The dark of the moonless night crowded in and made it more difficult to breathe. I had to focus in order to get any air.

"Stand by. Stand by." Kohl's tone lowered with each word.

His next words came out in a bark. "Now! Two-eleven in progress. Roll in. Roll in."

CHAPTER FIFTEEN

THIBODEAUX HIT THE gas. The patrol unit leaped forward into the darkness.

The headlights came on. Too bright at first.

We shot up Mona, headed for a red signal at Imperial Highway. I reached over to the Unitrol and flipped the switch for the overhead red-and-blue lights. We busted through the signal.

As we crossed Imperial Highway, in a brief snapshot of an image, I caught a glimpse of the gas station.

Ricky Blue had left the van in direct contradiction to orders and had come through the hole in the fence. He now stood at the lee side of the flatbed truck with a shotgun leveled. He confronted three people: one victim and two masked suspects.

The suspects fired at Blue with handguns. Blue let go with the shotgun that bellowed and spit out a bright flash.

In that same instant we crossed over Imperial, I instinctively brought my arm up for cover, half expecting shotgun pellets from Blue's gun to pepper the side of our patrol car and blast out the windows.

It all happened in less than a second.

We pulled into the alley, our assigned position. Gunfire continued in the parking lot of the gas station to the east and out of our view. I opened my door and jumped out before the car came to a complete stop. In my peripheral vision, Thibodeaux put the car in park and jumped out a half second behind me on his side.

With his left hand, he drew his gun and brought it up. In his haste, it hit the top frame of the open door. His gun skittered off into the darkness. He yelled, "My gun! My gun!"

He didn't go for the unit shotgun. He went down on his hands and knees in the dirt field that adjoined the alley. Frantic, he fumbled around in the dark.

The gun battle in the gas station parking lot went quiet.

Down the alley to the east, a masked suspect popped out of the hole in the fence and ran straight for us, trying to escape into the projects. Only he'd have to get by us first. He pulled his mask up. He didn't look ahead. He looked behind, running scared, running like a tiger chased him.

He ran right at us with a long-barreled revolver in his right hand. The game plan had gone to hell when the detectives in the van jumped their position and confronted the suspects in the gas station islands. We no longer had designated shooters. I brought my gun up to shoot just as Ricky Blue popped out of the hole in the fence. He swung his department-issue Ithaca Deerslayer shotgun around.

Leveled right at us.

I didn't have time to think. I dove for the ground, my eyes stuck on the approaching threat.

Blue held his finger down on the shotgun's trigger and racked it, firing again and again.

Some of the double-ought buck pellets slammed into the front of our patrol car.

The windshield shattered.

One headlight blinked out.

Glass tinkled to the ground close to my hand.

Pellets thumped into the crook's body. He let out a snort. His body spun around. He gasped for air and flew off balance. He fell and slid on the broken asphalt.

His inert form skidded to a stop two feet from me. His mouth opened and closed and opened and closed.

For the second time in two days, I smelled fresh blood, coppery and warm.

Blue walked toward us, thumbing shotgun shells into the breech, reloading.

Behind him, a second suspect popped out of the hole in the fence and ran north across the alley, into the field right by the van. He disappeared into the night. Detective Jenkins came out of the hole right behind him firing his handgun at the fleeing suspect.

Bam. Bam. Bam.

Blue didn't flinch or even turn. He racked a round into the shotgun and continued to walk toward the downed suspect, the one who lay too close to me for Blue to safely fire on.

I stood, my shaky gun pointed at the suspect on the ground. Bits of grit stuck in the palm of my other hand from the dive to the ground. Acrid gray smoke from Blue's shotgun hung in the still air.

Blue came up and nudged him with the barrel tip, the same as a hunter might do with dangerous prey. The crook didn't move. I didn't think he'd ever move again.

Blue looked up at me, his expression blank. He broke into a smile. "There isn't any workman's comp for armed robbers."

His words shocked me, his cynical coldness in the wake of such sudden violence.

Thibodeaux came around in front of the one working headlight, his found gun in hand, his words urgent. "You good, Blue?"

"*Sí, amigo.*"

Thibodeaux took off running straight up Mona in an attempt to cut off the suspect Jenkins chased, in case he decided to cut west toward the projects. I should've gone with him but couldn't get my legs to cooperate, or my knees to stop shaking.

Sirens filled the air, lots of them.

I forced myself to move. I took the couple of steps over to the suspect and got down on one knee beside him.

Blue stood close, not looking at the suspect. He scanned our surroundings as if danger still lurked in the shadows of the night. The one suspect could double back, or the people in the projects could come out en masse and cause a serious problem. It'd happened before.

Blue said, "Leave him be. Don't touch him."

I gently took hold of the suspect's shoulder. "I need to check his status. He might still be alive and need medical aid."

Blue looked down at me, his expression harsh. "You hear me, rookie? I said leave him be."

I pulled the suspect's shoulder and eased him over on his back. His black hoodie looked blacker with all the blood. And just like the night before with Pedro Armendez, in death, this guy's eyelids stayed hooded, showing only a slit of both eyes.

From the side, Blue stepped in quick and put his foot on the suspect's hand that still held the long-barreled handgun. "You're not going to make it out here, rookie. You need to listen to the people who know how to stay alive. You don't, you're gonna end up just like this poor slob, dead in some gutter, bleeding out. Now take his gun and secure the scene."

Blue took his foot off the suspect's hand. I did what he asked not because he'd asked, but because securing the gun followed protocol. I took it out of the suspect's warm hand and set it on the hood of the patrol car.

Blue stuck his shotgun out toward me in a nonthreatening manner, the gun pointed right at my gut. He used the barrel to move aside my green sheriff's windbreaker. When I'd bent over, he must've caught a glimpse of the model 59 Smith and Wesson in the shoulder holster. He smiled again. "Maybe you're not as green as you look." He didn't continue to scold me for carrying a ten-thirty weapon. And somehow, I knew he wouldn't tell anyone else about the policy violation.

Off in the distance, in the darkness of the night, three more gunshots echoed against the houses.

Blue brought the shotgun back up and let it rest casually against the top of his shoulder, the same as a bird hunter might after a long day of hunting quail or chucker. He smiled again. "Huh. Sounds like we might've just got ourselves a hat trick."

CHAPTER SIXTEEN

WITH THE SHOTGUN still resting on his shoulder, Blue walked by me and disappeared into the darkness toward Mona Boulevard. That's when I noticed his height, maybe five-seven or five-eight, short compared to my six-foot-three. I don't know why I thought he was taller.

Up close he looked like he might have a little Yaqui Indian mixed with Mexican. His nose stood out on his face a little too large in proportion. He also wore a sheriff's green windbreaker that couldn't disguise his muscular physique. He must've spent hours in the gym working the weight pile.

Our patrol unit, with the shot-out headlight and windshield, blocked the alley and sat next to the dead suspect, all of which became part of the crime scene and couldn't be moved. Ten minutes—or it might've been an hour later—yellow crime-scene tape surrounded the car and went all the way around the business on the corner where another cop car sat in the parking lot to keep pedestrians out. The shooting scene now took up the entire gas station, the alley, and the dirt field north of the alley.

All of a sudden I needed to get away from the dead guy next to the patrol car, so I walked east down the alley. I passed the expended green shotgun shells on the crumbling asphalt, the ones Blue fired at the fleeing suspect. I continued on to the fence where the detectives and the suspects came and went during the shooting. On the other side, a group of homicide detectives in rumpled suits stood talking with Sergeant Kohl. They stopped talking when they saw me. I froze. The gun under my windbreaker seemed to heat up, but it couldn't have been anything more than my imagination. No one could see the gun, and I had not even taken it out, let alone used it.

One of the homicide detectives waved his notebook at me. "Hey, you! Yeah you, ya dumbass. Get the hell outta that crime scene."

Kohl broke away and came over to the fence. "What's up, Bruno?"

"Nothing. I just . . . I can't . . . uh . . . our unit was involved in the shooting, and I'm going to need a ride back to the station."

"No problem. You're already here, so come on through." He pointed to the hole in the fence. I crouched down and slid through, making sure my windbreaker didn't come open or get hung up.

The same homicide dick said, "Hey, hey! What the hell?"

Kohl waved him off. "Come on," Kohl said to me. "I'll escort you to the street and get you a ride back to the station. You're gonna have to wait there to be interviewed. You're an eyewitness to the shooting."

"I understand, thanks." We walked by the group of detectives. The mouthy one shot us the stink eye.

I said to Kohl, "What's his problem?"

Kohl took my arm and guided us a little faster and farther away before he spoke. "That's the lieutenant from homicide, and he's pissed about the citizen getting smoked."

"The what? Are you kidding me? Really?"

A citizen caught in the crossfire, what a God-awful mess.

Kohl, still holding my elbow, looked over his shoulder and then steered us to the right and a little closer to the stake-bed truck.

On the dirty concrete, by the side of the truck, lay one crook still wearing his ski mask with an unsecured pistol next to him. Three feet away, rolled under the truck and on his side, lay the victim, the Hispanic male. He wore a tan work shirt soaked in blood. His eyes were frozen wide open in shock like his mouth, as if he couldn't believe what just happened to him.

He'd been shot point blank with a shotgun to the chest. His life winked out before he hit the ground.

I slowed, stunned and in awe of the scene. "Ah, shit."

"Exactly." Kohl guided us to the yellow tape at Imperial Highway and lifted it. I stepped under to the other side.

"What happened?"

Kohl lowered his voice almost to a whisper. "Ricky Blue jumped his position and confronted the two suspects and the victim on this side of the truck. I caught it all with the high-speed 35mm camera. The one suspect grabbed the victim and put a gun under his chin. That's when Blue came around with the shotgun."

"So, that's when it turned into a hostage situation."

Kohl shook his head. "The suspect took one look at Blue and didn't blink. He swung the victim around putting him in between, using the victim as a shield."

"Oh, man."

"Yeah. The suspect came over the victim's shoulder with his pistol to shoot Blue. Blue didn't have a choice. He fired and blew the victim right out of the suspect's hands. Bam! The victim goes down dead. The two suspects then open up on Blue."

"That's awful."

"You're telling me. I was up on that roof"—he pointed across the street—"and couldn't do a thing about it."

"I see what you mean. That's close quarters for a gunfight."

"They were maybe fifteen feet apart. And you're right, Blue's got balls the size of trash-can lids. He stands his ground and works the gauge. He takes out that one there"—Kohl pointed to the crook on the ground—"and then chases the second suspect through the hole in the fence and down the alley."

"That's where he shoots the other one right in front of me."

Kohl nods. "You're lucky you had the sense and state of mind to get the hell outta the way."

I tried to absorb and comprehend the hopeless tragedy of it all, though I really needed to put it aside for now, ponder it later. Someplace quiet and alone. That, or I'd end up standing on the street corner with a blank stare like some kind of zombie. I asked, "Is my lieutenant coming out?"

"I don't know. Haven't heard."

"How much shit is Blue in?"

"Right now, I couldn't tell ya. I don't know which way the cards are going to fall. He's easily justified in what he did once he confronted the robbers, but that's the rub. He shouldn't have moved from his position. I guess it's going to come down to how the report's written."

"What about the third suspect, did they get him?"

"Yeah, caught him hiding in a cockfighting ring in LAPD's area, just up that way a few blocks. Someone winged him with buckshot, but nothing serious."

So much for Blue's hat trick.

CHAPTER SEVENTEEN

THE SQUAD CAR came south on Mona and turned east on Imperial. Kohl saw it and flagged it down. The patrol deputy drove across the double yellow line on the wrong side of the street. Westbound traffic yielded for him. He came alongside us and stopped partially in the driveway of the gas station.

Kohl said to the deputy, "Hey, Mike, can you give Bruno here a ride back to the station?"

"Sure, Sarge. Hop in, Bruno."

I knew the driver, Michael Milts. We came out of the jail together and went through training at the same time in Lynwood. A good guy who did what needed to be done, and not much more. He went along to get along. He liked wearing the star on his chest, the idea of it. He didn't go out of his way to serve the public, and always jumped at the chance to claim "ghetto gunfighter" status when he'd yet to be involved in a shooting.

I opened the door and got in the front seat. Kohl bent down and said, "You know the routine, Bruno. Don't talk to anyone about what happened until homicide can interview you." He slapped the roof of the cop car, turned, and headed back.

I waved an acknowledgment too late. His words penetrated, but were again overcome by images of the dead that wouldn't leave me alone. The victim under the flatbed truck, the dead suspect in the alley, and, of course, Pedro Armendez. The worst part, though? I couldn't shake the phantom taste of Pedro's blood in my mouth. The way it kept coming back, warm and salty. I didn't know if I ever would.

I closed the door, and Milts took off driving across traffic to get back on the right side of the road.

In two and a half years on the street, I'd experienced plenty of death: car crashes; natural deaths; brutal, senseless murders. But I'd never experienced the cold, hard truth of death, not up close and personal like that. Nothing even came close in comparison. These last two sudden deaths hit me as a confused ambiguity that I couldn't rectify in my conscience, the moral right and wrong of them. All of this seemed needless, a terrible waste of human life, and played out as nothing more than a stupid game of cops and robbers.

Milts said nothing as he drove, which wasn't like him at all. I said, "Hey, what's been goin' on? You working late swing or the cover shift tonight? You here on OT?" With most of the shift working the shooting, the watch commander would have called in the next shift early.

He nodded toward the backseat. I turned and peered through the black mesh screen. Milts had another passenger who'd also needed a lift back to the station.

Ricky Blue.

Blue sat with his head back on the seat, his eyes closed. The passing streetlights flickered, revealing his face in flashes—the large nose, the black mustache, his shadowed eyes.

What he'd done came back in a rush and caused my anger to flare. The way he gunned down that kid without the smallest consideration for Thibodeaux or me, almost as if the killing of that kid meant more to him than the lives of his fellow deputies.

His lips moved. "Bruno. That's your name, right? Bruno Johnson?"

"That's right." I shouldn't have continued to stare at him, but with his eyes closed, he couldn't see me. And I somehow wanted to understand the man who could do what he did.

"I should've apologized out there in the alley," he said. "I shouldn't have fired like that with you on the other end of my gauge, not when you were so close to that asshole. I guess I just got all wrapped up in the moment. You know what I mean?"

"No, I don't. You could've hit me or your own partner, Thibodeaux."

He opened one eye, cocked his head to the side, and looked at me. "Or maybe I feared for *your* safety, and I didn't know if you'd have the nuts to drop the hammer on that little puke."

"Oh, is that right?" I said. "You're the one who jumped your position. You're the one who jeopardized the whole operation with that cowboy shit." I turned and faced front.

Milts, in a harsh whisper, said, "Holy shit, Bruno. Take it down a notch." He drove on, passing more streetlights and businesses closed for the night.

In truth, Blue had been right. I didn't know if I could've pulled the trigger, and that's where some of the anger came from: my inaction in the face of danger. I thought that I actually had been about to pull the trigger when Blue fired and I ducked to keep from getting hit.

I took several deep breaths and calmed, tried to think about something else and couldn't.

Even with the anger and acting like an ass, I still wanted to ask Blue some burning questions. I wanted to know how it felt to kill two human beings, what it did to his soul. It had to tear off a big chunk, a piece never to return, and that brought his soul closer to the edge of extinction. Which only served to bring up more questions: How much soul did one person have to risk? And how much did Blue have left?

I worked on a violent crimes team and Wicks had warned me specifically about what would happen. He'd been absolutely right. Only Blue handled it so casually, the same as if, sitting down to a big Sunday supper with lots of family, he had simply said, "Please pass the mashed potatoes." Maybe he'd already used up his allotment and didn't have any soul left.

I would never get that desensitized. If I did see it start to happen, I'd get out. If nothing else, I'd take a job delivering the mail.

Blue sucked his teeth, a sign of disrespect. "Johnson, just remember when they ask you, you be sure to tell 'em you saw the gun in his hand and he was running right at you. You tell 'em you were scared to death. That's all you gotta say. Just tell them the truth. You can do that much, can't you, kid? Tell the truth?"

"I've been ordered not to talk about it."

CHAPTER EIGHTEEN

SUNDAY AFTERNOON I caught the 91 Freeway and drove east, the window down, the warm wind on my face.

My muscles still moved with the slowness that comes with the fatigue of a marathon workday that had spanned almost seventy-two hours. My mind wallowed in a funk, still trying to catch up with all that had happened—with events that started from the moment Sonja knocked on my door.

I didn't get home from the shooting on Mona until five that morning, grabbed five hours' sleep—not near enough—had breakfast with Dad and my new daughter, and headed out to Lieutenant Wicks' barbecue.

I didn't want to go, not on my only day off. I needed more sleep and time to think. With this new job, I felt left far behind everyone else and had to continually run hard to catch up. I didn't know if it'd get any better or if it would always be like this. That's the part I had to think about. Did I want to run full speed without letup for the duration of my time on the violent crimes team? What kind of life would that be? And now I had a daughter to raise, another large responsibility to factor in. The largest.

Earlier that morning I'd awakened to Wicks' page. The beeper screech sliced into my raw nerves. I leaped out of bed, looking for my gun, looking for a suspect lurking in the shadowy recesses of my old room.

My old room?

What the hell was I doing there?

And then I remembered.

I shook off the sleep as best I could and, half-awake, shuffle-stepped into the kitchen to the phone mounted on the wall and called Wicks.

He answered. “Hey, Bruno? You still comin’ over this afternoon?”

“What?”

“You still in bed? Come on, man, wake up. You can’t be sleepin’ your life away. Get up and smell the coffee and get your ass over here.”

“What are you talking about?”

“The barbecue, remember? You said you’d come over and help celebrate the team’s first takedown. I’m grillin’ up some shark steaks. Get your ass in gear. The other guys are on their way.”

At least this time he didn’t refer to it as *the team’s first kill.*

“Yeah, sure, I’ll be there.”

No way would I be the only guy on the team who didn’t show up; otherwise I’d have gracefully declined.

He gave me the address.

When I hung up, guilt crept in. I needed to spend time with my daughter. How would I prioritize work with family? The logic of it seemed simple: without work, I couldn’t support my family, but if I worked all the time there wouldn’t be any family. I’d have to ask Dad. He’d know; he’d raised Noble and me. And that worked out, for the most part anyway. Not so much with Noble. There had to be some sort of easy formula to follow. Too many other people did it without any problem. How hard could it be?

After two freeway transitions, I got off in Whittier and made the turns I’d memorized from looking at the Thomas Guide.

He’d said one o’clock, and yet at one fifteen no other cars sat out front of the address. Had I gotten the numbers wrong? The house was in a predominantly white neighborhood and looked no different than the others on the block—a single-story wood-framed rambler, painted beige with brown trim and red brick that went from the ground to halfway up the wall. The front lawn needed mowing, and the composition shingle roof looked new. I didn't know what I expected from the great Robby Wicks' house, but this wasn't it. The place looked so ordinary.

Wicks' head appeared over the top of a cedar plank gate at the side, his hair perfectly combed. From the backyard, how had he known I'd pulled up out front? Had to be that predatory instinct of self-preservation that he couldn't turn off.

He waved, opened the gate, and stepped out. He smiled and again waved me in like an old friend just coming in from six months at sea. Neither of his arms moved like they'd taken a bullet just two nights prior in that alley off 123rd and Central.

I turned the truck off, grabbed the bottle of red wine from the seat, and walked over.

He wore starched and ironed denim pants with a sharp crease, a white long-sleeve shirt, and a blue apron that went down to just above his knees. He held a barbecue fork in one hand and a beer in the other. "Hey, good to see ya, Bruno. Thanks for comin'."

I looked around and held up my hands. "Where's everyone else?"

"Ah, screw 'em, if they can't take a joke. We don't need anyone else to have a kick-ass party." He spoke with a hint of a slur. His eyes stood out, bloodshot and watery. The odor of metabolized alcohol emitted from his breath and person. He'd been at it for a while. He turned to lead the way. On his right hip he wore an inside-the-belt holster with a Colt .45 Combat Commander sticking up. This one sported deerstag grips. He even carried heavy while in his own backyard. Part of that predatory instinct again.

"Hey," I said to his back.

He stopped and turned.

I pointed to the Colt. "You expecting trouble while you're barbecuing? Is there something I should know about?"

He came back, moved in close to me, smiling, his alcohol breath stronger and hoppy from the beer. He took another pull off his can, wiped his mouth on his sleeve. Something he would never have done sober. "Let me tell you something about me, my friend. You'll figure it out eventually, but here it is. I strongly subscribe to the theory that you never need a handgun until you *really* need a handgun. Words to live by, my friend. Words to live by."

Not me. I couldn't go through life with that level of paranoia.

He let that sink in, then said, "Hey, you wanna beer? Let me get you a beer, old buddy." He turned to yell, "Bar—"

A pretty woman in black slacks and a sleeveless yellow chiffon blouse appeared with two sweating beers. Her arms were muscular and lean, her smile the kind that lit up the world.

CHAPTER NINETEEN

WICKS SLUGGED DOWN the remainder of his beer, crumpled the can with one hand, and tossed the empty over by the barbecue amongst a pile of at least six others. He took the fresh one from her. "Thanks, babe. Oh, this is my favorite deputy, Bruno Johnson. Bruno, my lovely wife, Barbara. She's a patrol copper in Montclair."

She handed me the second beer and shook my hand. Her eyes stayed with mine as she continued to smile warmly. "Favorite? That's some title. You must really be something special."

My face flushed hot. "Your husband's just being nice. He hardly knows me."

Again, I didn't know what I expected for a wife, but she definitely seemed too nice for the likes of Wicks. Which wasn't really fair because I hardly knew him.

Wicks shoved his beer can in my direction. "Not true. Babe, you remember me telling you about this guy. He's the one that tracked that wounded car, chased it on foot for two-and-a-half, three miles, took down a murderer, a guy who ran down that child, that little girl in the crosswalk. Put the boot to him, too. Had to pull him off."

The shame from that incident returned. I'd lost control on that suspect and vowed that it would never happen again.

At the same time, his description also brought back the image of Jenny lying in the street and reminded me that I, too, now had a daughter at home who needed protection from a violent and dangerous world. The weight of that responsibility seemed insurmountable.

Barbara still held my hand and squeezed it again. "You should be honored. I'm serious, he doesn't often talk this way."

I tried to look away from her eyes and couldn't. "Ah, he's just drunk, ma'am."

Wicks put his hand with his beer on our two hands. "That's enough of that, Bruno. Unhand my wife." He laughed. "Come on. Come sit."

I followed them both to the picnic table and sat down. I opened the beer and drank. The taste reminded me of the last beer I had, the one on Holt Boulevard in Pomona, at the Pedro Armendez crime scene.

The beer tasted great on a hot summer afternoon. I could get used to it. I never drank a lot. Dad didn't go much for liquor. In fact, I'd only seen him drink one time, and after that I never wanted to see him drink again.

With the second beer, I quickly put aside all those other thoughts and started to decompress. I sat at the picnic table and dipped corn chips in salsa and talked with the lovely Barbara Wicks. She talked easily about working a patrol car for the Montclair police department, the mundane exploits of small-town law enforcement. But she spoke of them with excitement and verve. She told of how she met Robby two years ago at a domestic violence seminar, a POST—Peace Officers Standards and Training—update on mandated reporting, in San Diego. I just couldn't picture Robby going to a DV seminar.

Robby Wicks stood at his grill, and with the slight breeze, the smoke rose and swirled about him, giving the appearance of an apparition. His eyes watered enough to streak his face with tears. He laughed at his own jokes and continued to match me beer for beer. We crumpled the cans and tossed them onto the growing pile on the ground by the barbecue. He flipped the raw vegetables on the grill and forked the small sausages to us one at a time to munch before he put on the main course, thresher shark steaks. Big slabs of fish, stacked on a platter and covered in wax paper, sat on the wooden picnic table next to us.

After the third beer, the afternoon smoothed out. I didn't know how I'd drive home and no longer cared. With the warm sun and the camaraderie, all the ugliness from the last three days continued to just melt away. Maybe a barbecue after a takedown wasn't such a bad idea after all.

I helped Barbara bring out the plates and flatware. We set them on the picnic table already covered with a red-checked tablecloth. I tried not to act too much like an enamored puppy. I filled an ice chest with some Dr. Pepper, along with the rest of the beer, and brought it outside so we wouldn't have to walk so far to get resupplied. Barbara added a fifth of vodka, a bottle of vermouth, and a jar of olives.

I sat back down. She offered me another beer, and I waved her off. She also sat down.

"Hey," I said, "where's everyone else? Should we be worried about them?"

She sipped her dirty vodka martini, the first one of the afternoon, and leaned in a little, her eyes probing. "Robby called the other three and uninvited them."

Just that fast I lost my sense of humor and sat back, feeling like I'd somehow been ambushed and used. For some reason, they wanted to turn me into everybody's fool, and I couldn't fathom why. The beers filled my head with cotton and didn't help.

"Why?"

She sipped again, her eyes still not leaving mine. "You have to believe me, Bruno, this was beyond our control."

"What was?"

She'd said "our" as if she'd become a part of whatever was happening.

"Robby got a phone call," she said, "right after he talked to you." She paused and looked over at her husband at the grill.

"And?"

She looked back at me. "Let's just say this has turned into a working lunch."

"Ah, man, are you kiddin' me? What are you talking about here? Working? How?"

No way could she mean strapping a gun on and going after a violent felon, not with all the alcohol on board. They'd lured me there for a reason, to ask something of me. I didn't like the smell of it. They'd used the beautiful warm day, the beer, the camaraderie, to soften the blow.

"This is going to be real bad, isn't it?"

CHAPTER TWENTY

BARBARA SAID, "SILLY boy, of course not. Robby just wants to talk to you about something and it's better if no one else hears."

I should've felt honored. Instead, I felt betrayed. The afternoon's good cheer fled on shaky legs, and suddenly the intensity of the sun caused me to break out in a sweat. They'd turned me into a staked goat. The worst part, they didn't even have the common courtesy to ask. They just did it.

From over by the grill, Robby said, "You tell him yet, babe? You getting him all prepped like we talked about?"

The gall, talking about how they wanted to butter me up, doing it right out in the open as if I meant nothing more to them than a hand puppet. I stood. "What's going on? Tell me now."

Barbara just looked up at me, sipped some more of the cocktail. "It's okay, Bruno. Take it easy. This is a good thing. Trust me." Still sitting on the bench, she reached out and took hold of my hand, hers cool to the touch on the hot day.

I pulled away. She got up, hesitated, and went into the house to leave me alone with Wicks. I took the few steps over to him at the grill. "Tell me what this is all about. I don't like being blindsided."

Wicks smiled, his eyelids a little droopy from all the beer. "Take it easy, big man. Listen to my wife. Like she said, this is a good thing."

He picked up the platter, pulled off the wax paper, and used his fingers to lay the slabs of shark on the grill. He started to pull off the foil-wrapped corn on the cob, picking them up with bare fingers, jerking his hands and shaking them from the heat.

The fish sizzled.

He said nothing more as I waited for the explanation, too scared to walk away without it.

He picked up a plastic container with a brush and pasted on some thick and smooth white paste. He said, "The key to making great shark steaks on the grill is this concoction right here, baby. It's my old family secret recipe: mayonnaise, a dash of lemon, a dollop of sour cream, and just a hint of paprika. Keeps the steaks moist."

I stared at him as the smoke rose, carrying a marvelous aroma that made my stomach growl, embarrassing me further. Even my stomach took every opportunity to betray me. "Well, you gonna tell me, or am I gonna walk out?"

Robby didn't turn to see that Barbara had gone into the house. He said, "Hey, babe, I'm a little parched. Could you please get us a coupla beers?"

"She went inside. And I don't want to sound ungrateful, but you're going to tell me what's going on right now, or I'm leaving."

The gate at the side of the house scraped. I looked over to see a thin, gray-haired gentleman come into the backyard. I looked back at Robby, who didn't draw his .45. He didn't seem to care that this guy violated the sanctity of his inner kingdom.

The old guy, dressed in new khaki pants and a casual green polo shirt, came right over to me and offered his hand. "You must be Deputy Bruno Johnson. It's nice to finally meet you, son."

Wicks turned around, his eyes still weeping from the smoke, the barbecue fork in hand, and said, "Bruno, this is Deputy Chief Rudyard."

Deputy Chief? Ah, shit.

Wicks said, "Well, shake his hand, man."

I took his hand and shook. My next words came out softer than before. "What the hell's going on?"

Deputy Chief Rudyard laughed. "Not exactly the reaction I'd expect. Robby, I'm guessing you haven't told him."

"Not yet, boss. We were waiting on you."

"I see. Leave the dirty work for me. You have another one of those beers? Bruno, let's sit and take a load off."

Barbara came out of the house carrying a tray with a green leaf salad, a pasta salad, and a casserole of scalloped potatoes hot from the oven. The load made the muscles in her arms stand out. The Deputy Chief hurried over and relieved her of it. "Here, let me take that."

The chief ogled her. My mouth sagged open in shock. He made no attempt to cover it, leered at her right out in the open.

Barbara had to have seen it. "Why thank you, Bill. That's very gentlemanly of you." She handed him the tray.

I turned to look. Wicks had his back to us, working the shark steaks on the grill, or this might've been one of those instances where he "*really* needed a handgun" to dust off the chief with a couple of .45 slugs. Alcohol and firearms and another man's wife never mix well in anyone's backyard.

Wicks turned. "Hey, these babies are ready to eat. Get 'em while they're hot."

Barbara hustled over with the platter. He forked them on.

In a daze, I didn't know what to do and went along with them. There wasn't anything else for it. I sat down. Barbara put a steak on each of our plates and then sat down next to me and across from the chief. Wicks sat next to the chief.

Wicks handed me the pasta salad and smiled. I couldn't help thinking that it looked like the wolf smiling at the goat. I took the bowl from him and my gaze caught the contrast of his skin to mine. I usually didn't let that bother me. But under the circumstances, the fact that I was the only black man sitting at a table with three pasty whites, in a white neighborhood, with a dark secret among them that they were all afraid to give up, made me shiver a little.

Everyone loaded their plates and started to eat. I guessed we'd talk about it later when they were ready.

I took a bite of the shark. My mouth lit up with wonderful, mouth-watering sensations. The shark was nothing less than spectacular.

The chief spoke first. "I want to commend you boys on the great start with this new team. Truly amazing. You're really making me look good."

I stopped chewing and looked at him. I wanted to point out the senseless body count and would have, had the food not hit my stomach and started to sober me up enough to keep my comments to myself rather than commit career suicide.

Wicks said, "Thank you, Chief."

Barbara reached over and squeezed my arm. She smiled at me. I caught the chief looking at her hand on my arm, his mouth a straight line. He broke his gaze and redirected his attention to his plate.

One thing I knew for sure, I didn't belong there and needed to extricate myself as soon as possible. Hopefully with my career still intact.

CHAPTER TWENTY-ONE

THE CHIEF PUT a bite of shark in his mouth and then pointed his empty fork at me. "Bruno, Robby says you ran the op in Pomona and caught that escaped prisoner from CIM. Did it in about two hours flat. That's some good work, boy. Really great for the team's first effort."

I looked at Wicks, who smiled and took another swig of his beer, the food on his plate hardly touched. I nodded, afraid of commenting, afraid the words would get out of control.

I wished Armendez had not died at my hand.

The chief shook his head. "Then last night, *hmm*, that was really something else, too."

The emotions of the shooting in the alley, the confrontation with Blue, still burned hot in my memory. I fought the urge to complain about what had happened, how Blue failed to follow orders and ultimately got three people killed. How Wicks wasn't there to take care of his men. How I'd been forced to go back in uniform. That last one sounded petty even to me.

I said nothing.

Wicks took a pull off his can of beer and said, "That wasn't any of our guys who dropped the hammer on that one, Chief."

Wicks words came out as if disappointed we didn't shoot.

The chief looked at me when he spoke. "I know, and that's why we're here today, isn't it?"

I set my fork down. Now I knew why all the special treatment came my way. They wanted me to rat out Blue, speak to "Internal Affairs," tell them what really happened. But my statement wouldn't make a difference. They already knew exactly what happened. Nobody tried to cover anything up. Sure, Blue acted like some kinda arrogant asshole, but that wasn't a violation of policy.

Unless they intended to bang Blue for jumping his position, going against the plan and confronting the two suspects while the suspects held onto the victim.

Still, not a big deal—that violation of policy only rated, maybe, a letter of reprimand or a day or two on the bricks.

The chief looked down and stirred around some pasta salad while everyone waited for him to speak. He looked up and again pointed his fork at Wicks then at me. "There's something neither one of you knows about."

Disgusted, he let his fork drop and clatter on his plate. He took a napkin off his lap and wiped his mouth and shook his head. "I don't know. Blue, that bastard, I can't figure him. He's a walking contradiction."

Wicks asked, "What do you mean, Chief?"

The chief's eyes went to Barbara.

The awkward moment hung thick in the air. Barbara stood and picked up her plate. "Guess that's my cue." She gave us a cardboard smile. "I'll be inside. Call me when it's okay to come back out and rejoin the boys' club."

"No, wait," the chief said. "I didn't mean to make you feel that way. We can talk about this later, Barbara. I don't want to run you off and ruin your dinner."

Barbara just smiled and kept moving toward the door, the perfect hostess.

Wicks said, "Thanks, babe."

The chief waited until the door closed. "That's a good woman you have there, Robby."

"Don't I know it."

The chief looked across the table at me as if he didn't know how to start the conversation, and with him, I bet that didn't happen too often.

Wicks helped him out. "What is it that we don't know, Chief?"

The chief nodded as if he'd made up his mind. "Before I get to that, let me first get to the question. Bruno, we need to ask a big favor of you."

I leaned back, stared at the chief, the food in my stomach starting to sour. "I figured as much."

Wicks said, "Take it easy with the mouth, Bruno. This is a chief talking here."

"It's okay, Robby, I've got this. Bruno, we want you to go undercover."

"What?"

This wasn't at all what I expected. Undercover wouldn't be so bad. In fact, I'd always wanted to try it. Go deep undercover after the major narcotics dealers, the ones selling their poison to the kids on the street. Go after people like Papa Dee and Lucas Knight, really make an impact and improve the quality of life in the ghetto. "Who's the target and where?"

"There really isn't any easy way to say it," the chief said. "I'm going to reassign you to the narcotics street team at Lynwood. Temporarily. It'll just be for a week or two, maybe a little more. I don't think it'll go that long. But it'll have to look like a permanent assignment, so I don't want you to worry about that."

I got up, threw my napkin down on the table, and headed for the gate. I didn't care what the chief thought. No way would I work undercover as a rat. Even if it worked out perfectly, I could never come out of the assignment unscathed. I'd be labeled a pariah. No deputy anywhere would ever trust me again for anything. No one in any other agency would either.

Behind me, Wicks got up and said to the chief, "Let me talk to him." He hurried to catch up.

He caught my arm as I reached for the gate latch, his voice harsh. "What the hell's the matter with you, man? When a chief asks you for a favor, you never turn him down. You just do it and say, 'Thank you, sir, can I have another?' What you don't do is throw a childish little fit and stomp off."

"I'm nobody's rat."

"You haven't even heard him out. How do you know what's going down?"

"Well?"

"Well, what?"

"Is the plan for me to go undercover and catch Blue's team dirty, stealing dope and money or both?"

"No."

"What?"

Now I was confused. I looked him in the eye to see the lie and couldn't. "Why isn't IAB doing this? Why me?"

"It's because of what Blue said in the interview last night. That's what the chief was getting at before you threw your little hissy fit."

"I didn't throw any hissy fit. What did Blue say in the interview?"

I could only imagine what he'd told them after our confrontation in the cop car on the way back to the station. The nerve of the bastard saying he shot the kid to save my life and for me to be sure to tell the shooting team the kid was running at me with a gun in his hand.

"Blue said you showed more balls out there than he's seen in a long time. He said he'd trust you with his life, anytime. And since he needs a black undercover for his street team to do hand-to-hands, he called the chief and asked for you."

"He did what?"

"That's right, he asked for you. So, you see how perfectly it works out? This thing just fell right into our lap."

"What do you mean 'perfectly'?"

"Just come back and sit down. Listen to the whole pitch before you make a decision that'll torpedo your career. And when I say torpedo, that's an understatement. You'll blow it right out of the water for good."

I tried to make sense of everything he'd just said. "So, I'm not being kicked off the violent crimes team?" I knew that didn't make sense, either, but I needed a few more seconds to think and try and put it all together so I didn't sound like a total idiot. Only I couldn't put it together, not without all the information, the missing piece.

"No. No, of course you're not leaving the team. You just heard a part of it and then you jumped up and ran off half-cocked."

"I don't like being made a patsy and I don't think you would either. You wouldn't have sat there like some sort of chump. It doesn't really matter, it still doesn't sound like anything I want to do."

I tried to imagine what it would be like to stand up in court, raise my right hand, and testify against my fellow deputies. Or worse, testify against someone like Blue.

The lack of sleep, the warm sun, and the alcohol worked as contributing factors to my unruly behavior. I didn't want to give Wicks those excuses. He deserved a yes or a no.

Wicks nodded. "Okay, look, I handled this whole thing wrong from the beginning and I'm sorry. We should've been more up front with you. Come on back to the table, and we'll explain it all to you."

Even with the fatigue and alcohol as factors, the little voice in my head kept yelling, "Run away, run away. You want no part of this screwed-up mess."

"If it's not about the dope or the money, then what is it about?"

"There's a problem with answering that question, Bruno."

"Bullshit."

"No, I'm not allowed to tell you unless you say you're in. Are you in?"

"How do I know if I want to be 'in' if I don't know what 'in' entails?"

Wicks stared into my eyes and wouldn't answer. I wilted under his glare and looked away, down and to the left. My eyes caught a glimpse of something. On his white shirtsleeve, high up by the bicep, a small spot of fresh blood appeared. Not big, but one large enough to have seeped through a tightly wrapped bandage. The entire afternoon he'd not said a word about the amazing feat he'd accomplished. All alone, standing toe to toe with the armed and dangerous murderer Damien Frakes Jr. Going to guns with him close enough to feel the heat and concussion from Frakes' muzzle flash. If Wicks could do that, what the hell was I complaining about? All of a sudden I wanted to prove to him that I could do something worthy of his approval.

"Ah, shit, okay, okay, I'm in. Tell me."

He hesitated; the delay made me hold my breath.

"You sure?" he asked.

"Just tell me."

"It's murder for hire, Bruno. They're doing contract killings."

CHAPTER TWENTY-TWO

"MURDER FOR HIRE? Are you kidding me? No way. Not Los Angeles County sheriff's deputies."

"Come on." Wicks escorted me over to the picnic table where Deputy Chief Rudyard continued to eat his lunch. Life went on for him as if nothing at all had happened, as if no careers or innocent lives hung in the balance. Throughout his career, he must've heard a lot worse, been involved in the destruction of many deputies, and at the same time their families.

I again sat across from him.

He looked up, his congeniality gone, his expression grim. I'd screwed up and slipped over onto his bad side. That mattered to me. I'd have to work hard and try to fix it.

Wicks sat down next to him. "Everything's fine now, Chief. Bruno's on board; we're a go."

The chief stared at me as he stuck another piece of shark in his mouth and chewed. Finally, he nodded and smiled. But I didn't believe it to be genuine. He'd only smiled as a political ploy to get the job done. I understood the dynamic, understood I should apologize. Only I couldn't. My arrogance wouldn't allow for that breach in pride. So I waited.

He pointed his fork at Wicks. "Go on, tell him the rest." He waved his fork. "You know the part I'm talking about."

Wicks said to me, "Okay, look, here's what we know. Blue and Thibodeaux were working SPY. While operating in and around the prisons, they somehow got tangled up with EME, the Mexican mafia. They got in ass-deep and started answering to EME's shot caller, a guy named Sonny Quintero who's doing life without. From what we understand, they did small jobs at first until they moved up to the bigger paydays."

"And we know this how?"

Wicks looked at the chief, who shoveled scalloped potatoes into his mouth and nodded.

How did the man stay so thin and eat like that?

Wicks said, "This goes nowhere, you understand? There are only four people who know this, and you make five. So if it gets out, it won't be difficult to backtrack where it came from."

I didn't like being threatened, or having my integrity impugned, but no longer had a choice. I'd agreed to join them.

Wicks hesitated.

The information must've really been radioactive.

He said, "It's a wiretap."

I looked from the chief, who'd stopped chewing then back to Wicks, and in that moment of perfect clarity figured it all out.

I shook my head. "My God, it's a black bag wiretap, isn't it? That's why you can't bring in the DA or IAB."

The chief gave me another one of his Cheshire cat smiles and turned to Wicks. "You told me he's a smart son of a bitch and now I see what you mean."

Everything fell into place with those two simple words, the ones they'd been too afraid to say: black bag. I now understood why they'd treated me the way they had. Once I was told about the black bag job, I would forever hold sway over them, over their careers, over their freedom. Not a power you'd easily hand to someone you didn't know well, not even something you'd hand to your best friend. And yet they'd thought enough of me to trust with this huge bit of damning information.

"So, you have them on tape," I asked, "accepting a contract from EME to kill someone?"

The chief picked up his fork and pointed it at me. He opened his mouth to speak when Wicks stopped him by putting his hand on the chief's arm.

"Listen, Bruno, it's better if you don't know the whole thing. We trusted you enough to tell you this much. I'm asking *you* to trust *us* and not ask for specifics. What I want to do—that is, if it's okay with the chief—is give you a specific assignment: what to look for and what evidence we'll need. The less you know about the front end of this thing, the better it'll be for everyone. If you don't know, you can't testify about it."

It could also aid in plausible deniability for *them* as well.

"Why not shut it down right now, forget the criminal prosecution? Fire both of them and be done with it? If you let it run, you risk innocent people—the future victims of the contracts—getting killed."

The chief looked at Wicks, which meant for him to take this one.

Wicks said, "First off, none of the people EME are taking off the board are taxpayers. Don't get me wrong, that doesn't matter; victims are victims. And they're murderers, criminals. And that's what we do; we put people like them in jail for the rest of their lives. But still, those aren't the biggest reasons. The biggest reason here is that the chief and I believe there's someone else."

The chief said, "That's right, the dog heavy."

"The what?"

"We're pretty sure Blue is calling the shots for him and Thibodeaux. Pretty sure, but that's not an absolute. There's some reason to believe there's someone else above them. We need to let it run a little while longer to be sure there isn't anyone else. Or if there is, that we can identify him and take him down with the other two."

I let all this astounding information run in my head for a moment. "All right," I said, "I understand. But for now, let's focus on Blue and Thibodeaux and talk this through. Evidence requires a basis, a trail in how you came to have the information in order to use it in court. Say I get enough on Blue and Thibodeaux, how are we going to complete the chain of evidence and justify my transfer from the violent crimes team to a narcotics street team when I've only been on violent crimes a few days? It'll stink of a setup. People will start to ask . . . Ah, shit."

I marveled at the simplicity of it. "That's why you said it was perfect. Blue personally asked for me."

"Son of a bitch, Robby. This kid's sharp as a tack."

My mind spun out far ahead, trying to see how this could turn out any other way than in a major disaster.

And couldn't. Not one chance in hell.

Wicks read my mind. "We know this isn't the best setup and that it's going to be extremely dangerous."

That's what Sergeant Kohl said in the briefing for the Mona gas station surveillance, that it wasn't the best setup. Look how that ended. Another red flag that said I should just get up and leave. Take a flyer and run for it.

"Blue is smart," Wicks said. "Cunning, smart, and highly effective. In a way, I wish I were the one going up against him instead of you. But the way the cards fell, you're the best man for this job. You're also not married and you don't have any kids. You can devote all the time necessary to make this work. You won't have the responsibility of family influencing your decisions so you can step out onto that edge and—"

The chief pointed his fork at Wicks. "Ah, but that's no longer true. He does have a family now." He shifted and pointed the fork at me.

"Don't you, son? Just a couple of days ago, you found out you had a baby daughter, didn't you?"

The world spun as vertigo set in. I grabbed hold of the picnic table for balance. How in the hell did he know?

Wicks said, "What? What's he talking about, Bruno? You had a baby and didn't tell me about it?"

His words swirled around in my head and exited the same way they came in as I tried desperately to figure out how and where the chief got his information.

Click.

It came to me just like that.

Millie, the redhead from the shower, on the day Sonja knocked on my door. She was the captain's secretary at Lynwood Station. Of course, she was the only one who could've passed on that little gem of truth. That meant the captain and chief also knew I'd been messing around with Millie.

A white woman. Ah, man.

In this day and age that shouldn't still matter, but it did.

I waved my hand in an attempt at a casual dismissal. "My daughter won't affect my work product, I can promise you that." The words "my daughter" came out alien, as if someone else said them. How could I have a daughter?

One part of me wanted to turn down the assignment because of her. The other part wanted the excitement, the adventure of it. The kind of thrill I'd seen in Wicks' eyes just now as he described going after Blue. But I no longer had the option to decline. I'd already agreed. When I did, Wicks and the chief let the genie out of the bottle.

And everyone knows that once the genie's out, he won't ever go back in. Not without force.

Not without a lot of dead bodies.

CHAPTER TWENTY-THREE

"All right," I said. "Then, as we agreed, give me the details on my specific assignment."

Wicks smiled. "Good, good. So listen, we're going to come at this from a different angle. We're going to get a legal search warrant for the phone taps and we're depending on you to get us probable cause for that warrant. So it doesn't matter if the warrant is for dope, money skimming, or whatever, just get us that PC for the tap. They're doing contract killings; you can bet it doesn't stop there."

The chief stood. "I think it's time that I take my leave and let you two work out the particulars." He wiped his mouth and hands on the red-checked napkin. He offered me his hand. We shook. "Bruno, I'm proud to have you on board. I know you'll do a great job. And rest assured, you'll have the full backing of my office during this investigation." He turned to Wicks. "Give your lovely wife my thanks and make my excuses, would you, Robby?"

"Sure, Chief. Thanks for coming."

We both watched him walk to the gate and disappear into the front yard.

I turned back to Wicks and said, "The clean search warrant still won't allow you to use what you already have because the dates won't line up with when you obtained the information on the black bag wiretap. You'll have to start all over with this new tap. If they don't tumble to what I'm doing, you'll still have to wait for them to get another contract. That could cut it a little close for the next victim."

Another thought hit me.

"Just to be clear, there hasn't been a victim since you went up on the wiretap, right?"

"No. No one's been hurt. I give you my word on that."

"Good."

That would not only be our jobs, but it would also be a "failure to protect" lawsuit worth tens of millions of dollars. We'd also end up in federal court and then in the federal slam.

"Okay," I said. "How about this 'dog heavy' thing? I've never heard that used before."

"Believe me, I didn't know either. The chief had to explain it to me. The chief comes from a family of movie and TV people. His father was one of the cameramen on *I Love Lucy*. Before that, his grandfather directed silent movies. In the silent movies of the '20s and '30s, if the bad guy was the town banker, the mayor, or someone in a position of authority, this guy would kick a dog when no one was looking, to let the audience know he was the bad guy. Back then he became known in the trade as 'the dog heavy.'"

That made sense, sort of, but I'd only half-listened.

I'd never done anything like this, going outside the law, crossing over that defined line between black and white—going deep into the black—to grab a crook and scurry back across to file the case. I was amazed at how easily I fell in with this concept. Maybe it was because a cop was involved and was giving us—law enforcement—a black eye.

Or maybe it was because that cop was Blue.

Though I did know the truth of the matter, I didn't want to look at it head-on. I'd already gotten dirty, the night I pulled that drunk driver, Jenny's murderer, through the screen door and put the boot to him. He'd gotten what he deserved. No doubt. Only not in the way the law prescribed.

In any case, I'd made my decision to join up in this operation and needed to keep my head in the game.

"And you're right, we won't be able to use any of the past information, only the new stuff *you* dig up," Wicks said. "But if we do this right and we don't spook them, when they take another contract, you'll be in place to watch for the overt act."

"Overt act? So, we'll take them down for PC 182/187, conspiracy to commit murder, before they even get close to doing it?"

"Yes, of course. What else did you think we were going to do?"

Even as a new detective, this didn't sound right. First, I'd never worked undercover; second, these two guys, Blue and Thibodeaux, would never take a stranger into their confidence to commit one of the gravest of crimes. Not without some serious validation on my part. The kind where I committed felonies right alongside them until they had enough dirt on me to carry the load.

"And if we're real lucky," Wicks said, "and you do your job right, maybe they'll even invite you into the inner circle to take the contract or at least to assist." He shrugged. "Maybe this won't work at all, but when Blue asked the chief for you, it was just too sweet a deal to pass up."

He shoved away his plate of cold and congealed food. "What's this about a baby daughter? What the hell happened—you accidentally knock up some one-night stand?"

Sonja wasn't some "one-night stand." His accusation made my face flush hot.

I jumped up. "You're my boss and I have a great deal of respect for you, so I'm telling you right now, don't ever refer to her that way again."

"Whoa! Whoa there, buddy! I'm sorry. I stepped over the line. I didn't know the circumstances. I misspoke. Sorry. Take it easy, okay?"

I tried to control my breathing.

"I know a kid complicates things a lot," Wicks said. "And, of course, I want you to tell me when the job clashes with your family life. I'll do everything in my power to compensate for it. Deal?" He stuck out his hand. I took it and shook.

I sat back down. I, too, had lost my appetite, but I ate a little more as a distraction to think over all that had just transpired. To put all the pieces together to see if they fit the way they had been presented. I stopped chewing. "Hey, the chief never explained that thing that we didn't know."

"What are you talking about?"

"You know, when he was talking about Blue, and how he was a contradiction?"

"Oh, that. I think I know. What he meant to tell us was that when Blue got back to the station, and during the interview with homicide, right in the middle of it, he just casually stood up, took off his sheriff's windbreaker, took off his shirt, and showed the dicks his body armor. And get this: he'd taken two slugs to the chest. Homicide dick I talked to said it was the damnedest thing he'd ever seen."

"You're kidding."

I thought back to the ugly events: Blue walking toward me in the alley, a smoking shotgun in his hands, his words, the way he moved. I would never have guessed he'd just been shot. It wasn't like in the movies. Bullets to the chest with body armor caused trauma and a great deal of pain and in some cases even turned life threatening.

Wicks continued, "He never said a thing about it to anyone at the scene. Two huge bruises to his chest. He could've had a bruised heart or internal bleeding. He should've been transported right from the scene and checked out at the hospital. You believe it? Never told a soul and then just stood up right in that interview, showed those two homicide dicks as if it were no big deal at all. The slugs were still embedded in the vest."

I shook my head. How could someone, a cop who crosses the line to commit the most heinous of crimes, display such bravado?

"So, here's the deal," Wicks said. "The chief still looks at these two, Thibodeaux and Blue, as low-down dirty dogs for committing these types of crimes, especially under the color of authority. But to take two to the vest while taking down two asshole robbers . . . well, there's the contradiction he was talking about."

Something Thibodeaux had said just bubbled up. Words from a conversation the night before, while we sat in the car waiting for the robbery to go down. Those words echoed back in my brain, simple words that changed everything in the way I looked at my world.

CHAPTER TWENTY-FOUR

I STARED OFF into nothing as my mind ran full tilt to catch up, to calculate all the horrible ramifications.

Wicks must've seen it in my expression. "What? What's the matter?"

I looked at Wicks. "You're a lying asshole."

Wicks looked as if I'd slapped him. He recovered, shifted to anger. "Don't you talk to me like that. I'm a sheriff's lieutenant, *Deputy* Johnson."

I pointed at him. "Last night, Thibodeaux told me that Blue just randomly volunteered for the robbery surveillance. No warning, right out of thin air, a street narco team jumps into a robbery surveillance with station detectives and the violent crimes team. That just doesn't happen."

Wicks' expression shifted again to one of concern and then discomfort as he squirmed in his seat. He watched me closely to see if I'd put the whole thing together. "Don't, Bruno. Stop right there. Don't say another word. You don't want to say it. It's better for—"

"One of those two robbers Blue killed was a contract hit, wasn't it?"

"Shit, Bruno. Ah, shit." He slapped the picnic table with his hand. Everything bounced, the plates, the glasses, the condiments.

I said, “You, or somebody the chief has working this black bag, had the wire up and knew there was going to be a hit. You just didn’t know exactly when, right? So, you and the chief couldn’t stop it, right? Not without tipping your hand. That’s why you put the violent crimes team on the surveillance. That’s why I was put in the car with Thibodeaux. And Blue was put in the containment car to keep him out of the way, to keep him out of the action. But Blue changed his position at the last minute, something you didn’t know about because you weren’t there.”

“Bruno, you cannot, and I mean absolutely cannot, tell anyone about any of this.”

“Which one of the two robbers was it? Which one was the target?”

Wicks shook his head. “No, you don’t have a need to know.”

“Tell me. I’m in this now up to my neck. I have a right to know. Those two rounds to his vest give Blue some cover for the murder, right? Isn’t that right? That’s what the chief really meant. If you try to drag Blue into court, he looks too much like a hero going to guns against two armed suspects and getting shot twice in the process. How can anyone bring charges against him? No jury in the world would buy it. And worse, it’ll come out that the whole thing, the robbery surveillance, was mishandled. What a God-awful mess. Blue really put the screws to you.”

But at the same time there was a beauty to it, the cold brutality of it. The way Blue pulled off the perfect crime, with animal cunning and bravado. It gave me a little shiver.

Wicks said nothing.

I thought about it some more, plugging in these new pieces to the puzzle. “It was the kid in the alley, wasn’t it?” I asked. “The one running right at me. The one that almost got away. The one Blue chased down and gunned in the back with a shotgun.”

Blue's words sounded in my head: *Be sure to tell them he had a gun in his hand and that he was running right at you.*

Wicks said nothing.

"Tell me."

I read his blank expression as he tried to throw me off. But it didn't work.

"No."

"Wait," I said. Shock set in. "It wasn't either one of those two, was it? Then that means it has to be—Oh, you're kiddin' me. Not the other one, not the poor guy over by the truck hit in the chest with the shotgun? Not the robbery victim?"

"No. Stop it, Bruno. Just let it go."

"How did Blue know that guy would be at that gas station, driving that stake bed truck, on that particular night during our surveillance? Tell me or I'm out. Tell me right now." I stopped short before I said, "I'll take it to the press." I couldn't; Wicks and the chief trusted me. It didn't matter anyway. I'd been a part of the killing, a part of the plan to block the alley with our patrol car. If it did come out, no way would anyone believe I wasn't involved.

Wicks let out a long breath. "The EME, the Mexican Mafia, set that guy up, the guy driving the stake bed. They sent him there on some bullshit pretense, told him to go there to pick someone up, a heroin courier from Mexico. We didn't tumble to it until it was too late. We thought he actually was going there to meet with someone. You have to understand, we only had one end of the information and even that came to us cryptic. Blue could've just as easily been told to take down the courier in a dope arrest. He'd also been doing that sort of thing for EME, taking out the competition."

I sat there, stunned. "What a mess. Jesus, what a mess." And at the same time what a perfectly executed murder. Blue did it with such bravado that no one could question it. Amazing. I said, "Good thing you weren't there. You dodged a bullet that time."

But still, having the knowledge and not doing enough to stop it created an enormous liability problem.

If it got out.

"I would've been there," Wicks said, "but if something did happen, just like it did, then my name would be all over those reports. I couldn't risk it. Not when—"

I cut him off and finished it for him. "When you were supposed to be on five days' admin leave for the killing in the alley at 123rd and Central? The killing of Damien Frakes Jr.?"

That's the first time I mentioned that I knew about Frakes. Wicks did a great job finding Frakes, going after him, standing up to him. Only at what sacrifice?

If he'd been at the robbery surveillance, being the only one with the wiretap knowledge, he would have seen the error when Blue changed positions, setting himself up for the kill.

My boss, Lieutenant Wicks, nodded, "That's right, five days' admin leave."

CHAPTER TWENTY-FIVE

I GOT HOME from the barbecue late and opened the front door to my daughter crying. Dad held her and paced the small living room floor, gently bouncing her in his arms.

I hurried in. "Is something wrong? What's the matter with her?"

"Take it easy, Son. This little girl is just a little colicky, that's all. And she probably misses her mother, or at least a woman's touch."

"Here, let me have her."

So small and delicate. So small in my huge hands.

I loved to chase violent criminals on the street, but the idea of holding my own daughter scared the hell out of me. And yet, at the same time, I had the overwhelming need to be closer to her.

Dad pulled away. "No, no, why don't you get some rest and you can take the second shift in about three hours."

"Second shift? You think she's going to be crying that long?"

Dad just smiled and shook his head at my naïveté. "What time do you have to work?" He spoke over the wail of the baby.

"Tomorrow morning at eight."

"You've been burning the candle at both ends and you need to be sharp. Sometimes your life depends upon it. You better get some sleep. I just deliver the mail and that's not all that dangerous."

"I'm okay."

"I know what's best."

"I know you do."

"What is it? Something else is wrong."

Even with my daughter as a crying distraction, he'd been able to read me.

"Dad, I got transferred."

His expression shifted to one of concern. "What happened? Was it because of all that blood on your coat and shirt the night before last? Was that what it was? I'm real sorry, Son. I know how excited you were to have that new job."

Wicks told me not to tell anyone that the transfer wasn't real. The way he phrased it, "You can't tell one swingin' dick. And that means absolutely no one. It's a part of working undercover. That's part of the life of an undercover. It's the number-one thing you need to get into your head. You have to be playing the game every second. You can't trust anyone. No one. The word slips out and you're through. Dead. Are you getting my meaning here?"

I couldn't lie to my father—I wouldn't lie to my father.

"It's not a real transfer. I'm going undercover. I'm going to be working with the Lynwood narco street team." I raised my voice a little to be heard over my daughter.

"Ah, jeez, Son, that's not good."

"Why do you say that?"

I hadn't even told him the worst part, the part about going after two dirty cops. How did he know that it wasn't good? Did he know something I didn't?

"I don't know much about your job," he said, "but working undercover has got to be one of the most dangerous positions in the department. You're out there all by yourself, without a radio, without all your gear."

He hadn't figured it out after all. He'd cut me off before I could tell him about the who and the why of the assignment. And if he worried about just working undercover, he'd go ballistic if I told him the part about trying to build a case against two very dangerous cops. "I'll be all right, Dad. You don't have to worry about me."

"But I do. You know I do. And I always will."

"Here," I said, "let me have her." Her wailing cut through flesh and bone and sliced right down into the exposed nerves.

He handed her over.

All at once I was struck by her softness, her warmth, her tiny size—her delicate vulnerability. The realization finally set in that this was *my* daughter. My chest expanded, shoving out my ribs to make room for my bigger heart—for the love I now experienced for my baby girl. I gently bounced her, put my lips close to her ear, and cooed. She smelled of baby powder and of an unseen newness I automatically linked to innocence.

She stopped crying.

Dad smiled. "Well, I'll be a son of a gun."

Tears welled in my eyes. I turned to the side, away from Dad, a little ashamed of my weak emotional state. Dad reached out and put his hand on my shoulder.

"Why don't you go on to bed, Dad," I said. "I'll take the first watch."

CHAPTER TWENTY-SIX

I DROVE MY Ford Ranger into the employee lot, all the way around the back of Lynwood Station, and parked in a slot twenty yards or so away from the single-wide mobile home. The mobile, my new home until further notice.

I shut the truck down and sat watching. The truck ticked as it cooled. To the right, or west, over by the red-bricked station, black-and-white patrol cars drove in and out of the motor pool shed area, deputies going about their daily routine, all friends of mine. A large part of me already missed patrol, the simplicity of it. Just chasing standard everyday street crooks and murderers.

Wooden steps and a small landing painted green fronted a door at each end of the mobile home, one side for OSS—Operation Safe Streets—the other for the street narcotics team, with an interior wall in between. To the left of the mobile home, or east, a ten-foot-tall chain-link fence with coiled concertina wire at the top ran the entire perimeter of the parking lot. A sidewalk bordered the other side of the fence. Beyond the sidewalk, a residential street, and beyond that a well-manicured neighborhood, all with houses free of gang graffiti.

A short Hispanic male ran in from Bullis Road, the same way I'd entered. He came down the long drive and into the parking lot. He ran by with the two rows of cars in between for cover and went over to the mobile home, the narco side.

Blue.

Running in Lynwood wasn't a healthy proposition, not with all the gangs moving around shooting at each other, especially if you were a member of the opposing team: the cops. Foolish. True to form, though, for Blue: bold and foolish.

He wore green Miami Dolphins running shorts and a yellow tank top, LASD colors. His bodybuilder shoulders and arms, along with his face, glistened with sweat. A regular athletic tube sock covered his right hand. An odd place to wear a sock, it made him out as a puppet master on the cheap. Maybe he had a rash or dry skin and needed the sock to keep the aloe moist.

He climbed the steps and stopped on the stoop facing the parking lot. He looked over the two rows of cars, right at me—at least in my direction.

Could he really see me from that distance? Did he have that kind of tuned-in instinct? Did he know what kind of car I drove?

Seven thirty in the morning; I didn't need to report for another thirty minutes. Now I felt guilty. He'd arrived early to work out, conscientious and disciplined, another facet of the contradiction.

Still standing on the stoop, Blue turned and faced the direction of the ten-foot chain-link fence and the neighborhood on the other side. He pulled off the athletic tube sock revealing a small revolver. He set it on the railing.

Oh, a gun. That's how he could run with confidence on the streets of Lynwood. Lord help anyone who tried to mess with this guy, a Hispanic running in an all-black neighborhood with a puppet sock on his hand.

Without any pretense, he pulled down the front of his Dolphins shorts, took his penis in hand—one abnormally large for such a short man—and urinated off to the side of the landing.

I couldn't believe the balls of this guy, right out in the open, the public right across the street, in plain view through the chain-link fence. He finished, shook, put his penis away, grabbed his gun, and disappeared inside the open door.

I took a deep breath, sighed, got out, locked my door, and walked in between the cars to my new unit of assignment.

My feet thumped going up the four wooden steps to the landing. I hesitated and then entered. To the left, a row of filing cabinets abutted the end wall, filling the entire space, side to side. To the right, three desks on each side faced the outside walls and left a narrow aisle in between. Thibodeaux sat at the middle desk on the right. He looked up and glared. Blue stood by the last desk, naked, wiping his brown and muscular body down with a damp hand towel.

Two circular bruises, both loud and red inside purple star bursts the size of oranges, stood out like beacons, one high on his abdomen, the other higher, on his upper right chest. He didn't grimace or move with any favoritism to his injuries. At least he didn't let it show.

"Hey, Dirt, look who's here," Blue said, not slowing in his post-run hygiene. "It's Bruno, the Bad Boy Johnson, come to pay us a visit." He finished, took a pair of underwear off his desk, and stepped into them. "What can we do for you, Deputy Johnson?"

"I'm reporting for duty."

Surprised, Blue looked at Thibodeaux, took a folded pair of denim pants off his desk, shook them out, and stepped into them. "That right? You working here now?"

"That's right, didn't anyone tell you?"

"Nope, and it doesn't really matter; we can use you." He walked the short distance, buttoning up his pants, and offered his hand. "Welcome."

I didn't want to, but I took his hand and shook. I fought the urge to wipe my hand on my pants.

"Well," Thibodeaux said, "I, for one, don't think it's a good idea to have him working here with us."

Thibodeaux shot me a scowl. He couldn't get over that he'd dropped his gun in the dirt while an armed suspect ran right for us in the alley off Mona. He let his anger eat away at him, anger that I'd been the one to see his dangerous and almost deadly error. He was angry that I alone kept his embarrassing little secret.

"Ah, come on, Dirt," Blue said. "Stand up and shake the man's hand. Welcome him to the team."

I found it difficult to accept this nice and congenial Blue over the one I'd experienced Saturday night in the patrol car on the ride back to the station. This new Blue put me on my guard.

"Shit, Blue, we don't know diddly-squat about this guy. For all we know he could be—"

"Go on, shake his hand."

Thibodeaux stood and offered his hand. "Good to have you aboard." His tone didn't reflect his words. He dropped back into his county-issue chair, which creaked and rattled and threatened to break down.

I would've really liked to hear what he started to say before Blue cut him off. For all they knew I could be . . . what? Could Thibodeaux be that stupid, about to say something like that?

CHAPTER TWENTY-SEVEN

LIGHT FOOT TREADS on the wooden steps outside alerted us to a visitor. We all turned to look. A woman with lustrous hair stuck her head in. "Is this the Lynwood street narco team?" She had wild brown eyes, a color that matched her hair, and a small mouth with dimples at the corners of her smile. Her creamy smooth skin didn't have a blemish, except one. An obvious half-moon scar under her right eye added to her mystique. Her tight denim pants revealed slim hips and long legs. She wore a narrow brown leather belt with a pancake holster and a 4" blue steel .38 revolver, department issue.

Ah, a deputy sheriff.

Thibodeaux smiled and jumped up. "Sure is. How can we help you, my lovely lady?"

She came in the rest of the way and offered her hand to Thibodeaux. "Deputy Chelsea Miller, nice to meet you. I've been assigned to work here." Her eyes went right on past me to Blue's topless build. They hung there a beat too long.

With Blue's type, no other man stood a chance with women in his presence. Even with his abnormally large nose, he carried confidence like a weapon that women fed on.

"Ouch." Chelsea nodded to the gunshot injuries to his chest. "What happened there?"

Blue smiled. "What? This? I'm allergic to peanut butter."

Chelsea smiled at him, her eyes still locked with his.

Blue clapped his hands once and looked at me. "One day we don't have enough manpower to do the simplest buy-bust. Today we got enough to do a full-blown mobile surveillance. Look out, Lucas Knight, we're comin' for your black ass."

Thibodeaux continued to shake Chelsea's hand with vigor, his grin lecherous.

Blue, still looking at me in an odd way, said, "Dirt, give young Deputy Miller her hand back and roll your tongue back up into your mouth."

Thibodeaux let go but didn't stop looking at her.

Not a raving beauty by any standard, Deputy Miller still possessed a certain aura of intrigue that begged to be investigated further. The kind of woman that, the more you got to know her, the more beautiful she became.

Blue moved over to the water cooler. From the desk, he picked up a large plastic cup and filled it to the top. He drank while everyone watched, his throat doing all the work. He finished the entire cup.

"Okay," Blue said. "Before we can go out and have some fun, we have some boring busywork to finish." He wiped his mouth on the back of his arm. "The street narco team works as a support component of this station. So, we're tasked with processing all of patrol's dope. Every morning the stuff from their on-scene dope arrests the night before has to be tested and processed for the lab. Since you two are new fish, you now have that responsibility. Dirt will show you the ropes and hand it off to you. It'll be done every day when you first come in."

"Thank God," Thibodeaux said. "That's a thankless, piece-of-shit job. Maybe you're right—these guys will work out, after all."

The outside steps behind Chelsea thumped again, only louder and with purpose. Captain Gary Stubbs bulled his way in, his face flushed with anger.

I stepped back two steps, ready to physically defend myself. He knew I started work today and came out of the station to take his pound of flesh outta my ass for fooling around with Millie, his executive secretary. In that split second, I decided I would not put up with any physical or verbal abuse. I'd technically done nothing wrong. If I lost my job over it, so be it.

Captain Stubbs, a large, florid-faced man dressed in a tired brown suit, took us all in at once. His bloodshot, watery eyes fell on the shirtless Blue. He raised a fat finger at Blue and leaned into it as if on a pistol range. "Goddamn you, Blue. I just warned you the other day about pissin' off the back of this mobile. And what do you go and do, not two days later? Son of a bitch. This is your last warning. You do it again and I don't care how good your arrest stats are. I don't care what kind of juice you have downtown. You're going to find your brown ass in a sling and launched back to MCJ working graves, sniffin' ass and dirty feet. Do we understand each other?"

Blue gave him a half-guarded smile. "Oh, sorry, Cap, I thought you meant—"

Stubbs took a long step toward him, his finger moved into a fist. "Bullshit! You damn well know what I meant. Last chance, asshole. You got the balls, do it again. Just try me. Go on, take another piss out there."

He stopped himself and took in several long breaths, his lips silently counting down. None of us moved. Rumor around the station said that, due to his anger issues, Stubbs had caught a midnight transfer from a plum assignment at HQ to this last-resort outpost, Lynwood Station. That same rumor put him in anger management classes, and that if he didn't successfully complete them, he'd be asked to resign from the department.

The ironic thing about his outburst, using threats and talking that way, especially in front of a female employee, was that he'd just put himself at the same risk as "pissin'" off the landing. It gave Blue power over him. Now the captain couldn't take on Blue without the risk of Blue blowing the whistle on him.

Had that been Blue's intent from the beginning, to put a sheriff's captain in his pocket?

Blue took his cue. "Won't happen again, Captain. Scout's honor." He raised his hand in the three-finger salute of a scout.

"Put a shirt on, before you catch a sexual harassment beef." He pointed his finger again, this time at Blue's desk. "And I won't tell you twice, you're on five days' admin leave. You shouldn't even be here. You should be at home. You're riding that desk until Friday, no arguments."

"Thursday."

"Blue."

"Yes, sir, Friday."

Stubbs took another step back from his unchecked fury, calming even further, and finally noticed the rest of us. "Good to see you, Chelsea. Sorry you have to work with this bunch of shit-ass monkeys." He took another cleansing breath. "Please pardon my behavior; it was uncalled for."

He looked at me, his face flushed red all over again. "And you, you keep that dick of yours in your pants. Understand?"

"Yes, sir."

He turned heel and fled before the anger again took him by the throat and led him down the path to an unplanned retirement. His big wingtips pounded the wooden steps outside.

Blue came up behind me and put his hand on my shoulder. He leaned up and whispered. His congenial tone gone, he now spoke with that same hard edge from Saturday night in the patrol car. "Keep your dick in your pants, huh? You're going to fit in here just fine, Johnson."

CHAPTER TWENTY-EIGHT

STILL SHIRTLESS, HIS expression neutral, Blue turned to face his desk. He stayed that way, staring at the wall. Chelsea broke the trance that gripped us all. "Let's get started on that station dope evidence so we can get out there and throw some dirtbags in jail."

Her tone didn't match the words. She didn't want the busywork assignment either. The word "dirtbags" somehow didn't seem right coming from her lips. Not without knowing her better. I'd not yet accepted her as a deputy.

Thibodeaux held up his hand and said, "*Shh.*" He watched Blue carefully with a look of concern.

After a moment, with everyone still not moving, Blue picked up a white mug off his desk, one embossed with the gold letters "LASD." He rolled the mug around in his hands. All the pens and pencils fell to the desktop. He muttered, "Ride the fucking desk." He said it a second time, louder: "Ride the fucking desk."

He threw the mug against the cheap wood-paneled wall. The mug shattered. He grabbed at his chest with one hand; the other went to the edge of his desk for support. He closed his eyes, trying to eat the pain the sudden movement caused to the deep bruising in his gunshot injury.

He'd finally let his guard down and showed some evidence of vulnerability, some humanity. Without realizing it, I had begun to view him as a sort of super bad guy, the kind only Batman or the Green Hornet could take down.

He turned his back to us, pulled a folded t-shirt off the desk, and without turning around to face us said, "Dirt, tell those two about the thing. Have them go handle it." He shrugged into the worn-out Black Sabbath t-shirt and ran the fingers of both hands through his black hair, smoothing it straight back even more.

"Sure, Blue, whatever you want. What about the evidence? We have to get that stuff processed. The lab transport will be here in another coupla hours."

"You and me will handle that. I'm on the desk, remember?"

"Ah, shit, Blue."

He spun around, his eyes fierce. "What'd I just say?"

Thibodeaux held up his hands. "Okay, boss, okay. Whatever you want, man. I'm with you."

The two stood face-to-face for a moment until Blue broke, turned, and walked by us. Heat radiated off his body as he continued to cool down from his long run and now also from this new predicament he couldn't control, being shackled to his desk.

He stopped at the door. "I'll be on the pager." He disappeared outside, his footfalls on the steps light as a dancer's.

Thibodeaux kicked the desk, dented a drawer. "Shit."

Chelsea spoke first. "We can do the evidence. We need to learn it anyway."

"You just hear what Blue said? You'll figure out soon enough, little lady, that you do exactly what he says, when he says it, or you'll pay the price." He stepped over to a rack of handheld radios and pulled one out. He handed it to me. He pulled a piece of paper from his shirt pocket and handed it to Chelsea. "You two twits, go to this address and set up on it. Today, sometime before noon, a fat black chick is going to make a big delivery for Lucas Knight, aka Mo Mo. She'll be wearing purple. According to the snitch, she always wears purple.

She'll drop off a load of rock and pick up some cash. Hopefully a big chunk of cash." He smiled at the cash part. For a brief second, it shifted his whole personality.

"And if she shows up?" I asked. "What do you want us to do?"

He lost his smile and shifted back. "Get on the radio, dickhead, and call it in to us."

I didn't like his attitude or the petty name-calling. "What car do we take?"

"What car did you drive into work today, *dickhead*?"

I took a step closer to him, my fists clenched. I remembered the switchblade he kept in his boot and realized I shouldn't have moved in so close. Not against someone like Thibodeaux.

Chelsea reached up and put her hand on my shoulder. "Come on, big guy, let's get going."

I didn't break. My bad-self wanted to sock Dirt, knock his nose loose at the roots, shove some teeth down his rotten, murderous throat. Chelsea, from behind, pinched my shoulder in a pain compliance move.

"Ouch." I dropped my shoulder and broke away from her, still looking at the threat, Thibodeaux. From the sound of her steps, Chelsea had already turned and headed for the door. "Men and their stupid, testosterone-fueled bullshit. I'll never get used to it." Her light footfalls followed her on the wooden steps. I backed away, not breaking eye contact. He finally grinned. A grin, not a smile. I turned and left.

Twenty minutes later, we pulled up and parked a block from the house on Peach, in Fruit Town, a section of unincorporated Los Angeles. The drive over had come and gone in silence as we both pondered our new situation, working for a neurotic supervisor with a hair trigger—one who liked to pee in public.

The problem was more critical for me, though. From the moment I first walked in the door of the narco mobile home, I sensed a constant low-level hum of potential violence, one much different than the kind on the street. I hadn't realized it until after I stepped out of the presence of those two.

I shut off the Ford Ranger and reached across to get the binoculars out of the glove box. Chelsea reacted too fast and put both hands on my arm and pushed away so I wouldn't inadvertently touch her knees. Or give her a grope. I didn't know which.

I pulled back, looking at her, kind of shocked. What the hell? What she must think of me.

Then Captain Stubbs' words echoed back: *"Keep your dick in your pants."*

"Sorry," she said.

"Yeah, right."

CHAPTER TWENTY-NINE

I SHOVED THE glove box closed and leaned back in my seat, angry. I checked out the house through the binoculars.

I grew up in the Corner Pocket, not too far from Peach, in Fruit Town. I didn't recognize the numbers of the address but I recognized the house. Big Stevie used to live there. On the high school varsity team he could shoot from the corner, a flat jumper, no arc, and hit it at least 90 percent of the time. Kind of eerie, the way the ball went straight to the basket as if on a metal wire. No defender could shut him down. He definitely had what it took to get a full ride on a hot college team. UCLA and USC started to scout him at some of our games.

His family moved out of the Peach house after Big Stevie took a round in the spine while he sat in his car at the Big O donut shop. An errant rifle round meant for someone else. That happened one hot summer night, seven or eight years ago. They moved to Moreno Valley in Riverside County to get away from the gangs. I'd heard from his sister that he now resided in Chuckawalla State Prison. He'd caught a ten-year jolt for possession of two keys of rock.

Someone else now lived in Big Stevie's house. And if Blue got his information right, Lucas Knight had bought it as a stash house for distribution purposes.

"We might have as long as four hours sitting in this car together," Chelsea said. "Let's start over, okay? I am sorry about flinching like that."

I handed her the binocs and pointed. "It's that pink one with the black wrought iron on all the windows and the front door. They got a derelict hoopty, an old rust bucket Chevy, parked in the yard, to slow down any bullets from a drive-by."

She looked through the binoculars.

After a moment, I said, "I don't bite."

She brought them down. "I know. I said I was sorry. Don't be so thin-skinned."

I nodded and rubbed my shoulder, smiled. "What was that you did to me back there, some kind of Vulcan death grip?"

She smiled. "No, I grew up with three brothers and learned a few things in how to survive a dog pile."

"Where'd you do your street time?"

"Lomita."

I chuckled. "You mean, Slowmita."

Lomita, which was in an affluent section of Los Angeles, didn't have a lot of action. "What was your last assignment before you came here?"

"Public Affairs." She didn't hesitate and said it with confidence. Public Affairs, a know-nothing fluff job for those who couldn't handle the abrupt and violent vagaries of the street.

Perfect. She didn't have a lot of experience. Not the kind that counted, not the kind needed to work a street team in South Central Los Angeles, where if you let your guard down for one second, even a hundred-pound coke whore will shank a lung out of you.

"Did you put in for this team?" I asked.

"As a matter of fact, I did. This department is top heavy with good ol' boys who like to promote all the other good ol' boys. If I want the slimmest chance of moving up, I need to show them I can handle myself. And I *am* going to move up."

"Well, you came to the right place, that's for sure."

"Don't you worry about me." Her smile tarnished a bit.

"I didn't mean anything by it." I offered her my hand. "Bruno Johnson."

She took it. "Chelsea Miller, nice to meet you."

She looked at me for a moment more and then went back to looking through the glasses. She asked, "Who's this Lucas Knight we're watching?"

"They call him Mo Mo on the street. This is supposed to be one of his stash houses. Our goal here, in theory, is to take down this pad, grab up some of his cohorts, and flip 'em. Then, with each arrest we move up the line, flipping the next higher up until we get to Mo Mo."

With the glasses to her eyes she said, "I see, so we're going after the dog heavy."

"Ah, shit." The words slipped out before I could pull them back. I couldn't believe what she'd just said. I'd never heard that term used before and I'd just heard it twice in as many days. And I didn't believe in coincidence.

She pulled the glasses down to look at me. "What's the matter?"

No way would I tell her, and reveal what I just found out about her—that she hadn't just fluttered in like some delicate bird from Public Affairs. The motivation for her presence on the narc team just changed the entire game.

"Nothing," I said. "I think I left a burner on the stove at home. That's all, no big deal."

"We can't leave here to go check on it," she said.

"I know, don't worry about it. *I'm* not."

"You okay? You look a little pale all of a sudden."

"I'm fine. Tell me what you've heard about our new team leader." I needed to change the subject to give me time to think. And also try to find out exactly what she knew.

She said, "Ricky Blue? He's a real piece of work."

"That right? Why do you say that?"

"He—"

"One of us needs to watch the house," I said. "Let me have the glasses."

I didn't want her reading my expression. I had the feeling she knew a lot more about me than I knew about her. That she knew a lot more about everything going on than I did.

She handed them over.

"Go ahead," I said. "Fill me in. I only heard what Thibodeaux told me night before last."

I sensed her moving around in the small front seat, trying to get comfortable. She hesitated a moment, as if deciding exactly what to tell me. She said, "I only heard what's going around, you know, the rumors on the street."

"Okay, and . . . ?"

"Just that he's a shit-hot cop who's a little trigger-happy and has at least ten OIS's, five of them kills. That he's a piss-poor pistol shot and prefers to use a shotgun."

Did those numbers count the three from Saturday night? I didn't think so. That would put him at thirteen, with eight of them kills. Had some or all of those others been contract hits? Wicks hadn't said anything about them and he'd know of the shootings. He had to have been through Blue's file.

"I also heard," she said, "that he has a helluva rabbi, some heavy juice way up the chain of command that looks out for him."

I pulled the glasses down to look at her. "Who?"

But I thought I knew and didn't want to believe it.

CHAPTER THIRTY

SHE SHRUGGED. "IT'S only a rumor. But I also heard that whoever was protecting him is running scared."

"How can you know that if you don't know who's protecting him?"

"Why else would Blue be launched from SPY to this shithole of an assignment?"

"This place isn't so bad." She was right but I still didn't like her disparaging the area where I grew up.

I went back to watching the house just in time to see some activity. "Okay," I said, "write this down. A yellow Honda Civic just pulled up, no front license plate."

"Is it a heavyset black woman wearing purple? I hope to hell it is. I don't want to stay out here all day."

"Nope, a skinny Mexican chick wearing shorts and a tank top. She didn't stay long. They must be out of pocket, waiting on the delivery. Or they really have a good system to move the dope. I don't think this is a stash house. I think it's just a rock house. Go on, tell me more about Blue."

She again hesitated.

I pulled the glasses down to look at her.

"You can't tell anyone any of this," she said as she looked into my eyes. She shook her head. "Nah, I better not. I hardly know you. This is some pretty heavy stuff. Real personal, and I don't feel right talking smack about other people."

"Look, you and I are in the same boat with this new dope assignment. We need to help each other, right?" I smiled. "And the quickest way to get to trust someone is to tell each other some deep, dark secrets."

I'd never trust her, not for a moment. I didn't care what *she* told me.

She thought about that a moment. "All right, keep watching. But you have to promise you won't tell a soul."

I looked through the glasses at the house. "I promise."

"Once I found out that I got the assignment here at Lynwood with Blue running the team, I went looking for this sergeant, who's working Sybil Brand, the women's jail. Her name's Gale Taylor. I'd heard that at one time Gale was doing Blue on a regular basis, really tearing up the sheets. Blue broke up Gale's marriage. She was married to some other sergeant, and I guess that breakup got ugly. She got real tight with Blue and, when he got tired of her, he just kind of wadded her up and threw her away. Left her emotionally bankrupt. She's better now."

"Yeah?"

Chelsea talked like a street cop and not someone from Public Affairs.

"Would you just keep watching? I don't want to screw up my first assignment."

I looked back in the glasses. "Log another car," I said. "A gray Toyota, no front plate, Negro female about twenty, didn't stay long enough to make a deal. This definitely isn't a stash house. Okay, go ahead, continue."

"This Gale really didn't want to give it up, and it took me a while to get it out of her. The department put a lid on this thing. I don't know how they kept it from getting out. I guess it was easier back then."

"Get what out of her? Come on, give it up."

"Take it easy, big guy. I'm getting to it."

Another long pause. I had to let her tell it at her own speed.

"You promise you won't tell anyone?"

"Come on, we're partners."

"Okay, here it is. When Blue worked patrol in Pico Rivera, he got a call from dispatch to respond to his parents' house. His mom had called dispatch in a panic. Like I said, this was years ago when Blue was just a rookie. He goes home and finds his dad crazy-drunk. He's holding Blue's mom around the neck with a butcher knife to her head. Blue doesn't know what to do. His mom's bleeding from several cuts on her arms and what is later found to be a superficial stab wound to her stomach."

"You're kidding!"

I couldn't imagine a situation like that. My mom died before I could remember anything, and I just couldn't see Dad ever coming close to doing something that violent, especially to a loved one.

"What happened?"

"According to this female sergeant, Blue's dad had always been a mean drunk—half Scottish, half Mexican, so he came by the alcohol and meanness naturally. But Blue still loved him. He had to make a choice that day, a terrible choice.

"He kept yelling for his dad to drop the knife and let his mother go. When his dad looked like he was about to stab her again, Blue took the shot. Hit his dad right in the eye. Put him down for good."

I lowered the glasses. "Oh my God."

I hadn't known Blue long and never would've guessed he carried such a dark shadow like that, not one of that magnitude. I whispered, "What a horrible thing to live with."

"I know."

Chelsea's expression showed no emotion. For sure she didn't talk like any kind of Slowmita or Public Affairs deputy I knew.

"Jesus," I said. "Poor Blue. No wonder shooting people doesn't seem to bother him."

"What do you mean?"

"I was there the other night, Saturday, at the gas station on Imperial off of Mona."

"No kidding? You saw him gun one of those guys?"

She'd just slipped up, said the wrong thing. One wrong word just confirmed all that I suspected. She was not who she said she was.

With three shot by Blue at the gas station robbery, why would she think I only witnessed the *one*?

Unless she'd been briefed, and/or read the reports of the shooting.

"Yeah, I did see him shoot that kid and wish I hadn't." I put the glasses back up to my eyes just in time to see a white van pull a U-turn and park out in front of the Peach address. A large black woman got out and waddled toward the house. Her silken purple muumuu shone bright in the afternoon sun.

I grabbed up the radio, made sure the channel selector sat on the talk-around frequency, and called in: "25Nora4 to base."

Thibodeaux came right back. "Go."

"The primary just arrived at the location."

"Ten-four. Wait until she drives away and stop her. But don't stop her close to the location. Do not burn the location."

I looked at Chelsea then back at the radio. I keyed the mike. "This is my personal truck. We don't have any emergency equipment, no red light. How are we supposed to stop her?"

Chelsea shrugged. She didn't know either.

Yeah, thanks for the help.

Thibodeaux didn't answer, and I didn't know if they heard me. I keyed the mike again. "How are we supposed to stop her?"

This time Blue came back on. "We're suiting up now. You do whatever you have to do to stop that vehicle. Once you do, give us your location. Out."

I started the truck.

"Well," Chelsea said, "what are we going to do?"

"You heard the man, we do whatever we have to. Get ready."

CHAPTER THIRTY-ONE

MINUTES LATER, THE woman came out of the pink house with a rolled-up brown paper grocery bag under her elbow, pinned to her side. She opened the van door and climbed in. The driver's side dipped under the added strain. She started the van and whipped a U-turn, headed west on Peach.

I started up, shifted into first, and followed. She made the first left, headed south toward Rosecrans.

"Talk to me, Bruno. What are you thinking?" Chelsea's voice, calm and in control.

"If she runs, we can't chase her, not in this. We'd violate ten different department policies and vehicle codes."

"Okay, and . . . ?"

"We're going to get behind her and wait until she gets into some traffic and she stops at a red light. Then we'll get out, walk up, and throw down on her."

"Not good. We'll be on foot and she'll be in her car."

"I'm open for suggestions. She's not carrying the dope anymore and only carrying money. There's a good chance she'll think—"

Out in front, she pulled up behind two cars at a fresh red at Rosecrans. No time to discuss it. I shifted to neutral, put on the emergency brake, and bailed out.

I walked casually up alongside of the van, my gun drawn and held down at my side. I focused at the task at hand and lost track of Chelsea. I made it to the window. The woman missed my approach in her side mirror. She jumped when she saw my gun pointed right at her. I held the badge up for her to see. "Sheriff's Department. Turn your car off and step out."

The red signal changed to green; the cars in front of her started to move. She recovered too quickly from the shock of my appearance, smiled, and hit the door locks. She raised her hand and waved bye with just her fingers.

Chelsea appeared, standing right in front of the van, gun drawn in a two-handed Weaver stance. She yelled, "Don't move. Don't you move." She pointed her gun at the woman, who now looked scared.

But she again recovered quickly, put her foot on the gas, and bumped the van forward.

Chelsea didn't move her position. She swung her gun up and fired one round in the air. The crack echoed off the windshield and bounced around the neighborhood. She brought the gun back down, the barrel smoking, and aimed it at the woman's forehead.

I pulled back my gun and smashed out the driver's window. The woman screamed, raised her hands, and waved them in front of her face. Little cubes of safety glass covered her dress and arms and hair, their brilliant facets reflecting the sunlight.

I reached in, turned off the van, took the keys, and opened the door. "We're not going to hurt you. You're under arrest. Get out."

"Okay, okay. Just don't shoot me, you chickenshit bastard. Don't shoot." She slid out of the seat to the ground. The van rocked.

Chelsea came around, going for her handcuffs, and escorted her over to the curb. I got in and pulled the van to the side of the road. Chelsea yelled, "Toss me your cuffs. I need two pair to cuff her."

I tossed her my cuffs and ran to move my truck out of traffic and over to the curb behind the van. Then I opened my ashtray where I kept loose .38 bullets. I took one and shoved it into my pocket. I walked back to where Chelsea stood over the woman sitting on the curb, cuffed behind her back.

"This is Ollie Bell, and she doesn't have any idea why we stopped her."

"That's right, and I want my attorney. You two little shitasses have done gone and shit the bed for sure, this time. I haven't done nothin' wrong. I'm gonna own your asses. When my attorney's done with you, it's gonna be The Ollie Bell Sheriff's Department." She laughed and it came out a cackle.

Blue and Thibodeaux slid up to the curb in the undercover car, a maroon '79 Chevy Nova, the brakes smoking. They'd made remarkable time. They got out, dressed in green sheriff windbreakers with body armor underneath. They wore their black Sam Brown holsters with all their gear. Blue just violated Captain Stubbs' direct order about riding the desk.

He came over to us. Ollie saw him. "Ah, shit on a Ritz."

"Hey, Ollie, how's it hangin'?" Blue said.

"I was havin' myself a good day until your sorry ass showed up."

"Don't be that way. I thought we were friends."

"That right? Last time you harassed me like this, you took my nephew off ta prison. He's doin' twenty-five ta life. Never gonna see the light a day, not ever again. All his lil' chillrens will never know their daddy."

"That's real tough. A double murder over dope will do that to a person. I'm only gonna ask you this once, you understand?"

She nodded. "Yeah, I figured it'd be somthin' like that."

"What's goin' on back at the pad on Peach?"

She opened her mouth to speak.

Blue stepped closer to her, his finger pointed right at her eye. "Don't you lie to me. You know what happens to people who lie to me."

She nodded again, swallowed hard. "Dat's Mo Mo's place back there. But you already know dat or I wouldn't be sittin' here."

"Where's Mo Mo?"

"He ain't there."

"I asked you, where's Mo Mo?"

"I don't know. Dat's the honest ta God's truth. I swear to you, Blue, I don't know."

"You know the game. You gotta tell me something good if you wanna walk on this."

"You ain't got me on nothin'."

Thibodeaux backed out of the passenger side of the van with the brown paper bag. "Looks like close to fifty K here."

"What about the money?" Blue asked.

"Ain't against the law ta have all dat money."

"Dirt, call for a dog to sniff it. There'll be coke on—"

She said, "All right. All right."

"Where's Mo Mo?"

"He's supposed to be over ta the house later on, ta check on the operation. He thinks the nigga there, Tarkington—Tark, they call him, the boy Mo Mo's got there slingin' his cain—Mo Mo thinks he's on the skim."

"When's he comin'?"

"I don't know that for sure. Soon enough, though."

Blue waved to us to follow him. We left Ollie sitting on the curb and moved out of earshot down the sidewalk several feet away. Blue said, "We're going to take down the pad and wait for Mo Mo to show."

Thibodeaux clapped his hands. "Hot damn. Now we're talkin'."

Blue ignored him. "This place is tough, though. I've heard about it from a couple of different sources. It's got a birdcage on the inside. You two know what that is?"

I hated being ignorant in front of this man, but I wasn't going to risk the safety of the team. "No."

Chelsea shook her head.

"It's a custom-built cage just inside the door, heavy wrought iron with a gate at the end and a dead bolt. The buyers come into the house and are in the cage when they make the buys. It keeps Mo Mo's operation from getting ripped by street thugs. It also makes it extremely dangerous for us. So, here's what we're going to do. We're going to do a Trojan Horse in this van and drive right up into the driveway. Bruno, you and Ollie will go to the door. The rest of us will be in the back of the van waiting. You get inside, get the cage gate open, and we'll flood in right behind you. Got it?"

He talked like his plan was some sort of harmless football play in a game with nothing of importance at stake, nothing besides some bumps and bruises from the other team. He didn't consider Ollie and me there, inside and under the gun. He also didn't consider taking an arrestee as cover, as a shield, into a highly dangerous situation, yet another huge violation of department policy. If Ollie got hurt, everyone involved would lose their jobs.

I wanted to ask, Why me? But I knew. My skin matched Ollie's. And to be fair, if this Tark guy saw Thibodeaux, Chelsea, or even Blue with Ollie, he'd never open the inside gate to the cage.

"What if we can't get the inside cage gate open?" I asked. "And you flood in right behind us? We're all going to be sitting ducks."

"Don't worry about that. You tell Ollie what's at stake, and she'll get that gate open. She's got the gift of gab."

Chelsea said, "What are you talking about? What's at stake?"

I answered so Blue didn't bite her head off. "Her life. Ollie doesn't get the door opened, she'll get gunned right alongside us."

"Oh . . . oh." Chelsea looked surprised.

Blue came into my space, close enough for me to feel the warmth of his breath on my chin as he looked at me. "You ready for this, big man?"

I fought the urge to step back. "You don't need to worry. I'll always do what's expected of me."

"Good." He reached under my shirt and pulled the Smith and Wesson 9mm from my shoulder holster, the one Wicks gave me as a backup. "Think I'll keep this just in case. I'll be battin' cleanup if this thing goes wrong. I'll need that little bit extra. You know what I mean? You got a problem with that?"

I did but wouldn't give him the satisfaction of voicing it, especially not in front of Chelsea.

When I said nothing, he smiled and said, "Then let's saddle up, boys and girls, and do this thing."

CHAPTER THIRTY-TWO

OLLIE CLIMBED INTO the driver's side. I sat on the passenger side. Blue, Thibodeaux, and Chelsea sat flat on the carpet in back, on top of the cubed glass from the broken-out driver's window. The inside smelled of chemicals from Jeri-curl, body odor, and stale sex.

My heart rose up in my throat with the excitement of stepping into a confined cage, a trapped target for a known drug dealer to shoot at will.

I tried to think if I'd ever run into Tark on the street, an important question Blue should've asked before shoving me out there like a staked goat. If I *had* run into Tark, and just didn't remember, well, he'd probably chuckle at my stupidity as he pulled the trigger and dropped the hammer on my dumb ass. I also couldn't stop thinking about the secondary threat: What if Ollie gave me up? Shoved over to one side of the cage away from me and yelled, *"Shoot him, shoot him! He's Five-O. He's Five-O."* Nobody, not even the great and thrill-hungry Ricky Blue, would get there in time to keep me from getting gunned.

Ollie started up, stuck the van in drive, and shook her head. "Hope nobody saw me sittin' on the side of the road in them handcuffs with all you all. If they did, they'll for sure pop a cap in both our asses. Do it 'fore I even get out a 'Wusup?'"

From the back, Blue said in a deadpan tone, "Don't worry, Ollie. Then I'll have them for murder one. They'll get a lot more time that way."

Thibodeaux laughed.

Blue smiled.

Chelsea caught me watching, and she shook her head in disgust at the two mental midgets. But were they actually ignorant? Or had they set this whole thing up as a way to take out a rat amongst them?

Me.

Or was this their test to see if I'd play along, dirty me up a little? Or to see if I'd call foul and turn them in?

Ollie threw her head back and cackled as she drove straight into the intersection at Rosecrans. She horsed the wheel in an abrupt U-turn to head back north, barely missing the other cars also going north. The maneuver knocked around the passengers, who lost their smiles.

I didn't like that, not one bit.

Ollie pulled to the side of the road and pivoted in her seat as best she could with her bulk. "Blue, be a peach and at least gimme a gun to take in wit me."

"Not a chance," Blue said. "You get Bruno. He's your gun. Bruno won't let anything happen to you. Will you, Bruno?"

I said nothing. I reached into my pocket, took out the spare .38 I'd taken from the ashtray in my truck, and flipped it to Chelsea. She caught it. She pulled out her gun, broke open the cylinder, plucked out the expended cartridge, and loaded the live one. She snapped the cylinder shut with a jerk of her wrist and tossed me the empty. I caught it.

Blue watched the little display and said nothing. Warning shots were strictly forbidden, especially in the manner that Chelsea had done it. I gave her the cartridge in that way to send a message to Blue that we'd already stepped over the edge and dirtied up. The maneuver didn't seem to make a difference with him.

I took off my holster and shoved my gun in my front waistband so the crooks in the house could see it. I took my badge on a chain from around my neck and tossed it to Chelsea.

Blue nodded his approval.

Ollie took off from the curb, the distance to the house far too short for my liking. She said, "Holy shit on a Ritz."

I tried to regulate my breathing so I didn't hyperventilate.

Two minutes later, she pulled into the driveway just as planned.

Chelsea leaned up behind the seat and whispered to me, "Good luck, partner."

I hadn't known her long, but her words warmed my insides, gave me a boost in confidence, and put some steel back in my spine.

I got out, slamming the door so the folks inside the house didn't think we were trying to sneak up on them. I tried to keep my knees from quaking, and hoped Chelsea didn't see the cold fear that gripped my stomach and made me walk a little bowlegged and hunched.

Ollie knocked on the first door. A muffled voice barely made it out to us. Ollie yelled, "Open the damn door, Tark, ya candyass lil' pooh-butt."

The door buzzed on a solenoid.

"Shit," I whispered under my breath. "You didn't say anything about a solenoid entry."

She pulled the door open. "Say what, nigga? What's that? I know nothin' about no noid." She stepped in.

I took a deep breath and followed.

Just like Blue described, we stepped into a wrought-iron cage, one big enough to house a couple of tigers in a traveling circus. The door behind us slammed closed with a finality that caused me to give a little jump.

Trapped.

The air turned thin and made it even more difficult to breathe.

We couldn't get out and no one behind us could get in.

On the other side of the cage bars, in the living room, stood a shirtless Tark. He wore denim pants, hung halfway down his hips, exposing boxer shorts. A Dodgers ball cap sat on his head, cocked sideways, and the laces to his oversized hundred-dollar basketball shoes hung untied and loose. Black ink tattoos depicted his gang, with a double-barreled shotgun; the bust of a beautiful naked black woman with perfect huge breasts; and a street sign that read "Piru." In his hand down at his side he held a Tech-9, a poor man's machine pistol.

"Wusup, Ollie? Why you back?"

I stepped close to the bars. "Open this gate."

"Who the hell you think you are, nigga? Don't you step up on me."

"He works for Mo Mo," Ollie said. "Your bag came up short."

"Bullshit. I gave you sixty-two-five jus' like I told Mo Mo when he called. It ain't my fault you didn't count it here. I tolt ya to count it here, ya crazy ol' fat bitch."

I looked him in the eye. "I said, open this gate. I'm not gonna ask again."

I didn't know where I found the guts to bluff and bluster.

Tark looked me in the eye and then at the .38 in my waistband. Behind his eyes, his mind worked the odds.

"Don't you raise that gun," I said. "You might get one or two off, but I'll pull and drop you where you stand. Now, last time I'm gonna say it: open this damn gate."

He hesitated, thinking over his options. Then he sighed. His shoulders relaxed. He shuffle-stepped over, put the Tech-9 under his arm, and held it there, pinned. He pulled up a chain that hung from his waist, chose a key, and unlocked the gate.

I burst out of the confines and slapped his gun to the ground. I grabbed him and shoved him up against the bars.

I didn't have to tell Ollie; she waddled over to the entryway to the next room, reached around the corner, and hit the solenoid release on the inside wall. The front door popped open. Three cops, members of my team, flooded in, guns at the ready. They moved right past me and disappeared into the next room. They all started yelling. "Sheriff's Department. Get down. Get down."

Tark turned his head back to Ollie. "You're dead, bitch. You're dead."

CHAPTER THIRTY-THREE

I SHOVED TARK'S face into the bars, a little too hard.

Ollie came over. "Shut yore fat ass. They made me do it. And I'll tell Mo Mo the same thing, right to his face. He'll understand."

Only in her world. No way could Mo Mo let her get away with being a rat, no matter how much he liked her.

She reached up and again shoved his head into the bars. His face thumped harder this time. Tark brought his free hand up and covered his face. "Hey, hey. Damn, girl."

I liked Ollie.

Blue stuck his head around the corner. "Bruno, bring his skinny ass in here."

I held him in a wristlock, bent over and picked up his gun, and escorted the both of them into the other room.

The doorway opened to a den on the right and a kitchen to the left, the counters invisible with clutter: discarded take-out Chinese cartons, Old English Eight Hundred 40-ounce bottles, and a tall stack of empty Arm & Hammer baking soda boxes used in converting the cocaine hydrochloride to base, or rock, cocaine.

On the floor, stacked in the corner, I recognized grease-laden pizza cartons from Central Ave Pizza, the same place Dad sometimes used when I stayed over. On the stove, two deep-dish Pyrex cake pans held a couple of pounds of rock coke in the final process of drying before being cut into retail sizes, two-five and five-oh rocks. Two pounds of rock cocaine, a helluva bust for a major's crew, let alone a brand-new street team. Captain Stubbs couldn't say boo about this takedown. We'd stepped out on the edge, risked it all, and now reaped the benefit. What an exhilarating feeling.

To the right, a short room addition kicked out one wall and opened the house a little. Two more street thugs lay facedown on the carpeted floor, handcuffed in front of a seventy-inch television screen, the real expensive state-of-the-art kind with the rear projection. The team interrupted a movie still playing, *Mississippi Burning*.

Thibodeaux took Tark, cuffed him, and laid him down next to the others.

Just as the doorbell rang.

"Bruno," Blue said. "Get out there and sell them some rock."

"What? Are you kiddin' me?"

"Word gets out this place is closed to business, no way will Mo Mo make an appearance. Get your ass out there. Chelsea, cut a piece of rock off that cookie and give it to him. Bruno, when the hand-to-hand goes down, pull your gun on him and we'll come out and take him down."

"Cookie?" Chelsea said.

"In the cake pan on the stove."

The doorbell rang again.

Thibodeaux didn't wait for her to move. He looked put out. He hurried into the kitchen area, reached into his boot, took out his switchblade, flicked it open, and carved off a chunk. He pared it down into smaller multiple chunks. He came over and held them out to me. I looked at Chelsea. She shrugged.

"What the hell." I took them.

Blue moved over and stood in the middle of the thugs on the floor. "Any one of you turds yells or so much as farts and I'm gonna kick your teeth in. You boys understand?"

None of them said a thing.

"Get out there," Blue said.

I'd never sold rock before. Didn't have the first inkling in how to do it. Why would I? It went against everything I believed in.

What would Dad think?

I went into the living room just as someone behind me buzzed the outside door open. In came two street urchins in ratty clothes. I'd seen their kind before, arrested similar dopers of their ilk. They probably spent the entire previous day doing small-time rip-offs, or collecting bottles and aluminum cans, or pulling out copper from derelict buildings, all to get enough cash to come and cop some rock. Both males stood in the cage, their faces and hands dirty. They looked like they hadn't eaten in several days. They didn't care at all about food; they only cared about chasing the glass pipe.

"Whattaya need?" I asked, the rocks in my fist starting to sweat.

"I want a two-five. Gimme a two-five." He twitched and wiggled, sketching to the tenth power.

The other guy, not nearly as wired, eyed me suspiciously. "Who the hell are you? Where's Tark?"

"He took the day off. You want some of this or not?" I opened my hand and showed them the goodies. Their eyes went round as they both lost all thought of anything else. Lust and greed overpowered paranoia. Thibodeaux, in his rush, had cut the rocks too large.

"I don't see any two-fives there," the twitchy one said.

The other one elbowed his partner. "Shut up." He stuck his grubby hand through the bars with a handful of crumpled bills, twenty-five hard-earned dollars. "Gimme that one right there."

I gave him the rock he wanted and took his money. The second one took longer to choose. He finally made his choice. I gave him the rock and took his money. I drew my gun and threw down on them. They backed up to the other wall, their hands up.

The more coherent one said, "Hey, hey, man. What's goin' on? Don't shoot. Don't shoot."

Blue hurried into the room with the key.

They saw his green sheriff's raid jacket. "Ah, man, Five-O. It's Five-O."

Blue unlocked the gate, took the rocks from them, and ushered them into the room with the others, their hands still in the air.

I let out a sigh of relief and followed.

Blue patted them down for weapons and set them on the floor without handcuffs.

"Dirt," Blue said, "take the van back to where we all parked. Take Chelsea with you to bring back Bruno's truck. You take the Nova and run the money to HQ and get a count, get that money secured. Bruno and I will hold down the fort here."

The doorbell rang.

Blue said, "The both of you wait until Bruno hooks this next one up and then you haul ass. You understand?"

Thibodeaux said, "You got it, boss."

Chelsea nodded and looked as confused with this whole business as I did.

I stepped into the living room as the door buzzed open. In stepped a beautiful black girl I instantly recognized. Her name was Chocolate, a street hooker I'd arrested a few times in the past. She looked up, saw me, and tried to bolt back out the door.

Too late; it had latched shut.

She turned back around and smiled. "You slingin' rock now, Deputy Johnson?"

"Sorry, Chocolate. I guess it's not your day. Blue?"

Blue came out with the key, unlocked the gate, and took Chocolate by the arm as Chelsea and Thibodeaux went by and into the cage. Blue closed the gate and escorted Chocolate to the kitchen entry, where he buzzed Chelsea and Thibodeaux out. Blue patted Chocolate down for weapons, even her breasts and crotch, none too lightly, and set her on the floor. I didn't like him for touching Chocolate, not in that way.

She'd worked for me in the past, fed me a couple of crooks wanted for violent offenses that really made me look good with the station. We got along well, but I wouldn't let on about it, not in front of the other thugs and sketchers. Not in front of Blue.

I caught her eye and barely shook my head. She gave a little nod and half-smile.

Blue caught the exchange and said to her, "You sit quiet and don't give us any problem. We don't have anything on you, and when we're done here, you can leave."

One of the rank-smelling sketchers said, "What about us?"

"You're a dumbass. You bought dope from a cop. You're going to the can for possession."

"Ah, man, dat ain't right. He's supposed to tell us he's a cop. Ain't he? Ain't he supposed to tell us he's a cop, 'fore he sells us the rock? Dat was straight up, what's you call it? Entrapment. I know it was."

Blue ignored him.

Five minutes later, the doorbell rang again. I went out front and Blue buzzed the outside door. In came Chelsea. "I parked your truck down the street. I hope it's still there when we get done."

We stood close on opposite sides of the bars looking at each other. She whispered, "Thanks for the cartridge. Your timing was perfect."

"No problem," I whispered back.

"We're a good team," she said.

I reached in and gave her shoulder a squeeze. This time she didn't flinch. Her eyes never left mine.

Blue came from the kitchen and let her out of the cage with the key. "You two should get a room."

I spun on him. "It's not like that, and fair warning, Blue, I won't put up with that kind of talk. I'll take all the other shit you feed me, but not that. You understand?"

"Fair enough, big man. I know how to color inside the lines." He winked and turned serious. "If Mo Mo doesn't get here soon, we're gonna have a full house."

Chelsea tried to further change the mood. "I gotta tell ya, this is the most fun I've had in a long time. But I'm not sure about this other part. Is it legal to sell dope you just seized and then arrest someone else for the same dope? How are we going to use the same evidence for two separate cases in court?"

Blue smiled and shrugged. "How should I know? That's what the attorneys get the big bucks for."

We all chuckled and headed back into the kitchen.

And didn't make it there before the doorbell rang.

CHAPTER THIRTY-FOUR

IN THE NEXT forty-five minutes, the floor in the den off the kitchen filled with every variety of cocaine user, from the street urchins to hookers to college students, and even one guy in a suit on his way back to work from lunch. We kept all the property and the cocaine they purchased from me separate, in clear plastic bags and brown paper lunch sacks. With each new addition to the horde, the noise level rose a little more. If they wanted to rebel, they could easily overpower us.

Blue selected a movie and shoved it into the VCR hooked up to the huge television. The audience cheered and clapped when the lead-in for the movie came on, *Scarface,* with Al Pacino. Blue reached into the sack containing Tark's property that came off his person, and pulled out a handful of cash. "Here"—he shoved it toward Chelsea—"run out and get cheeseburgers and chocolate malts for everyone."

She looked stunned.

I reached to take the money from him. "I'll go."

"No, we need you here to sell the dope."

I pointed to Ollie. "She could sell the rock a lot easier than I can."

"Think about what you're sayin'," Blue said. "She's a criminal. How's she going to testify in court with any credibility? And what will that do to *her* case?"

I couldn't help but smile at the irony. "We're cops sellin' dope to crooks and then arresting them. Don't you see a problem with that? Let Ollie go after we're done with this. She only carried the money. We only caught her with the money and she did help us get in here."

"We'll see how things go."

Chelsea said, "No problem, I'll go. Just tell me where the closest burger place is."

Ollie, who had been eavesdropping, struggled to her feet and came over. "I'll go wit her. There's a good place over on Compton right off 'n Willowbrook. Got some great chicken wings."

Blue said, "Can you handle Ollie?"

"Of course."

"Go on, take her and hurry back, but only cheeseburgers and chocolate malts. We don't need a riot over the food. Bring extra because the body count's still rising."

In another forty-five minutes the number of suspects doubled, and they now sat shoulder to shoulder, ass cheek to ass cheek, eating cheeseburgers and drinking chocolate malts, cheering for the bad guys on the big screen. One of the less-than-mentally gifted street urchins kept standing up and mimicking a line from the end of the movie that had yet to play: "*Say hello to my little friend.*" The crowd yelled and cussed him, pulled him back down and pelted him with French fries.

Blue looked at Chelsea. "That's why I said only cheeseburgers."

Finally, the doorbell stopped ringing. Fifteen minutes after that, the phone on the wall rang. Blue picked it up and stepped around the corner into the living room, where I stood ready to meet the customers, who, without good cause, had petered out. I put my head up to Blue's to listen.

Blue said, "Yeah?"

"Well, hellooo, Mister Poooleeseman. What are you doing in my crib?"

Word on the street had gotten back to Mo Mo. Of course, it would. Just a matter of time really, and ours had run out.

Blue didn't even try to bullshit his way out of it. "Hey, Mo Mo, we're here throwing a little party in your honor and you're late."

"Nice try, Mr. Pooleese. Who is this? Is this my good friend, the guy who's been all over my ass trying to catch me dirty? My sworn enemy, Deputy Black 'n Blue?"

"We're here waiting to cut the cake," Blue said. "But I guess you're going to be rude about it and not show up to your own party."

"I have to say no to that, but if you don't mind, I'll have my people call your people to set up a meet for some other time. Thank you, Officer. Please clean up and lock the door after you're done." He clicked off.

Blue threw the phone against the wall and kicked three holes in the plasterboard before his rage subsided. He stood there breathing hard, his eyes fierce as he pondered his next move. He'd given it a helluva shot and lost.

And Mo Mo had just rubbed his face in it.

That was the first I'd heard of his nickname, Black 'n Blue.

I couldn't help but feel sorry for him. In the short time of the caper on Peach, I'd come to respect and admire him. At least a little, anyway. As stupid as that sounded under the circumstances.

"Hey," I said, "at least we wounded him. We took a couple of pounds of rock off the street and that cost him. We also took down some of his main people. We definitely put a dent in his operation."

"I don't want to just dent his operation, I want to blow it up."

He picked up the phone and handed it to me. "Call dispatch, have them assign at least three patrol units to shuttle all of these mutants here back to the station. You and Chelsea are gonna have to help the jailer booking these fools. I'll stand by here with Dirt until they're all gone then meet you back at the station. Leave Tark and Ollie till last. I want to interview them back in the trailer."

I did as he asked and made the call.

Each Lynwood Station cop car took five crooks, and if you jammed them in and shoved hard on the door to get it latched, sometimes six. We loaded the cars twice before we reached the halfway point.

Blue didn't help with the mundane job of handling the crooks. He retrieved a sledgehammer from the trunk of the maroon Chevy undercover car, the sledge used to knock down doors on search warrants, and he went to work dismantling the inside birdcage. He took his shirt off, really put his back into it, and got out a lot of frustration. He violated policy taking down the cage, damaging personal property, but I agreed with him going outside the rules on this one. I never wanted to make entry on another cage.

In between shuttling the crooks out to the patrol cars, I caught Chelsea twice staring at Blue swinging the sledge as his muscles bulged and his brown skin glistened.

Blue paused. The clanging stopped but still rang in our ears. He turned to me, breathing hard and sweating. "Okay, you two head back to the station and help get started with the booking and fingerprints so the captain doesn't blow a blood vessel. We'll finish up here."

I nodded. He picked up his sledge and went back at the wrought-iron cage with renewed vigor and rage.

Blue didn't have to tell us not to say anything to the captain about Blue being out in the field against direct orders.

I escorted Chocolate out of the den, through the mangled and semi-dismantled cage and into the front yard. "You owe me for this one," I said.

She smiled. "I don't think so, Deputy Johnson. I didn't do anything wrong this time. But I'll be happy to give you a free one, anytime." She leaned up and kissed me on the cheek before I could stop her.

"That's not what I meant." I turned to Chelsea. "That's not what I meant."

Chelsea just smiled and shook her head.

I watched Chocolate walk down the street. She exuded a sexy eroticism that radiated like an aura and a tractor beam for all things male.

I got in my truck and started up. Chelsea said, "That was a kick in the ass, arresting that many dopers at one time, all for possession. You ever do anything like that before?"

"No, not even close. I know one thing for sure, though. If we keep hangin' out with Blue, we're going to be doing a lot more of that, rule book be damned."

"Yeah, he's really something, isn't he? I'm going to like working here. I really am."

I didn't have any reason to, and it didn't make sense, but I was a little jealous of Blue. An odd thought popped into my head that I needed to increase the number of sets in my daily regimen of push-ups and sit-ups.

I nodded, put it in gear, and drove down Peach. We passed Chocolate, who waved.

"Hey." Chelsea smiled big. "Why don't we stop by your house to check and see if you left the stove on?"

CHAPTER THIRTY-FIVE

"MY HOUSE?" I said. "Oh, my house. Sure, we can stop by there."

I'd agreed too soon. She'd only been playing with me, and I hadn't seen it in time. I didn't want her to experience our little shabby house in The Corner Pocket, in the ghetto. What did it matter, though? Sure, I'd show it to her.

Minutes later, I turned down Nord and jerked the wheel hard, pulled right over to the curb, seven or eight houses down from our house. I sat there, a little stunned. Up on the porch to Dad's house stood a woman I'd never seen before. About the same age as Dad, dressed nice in business attire, a conservative navy blue pantsuit.

And . . . and Dad stood there hugging her with one arm, the baby held in the other. As he . . . as . . . as he kissed this strange woman.

Not a simple, chaste good-bye kiss, either. He really leaned into it. The kiss went on and on. I squirmed in my seat as I watched. I'd never seen Dad with a woman other than Mom. I never even pictured him with one. While Noble and I were growing up, Dad had put us first, his job second, and the rest of his time, his personal life, he put on hold . . . for us. I never truly realized the enormity of his sacrifice until that moment with the woman in his arm. And my child in the other, a child I would now have to make the same kind of sacrifice for.

Chelsea looked at me, then followed my gaze. "Who's that?"

"That . . . that's my dad."

"Boy, that's some kiss. He's a regular Don Juan."

I broke focus and looked at her. "Dad doesn't have a girlfriend. He's never had a girlfriend." The statement sounded odd even to me. Why wouldn't he have a girlfriend? Then, more strange thoughts crowded in. Had he had one all these years and I just didn't know about it? And why in the world would I say that to Chelsea?

Maybe because the woman was white.

Chelsea said, "Well, I guess he's got one now. I'm not kidding, that's really some kinda kiss."

I blushed for my father. I couldn't drive up while they stood on the porch, not even if I wanted to; my hands wouldn't obey any commands.

My dad had a girlfriend, and far off in the back of my brain, a little twinge made me think she looked vaguely familiar, like I'd seen her before. The way my mind worked, her name would bubble up in my brain later on, after I'd calmed down.

I waited until the woman gave Dad a final squeeze on his hand, climbed down the steps from the stoop, and headed for her car, a nice late-model, midnight-blue Cadillac Eldorado parked at the curb. The Caddy drove off down the street, headed west.

Dad went inside without ever looking east toward us. I shifted into first gear and drove up to the house. "We can only stay a minute," I said. "We have to get back to the station to help out."

Chelsea had already opened her door. She got out and stood looking back through the truck. "I know. I guess with your dad home, you didn't have to worry about that burner on the stove, after all. Is that your kid he's holding?"

"Yes."

"What's its name?"

"I . . . ah, well, we haven't named her yet."

She shut the door and came around the front of the truck to my side, her expression confused. We started walking up to the house.

"She's a girl then? How could you not have named her?"

"It's a long story. Where did *you* grow up?"

"Oh no, buddy boy, you're not going to change the subject that easily. Come on, give."

We stopped at the foot of the steps, my anger starting to rise at her sticking her nose into my personal business. I took a breath and tried to calm down. Would I have been as mad if my daughter had not been the product of an inappropriate liaison with a female deputy, a deputy I'd been assigned to train? Or if my daughter had come to me in a more conventional manner with a name and a mother who was the least bit interested in the child's welfare? Or if my daughter weren't half white, an unfair social handicap she'd have to live with the rest of her life? Something Chelsea would never understand.

Dad must've heard us talking. He opened the door and looked surprised to see us. He stuck his head out and checked the street, looked to the west to see if his Eldorado lady had made a clean getaway without me seeing her. Too bad, old man; no such luck. You're busted.

"Dad, this is my new partner, Chelsea Miller. Chelsea, this is my dad, Xander Johnson."

She took the three wood steps up, gave Dad a big smile, and shook his hand. "Nice to meet you, Mr. Johnson."

Dad pulled on her hand. "Come in. Come in. Can I get you something—some coffee, a soda?"

"We can't stay," I said, following them inside. "We only stopped in for a minute, to see if you needed anything. We have to get back to the station. We have a ton of paperwork ahead of us that has to be finished tonight. They're all in-custodies."

The small house I grew up in smelled of baby powder with a hint of sour—a hint of baby throw-up. What a contrast to Ollie's van and the rock house not all that far away, three or five miles at the most.

I moved in close. "Here, let me hold her."

He handed her over and kept his hands in the air close to her as if his mind hadn't fully agreed to let her go. I took her and supported her head like he taught me.

"Dad, what's that on your cheek? Is that lipstick?" I didn't see anything on his cheek, I just wanted to game him a little, see what he'd do. And instantly felt guilty about it.

He wiped the side of his face. "Huh? What? Oh, no, no, probably something from Olivia."

"Olivia?" I couldn't believe he'd copped out to his girlfriend so easily. I didn't know anyone named Olivia.

"That's right, I named your daughter. You said I could. And I know I said I wouldn't. I wanted you to do it, but it wasn't right that this beautiful little girl didn't have a name."

He shook my world with his simple words about my child's name.

"Olivia," Chelsea, said. "What a beautiful name. Here, Bruno, let me hold her."

I didn't want to give her up, but the name thing hit me like a kick to the stomach. I handed her over to Chelsea, who took her and gently bounced her and cooed to her, a big smile on her face.

"Son, you okay with the name Olivia?"

"Of course I am. Is there a reason why you chose that particular name?" I couldn't help the horrible thoughts that pinged around in my brain. That he'd named her after the woman who'd just left. A woman I didn't know. "You know someone named Olivia?"

The concern in his expression shifted to suspicion and a little anger. "Yes. That was your mother's middle name."

Of course, how could I have forgotten? What a fool for not seeing it right off.

"Then that's a perfect name for my daughter. Thank you, Dad."

He beamed.

"Chels, we really should be going."

She stopped bouncing when she heard me use a too-familiar nickname, one I hadn't yet earned.

"Yeah," she said, "let's get moving."

She placed Olivia in Dad's arms and headed for the door. She stepped out on the porch. I lowered my voice. "Hey, Dad, stay out of Fruit Town for a few days, okay?"

He nodded and hurried over, lowering his voice. "I heard what went on over on Peach. That was really something. I'm proud that you had something to do with it."

"You heard about that already? That quick?"

He nodded again. "It's all over town."

Why was I surprised? The grapevine in the ghetto traveled at the speed of light.

Dad nodded toward the door where Chelsea stood outside on the stoop. "She's really cute and she took right to—"

"Stop it, Dad. Don't start doing that."

He smiled and punched me in the shoulder. "Riiight. But I saw the way you looked at that sweet little girl. Just promise me to take it slow this time and don't scare her off. She's a keeper."

"It's not like that. And go on and tell me how you, with your Great Carnac ability, can see that she's a keeper in the short time she was in our house?"

"That's right, I can. I know women, Son. You might not believe it, but I know women."

"I'll bet you do."

"What?"

"We'll talk when I get home."

From outside, Chelsea yelled, "Come on, Bruno, we have to roll."

"Coming."

"See you later tonight, Dad."

"Be careful, Son, and keep your head down."

"I will, Dad."

CHAPTER THIRTY-SIX

THE NEXT DAY, I arrived early to the mobile home set in the back of Lynwood Station. My footsteps thumped up the wooden steps. I peeked inside. Empty. I went in the rest of the way. Blue's clothes—his jeans, t-shirt, underwear, and change of socks—sat folded neatly on his desk, just like the day before. Right alongside sat the Smith and Wesson 9mm, the one Wicks gave me to carry. The one he entrusted to me. I took it back and stuck it in my waistband. I chose one of the four unoccupied, unassigned desks and sat down. I spun around and around in the desk chair. I got up, went over to Blue's desk and the overflowing "in" basket filled with the previous night's rockhouse arrests.

For the first time, with no one else present, I had a chance to really look around. Taped to the cheap wood paneling over Blue's desk was a Xerox copy of a quote:

There is no hunting like the hunting of man, and those
who have hunted armed men long enough and liked it,
never care for anything else thereafter.
Ernest Hemingway

The quote fit Blue too perfectly.

I picked up the whole bundle of arrest packages, sixty-seven of them, and took them back to my desk. Each one needed a CR-1, a

CR-2, and a CR-3, a crime report face page, the narrative describing the arrest, and an evidence form. Hours and hours of work. I started to fill in the first one, transferring the information from the booking slip.

The steps outside thumped. In popped Blue, out of breath, dressed in his Dolphins running shorts, his sweat-soaked t-shirt, and the sock on his hand covering the small .38. "Morning, Bruno."

"Good morning."

He went right to his desk, paused for a second, and then picked up a tall yellow plastic cup. He pulled his shorts down and peed in the cup right in front of me. The man had no shame.

He walked back to the door, stepped out on the stoop, and tossed the urine toward the street and the people who'd ratted him out to the captain the day before. He came back in and set the cup on top of the filing cabinet by the door.

I worked on the reports and without looking at him said, "Somebody might want a drink of water and use that cup."

Blue walked by me to his desk. He opened his top drawer, took something out, and went back to the cup. He tinkered with it for a minute. "There." He set the cup back down on the filing cabinet. He'd added a "*Danger—Biohazard/Biowaste*" sticker to the cup, stickers we used to label blood evidence when we sent it to the lab. "You happy now?"

"Yes, thank you."

He came back over to me and stood by my desk chair. "Stand up."

"Please stand up?" I said.

He stood there and said nothing.

I slowly stood.

He took Wicks' 9mm from my waistband and went back to his desk. He stripped down naked and wiped his glistening body off with a towel from his gym bag.

I'd given in to his possession. Wicks would just have to live with it or get his own gun back. "You know," I said, "that gun has a magazine safety. If you take the magazine out, it won't fire the one still in the chamber."

He picked up the gun and looked at it. "Huh. Thanks. I'll remember that. I've never used an auto loader."

He'd just donned his clean briefs when Chelsea walked in. She pretended not to notice the semi-naked Blue, came over, took the desk next to mine, and grabbed half of the booking packages from my desk. "Hey, Bruno," she said. "You get enough sleep?"

We'd stayed past midnight booking all the prisoners. By the time I got home, Dad was asleep in the recliner with Olivia in his arms, also asleep. I'd wanted to talk to him about the lady with the Eldorado, but didn't want to wake him.

"I got a solid five hours before Dad had to go to work and I took over the baby duties."

"You've got a really cute little girl. You have to be really proud of her."

"You have no idea."

I really hadn't had too much of a chance to think about being a proud father until she'd said something. The truth of it made my heart swell, and I sat up a little straighter.

The steps outside thumped. In came an unhappy Thibodeaux with a box loaded with all of patrol's evidence from the night before, as well as the sixty-seven envelopes of rock cocaine from our arrests. On his way by my desk, he dropped a slip of scratch paper onto my pile of reports. "Use that DR number as the master and refer all of those other cases to that number."

I said, "Roger."

"Don't get smart with me, asshole."

I stood. "Look, I don't know what I did to piss you off, but let's end it right here. I'm sorry for whatever I did that upset you." I offered him my hand.

He looked me in the eye and didn't move.

Outside, the steps thumped again. On the other side of Thibodeaux, Blue hurried to finish buttoning his Levi's and quickly slipped the out-of-policy 9mm that belonged to Wicks under his t-shirt on his desk.

Just as Captain Stubbs entered our office.

This time, he smiled hugely as he stood for a moment, taking us all in. "I just wanted to come out to personally tell the team here what a great job you did yesterday."

Blue said, "Thanks, Captain. But I feel bad that my team filled up your jail and caused all of that extra work."

Stubbs held up his hand. "No, no, I love it. A full jail is a happy jail. That was a helluva bust, a helluva bust. Keep up the good work."

"We missed Mo Mo . . . Lucas Knight," Blue said.

"You'll get him, I have every faith in you. You need something, anything, you let me know." He turned to leave.

Blue said, "How about raising our overtime limit?"

Stubbs' shoulders came back as he froze and didn't turn around. "I can do that. Just don't abuse it." He continued on out.

Thibodeaux whispered, "Pompous ass."

Blue put on his t-shirt. "Knock it off. And get your head right about Bruno, too, or you and I are going to have a problem. We're a team now, so get used to it."

Thibodeaux tossed the box of evidence on his desk and headed back to the door.

"Where you going?" Blue asked.

"Ta get some coffee and some fresh air. This place stinks like a dinge."

"Get back here."

By dinge, he meant me.

Thibodeaux kept going. Outside, he got in his car, an ugly lime-green Thunderbird, started up, and chirped the tires backing out.

My bearing witness to Thibodeaux's embarrassment when he dropped his gun on the Mona armed robbery didn't justify this level of anger, not even close. Something else was in play. I turned to Blue. "What'd I do to piss him off?"

Blue grinned and hesitated. "Some of us just rub others of us the wrong way. Don't worry about it, he'll come around."

The grin, the way he said it, sent a long shiver up my back. Maybe I imagined it, but I thought the two of them had somehow figured out the reason for my assignment to their team. I shook the feeling off with a shudder and went back to work.

CHAPTER THIRTY-SEVEN

THIBODEAUX NEVER CAME back. Blue didn't seem to mind. He never paged Thibodeaux to ask him what the hell happened to him. Partners knew and trusted each other that way.

The arrest reports took the rest of the day, and we still needed a few more hours to finish. At four thirty, my pager went off: three sevens, a designated code. Robby Wicks wanted to meet.

Blue didn't look up and continued to write. "Who's that?"

"It's just my dad." I picked up the phone and dialed Wicks. The phone on the other end picked up on the first ring. I said, "It's me, Dad."

Wicks said, "Meet me, location three, in thirty minutes. Make sure you're not tailed." He hung up.

"Did you change her diaper?" I said into the dead phone. "Try burping her. Okay, okay, no problem, I'm leaving now. Thanks, Dad. I'll be right home." I hung up.

Blue looked up from his paperwork. "If you need to go, take off. Me and Miller can handle the rest of these reports."

Chelsea said, "Sure, Bruno. We got it. Go ahead."

"Thanks. It won't always be like this, I promise." Lying to these two stuck in my throat like a sideways stick.

"No, it's cool. Don't worry about it," Blue said. "I have two boys of my own. I know what it's like. What's the matter?"

He'd read my reaction to the information that he had two boys. I just never thought that he'd have a family, not a contract killer. The morally incongruent nature of his fatherhood, juxtaposed with his being a cold-blooded murderer, sucked the wind out of me. What would those boys do when we finally took down their dad and he went to prison forever? I wasn't sure it would've bothered me as much if I didn't have Olivia at home waiting on me, depending on me. "Great. Thanks again. See you both tomorrow."

Blue went back to writing and just raised his hand in a wave. Chelsea stared at me. "Yeah, see you tomorrow."

Her words trailed off a little as if she wanted to say something else. I waited a moment more to give her a chance to say it, and when she didn't, I got up and left. I made it down the steps and halfway across the parking lot when Chelsea called to me from the stoop. "Bruno?"

I stopped. The afternoon had turned hot and I hadn't really noticed it.

She walked down the steps and quickly over to me. And maybe she stood a little closer than she should have. Or I could've just been imagining that part in a wishful thinking sort of way.

"What's the matter?" I asked.

"Nothing. Nothing really, I mean—"

"Are you okay staying here with Blue? Is there a problem?"

"What? Oh, no. It's not that at all. It's just that . . . I was wondering if I could meet you later."

"What?"

"No, no, it's not like that." She shot a quick glance back over her shoulder at the mobile home. "I just want to talk about some work stuff."

"Sure, of course, no problem. Page me later."

"Thanks, Bruno, maybe in an hour or so. Maybe I'll just come by your house."

"Page me first."

"Oh, okay, I will. Thanks." She turned and walked back to the office slower than she had come out. I watched her go and shouldn't have. Blue would be watching me from the office, watching her.

Why had I insisted that she page me before she came over? Was I worried Sonja would snap out of her funk and right out of the blue show up at Dad's? Try and pick up where we'd left off over seven months ago? Start up again as if nothing had happened?

I stood in the parking lot a moment longer trying to check my feelings for Sonja and realized I didn't think I loved her anymore. Not after what she'd done. She didn't tell me about her pregnancy. She hid out from me and didn't leave any way to contact her. I'd worried about her night and day for months, until that worry finally started to fade. Millie had been the first woman I'd dated after Sonja. If Sonja truly loved me as I'd loved her, how could she do those things? And the worst part was how she'd treated little Olivia at a time when Olivia needed her the most.

No, I didn't think I loved Sonja anymore. Didn't think I could if I wanted to.

The bad little Bruno on my shoulder rang in: *Or, are all of these new negative feelings about Sonja bullshit, because you got eyes for this new girl, Chelsea?*

"Don't be ridiculous," I said to no one at all. But even I didn't believe my own words.

I drove over to Stops, a barbecue joint on Imperial across from the Nickerson Courts housing projects. On the way, I made a couple of abrupt turns into culs-de-sac, stopping and waiting to see if anyone followed. I didn't know anything about countersurveillance. They hadn't trained me for it. In fact, they hadn't given me any training at all for this undercover job.

Finally, I drove around back, parked, and went inside. My stomach growled when it caught a whiff of the heavenly aroma that wafted on the air. I closed my eyes and stuck my nose up.

I ordered a hot-link sandwich with extra sauce, some chili fries, and a Coke from Nancy, the nice girl at the counter. She wore her long black hair down and always had a smile for me. After Sonja, I'd thought about asking Nancy out, but before I had the chance, she slipped into the conversation that she was married to a fireman.

I took the food to a table outside.

Dad used to bring Noble and me to Stops for special occasions. Those memories of the good times, before Noble slipped over to the dark side, came flooding back and caused a little ache in my chest. An ache for something lost forever that could never return. Those times had also been so much simpler, without all the drama and stress. More and more, it seemed like life added higher levels of conflict and complications. Would it ever level off and stay constant?

Wicks showed up ten minutes later, just as I ate the last fry and wiped my mouth one last time with the napkin. He didn't wave or even acknowledge my presence and walked into the take-out restaurant to order. I got up, threw my trash in the can, and moved to a picnic table on the south side, out of view of Imperial Highway, out of view of any prying eyes in the cars driving by.

Wicks came out, looked at the table where I'd been sitting, looked around, spotted the new location, and came over. He stood next to the table and took a bite of his sandwich. He leaned over to keep the sauce from dripping on his suit. He spoke around the food in his mouth. "Where'd Thibodeaux go today?"

"You have a surveillance up on the narco office?"

How hard would that be? Put a car on the street behind the station, you could see right through the chain-link fence—see the narco trailer, the parking lot, the whole thing.

He said nothing. He chewed and looked at me.

"Thibodeaux's carrying some kinda grudge against me. We had words. He got in his car and split about eight o'clock this morning and never came back. He never said where he was going and Blue didn't let on if he knew either."

Wicks nodded, swallowed. "Did you ever think that this dustup between him and you is nothing more than a ruse so he could get away from the office?"

"What are you talking about? Why would he—?"

My mind spun at this new wrinkle. Why would he need a good reason to leave the office?

CHAPTER THIRTY-EIGHT

I SAT ON the picnic table and put my feet on the bench as the summer sun dropped lower in the sky. "No, I hadn't thought of that." I played back from memory the little snit Thibodeaux threw in the office. I shook my head. "If he did use the argument as a ruse, he's a pretty good actor. I didn't see it that way at the time."

My pager went off. I checked it. It was the code for Dad; he wanted me to come home for something. He probably needed more diapers or formula. Or maybe he'd just gotten tired of caring for such a small child.

Wicks took another bite and said, "Tell me about yesterday. How'd that go down?"

"You know about the stash house?"

He took another bite and gave me the eye.

"Blue sent me and Chelsea out to watch this house in Fruit Town."

"The one on Peach?"

"That's right. We took down a woman named Ollie Bell who made a delivery. We called Blue and Thibodeaux on the radio. They came out, we hit the place and took it down."

"Yeah, and I bet your butthole really puckered when you went inside that birdcage, didn't it?"

He'd seen everything, knew everything that went on. My God, had he seen my fear when Ollie and I walked up to that metal door on Peach? Seen it in my body language?

I suppressed my embarrassment. "If you already know all of this," I said, "why are you asking me?"

"Keep talking."

I watched him for a moment. He nodded for me to continue as he took another bite.

"We missed Mo Mo. His real name's Lucas Knight. So we waited for him."

He pointed his hot-link sandwich at me. "Selling rock and yanking the good citizens of Fruit Town into the house. That was a good caper, very creative. Blue really knows how to think outside the box."

He said it as if he admired his adversary. Our adversary.

"What exactly is it that you want to know?" I asked. "Why'd you risk calling this meeting if you already know all of this?"

He took another bite and wiped his mouth with a napkin, eating the hot link way too fast. "Because I think you already have the information, the probable cause for the search warrant."

"What?" My mind whipped back over all that happened yesterday, and I still didn't see what he could possibly be talking about.

"You mean because Blue left his desk against direct orders from the captain?"

"Nah. Come on, Bruno, you're better than that. Violation of a direct order is human resources shit and in no way rises to the level of criminal probable cause."

"What then? Tell me." I didn't like the way he talked down to me. I'd tell him about it soon, give him an ultimatum.

"No, you tell me about the money."

"The money?"

He nodded and took another bite. He ate like a ravenous caveman.

"Ollie Bell dropped off the coke. Least that's what we assumed. They rock it up right there in the house."

Wicks waved at me to keep going.

"We stopped her going away from the location. She had a bag of... money."

Wicks wagged his finger at me. "Riiight. How much?"

"We didn't count it."

"Ah, man, you're kiddin' me."

I shrugged as the guilt for screwing up started to sour my stomach. "How was I supposed to do that?"

"Did you try to count it and Blue or Thibodeaux stopped you?" He winked, as if he wanted me to lie to attain the probable cause.

"No. I really blew it, didn't I? Blue told Thibodeaux to run the money into narcotics headquarters to get a hard count."

Wicks shook his head. "Just take it easy. Maybe this can be salvaged. Did you get a look at the money?"

"Yeah."

"Estimate. How much would you say was there?"

I closed my eyes and tried to conjure up the scene. I opened my eyes. "No chance. I couldn't even come close to guesstimating the amount. That'd be like guessing how many jelly beans in a pickle jar. No, no chance, I'm sorry."

Wicks smiled and shook his head. "You buy him books, send him to school, and he eats the covers. Well, it was a shot anyway."

Dad paged again. I checked the readout. This time he added the code "911." An emergency.

With this new distraction, my mind relaxed on the other problem about the money screwup and locked in on something said the day before on Peach. "Wait a minute. I went with Ollie to the door."

I paused as I ran it back in my head to be sure.

"Yeah, and—"

"She was the one who got us in on a ruse. She told Tark that his bag came up short. She used that as an excuse to get us on the other side of the birdcage gate."

"Yeah, what did she say exactly?"

"She said the bag only had fifty thousand in it."

"And what did this Tark say?"

"He said that he'd already called in the amount to Mo Mo."

"How much?"

"He said that he told Mo Mo there was sixty-two five."

Wicks clenched his fist and jerked his arm back. "Got you, asshole."

"Why? How much money did Thibodeaux log in?"

"An even forty K."

"They skimmed twenty-two five? You're kiddin' me! Right in front of us like that? In front of me and Chelsea?"

"Looks that way. Even if they didn't really do it and there really was only 40K, there's still probable cause to legally start up the investigation. But there's no doubt in my mind that they took it. Now we can get the wiretap up and running. Listen, now they're going to figure you're suspicious about the money. They're going to assume you know. That's what I'd assume. And that makes you a liability. They're probably going to—"

My pager went off again. Dad. This time with two "911s."

"Am I keeping you from something, Deputy?"

"Sorry, I really need to go."

He locked his jaw and stared at me.

"It's my kid."

"I figured. What I was saying is that they're going to come at you now."

"What do you mean?"

"They need to get you dirty more than ever. They're probably going to offer you a chunk of that skim. If they do, you hem and haw a little, just enough to make it look good. You say something about having a new kid, and all the added costs. Yada, yada, like that, and then you take it. You understand you take the skim and report it to me as soon as you can. Without risking your cover."

"Okay, I got it. But I'm sorry. I really have to run. My dad doesn't put 911 in the pager lightly. Something's really wrong."

He slapped me on the shoulder. "Okay, go, go. Let me know what's goin' on with your kid. If you need me to help with anything at all, and I mean anything, you call me. I'm here for you."

"Thanks."

His offer didn't sound too genuine, as if he'd only said it as a manner of etiquette. I ran to my truck.

He yelled at my back. "I need the supplement report on what you just told me, ASAP. So I can get that tap up and running."

"Got it. Will do."

I got in, started up, and spun the tires leaving the parking lot.

CHAPTER THIRTY-NINE

MY MIND SPUN in all directions as I wove in and out of the neighborhood streets where I'd run barefoot as a youngster on hot summer afternoons, dodging in and out of alleys on full alert for gang members who continually tried to recruit me. Happy times for the memory, not so much back then living the reality of it.

Of course, I worried about what could possibly be going wrong at home with Dad and Olivia. But important thoughts of the job also horned in. The things Wicks said about Thibodeaux putting on an act and that I'd somehow missed the read on him. How could Wicks possibly know that Thibodeaux wasn't truly angry with me, and was putting up a façade? Wicks wasn't there when Thibodeaux threw his fit. And Wicks didn't know Thibodeaux well enough to guess either. Not on that kind of personal level.

I did though. I sat in the cop car with him during the robbery surveillance on Mona. He and I went through a harrowing officer-involved shooting where someone got gunned down mere feet from us. I'd worked the caper on Peach Street with him where we'd arrested sixty-seven suspects. You tended to learn about someone during these types of events, during the hours and hours they involved.

Then my mind all of a sudden clicked over to Chelsea. I'd fully intended to tell Wicks what I'd learned about her, that I thought she wasn't who she said she was. Tell him about how she used the term "dog heavy" and ask him to look into her background. Ask him to try and confirm her story as to why she now worked on the Lynwood narco team.

Why didn't I tell him about Chelsea?

All of that went through my head on the short ten-minute drive.

Until I turned onto Nord Street.

Then my mind went crazy with panic. Two black-and-white sheriff's cars sat in front of Dad's house.

I hit the gas, wound out the engine on the Ford Ranger, and skidded to a stop, the tires smoking. I jumped out and ran as the truck still lurched forward and jerked to a stop. On my way to the open front door, a muffled yell caught my attention. I stopped and looked back toward the street. Dad sat in the back of one of the black-and-whites, his face partially mashed up against the window as he yelled to me for help.

Dad, arrested?

"What the hell? Dad?"

I ran back to the street and to the back door of the cop car. I pulled it open just as two uniformed deputies appeared out of nowhere and grabbed my arms. They pulled me away and kicked the door shut. The deputy named Good Johnson got me in a wristlock and wrestled me to the ground with the help of his trainee, who grappled my knees and moved up to put his knees in my back to hold me down.

I worked patrol with Good Johnson. I became the second Johnson assigned to Lynwood. Two Johnsons at the same station became confusing. Cops called each other by their last names. The other Johnson, a prejudiced bigot, called me Boy. All the other regular deputies christened him The Good Johnson and me The Bad Johnson. Only Good was anything but.

Anger like I never experienced surged. Using my knees, I lifted them both off the ground in a one-armed push-up.

Another set of shoes appeared on the ground in front of my face, black wingtips. Lynwood detective Sergeant Kohl yelled, "Johnson, get up off of Johnson." Two more detectives jumped in and separated us. I struggled to my feet and lunged at Good, wanting to rip his throat out for arresting Dad. They restrained me.

Good stood, his sheriff's star torn loose and hanging from his uniform as he yelled, "Let him go. Let the son of a bitch go. I'll give him what he's got comin'. Let the bastard go." He stood with his black baton in his hand, his face bloated with rage.

"That's enough," Kohl said. "Stand down or I'll write your ass up."

Good's wild-eyed expression gradually calmed. He bent over and scooped up his handcuffs from the ground where he'd lost them in the melee. He'd tried to handcuff me as well, to make it a family affair.

Kohl said to him, "Go sit in the car. Now, Johnson, do it."

Good hesitated, giving me the stink eye, then turned and did as the sergeant ordered. His trainee stood there looking confused. Kohl said to him, "You, too, FNG."

I tried to control my breathing and jerked my arm out of Kohl's grasp. "Why's my father under arrest? What happened? What is it you think he did?"

"Take it easy, Bruno."

"Don't you tell me to take it easy. Tell me what happened. And then let him out and take the cuffs off. Whatever it is you think he did, he didn't do it."

Kohl straightened up as his expression turned angry. "Don't you dare tell me what to do, Johnson. You understand?"

He'd always been a friend, and I'd just disrespected him. I calmed even more, took in some deep breaths. "I'm sorry. This is a crazy situation. Please, tell me what's happened. Hey, where's my daughter?"

"She's okay. She's in the house with a neighbor lady, Mrs. Espinoza."

I looked back at the house. Mrs. Espinoza stood in the doorway, gently bouncing little Olivia in her arms. I waved. "It's okay, Mrs. Espinoza. I'm here now. I'll get this all straightened out."

She didn't smile as she usually did. She just went inside and closed the door. Closed the door as if she didn't want little Olivia exposed to this type of embarrassing family degradation.

I took another couple of deep breaths. "Okay, now tell me."

"Bruno, your father's been accused of rape."

"What? No way. No chance. That's not possible." I turned to head to the cop car with Dad in the back. Kohl grabbed my arm. I tried to shrug him off.

"Bruno, you need to calm down and listen to me. We're friends, but I'll arrest you if you try to intercede. You understand? You won't give me any choice."

"Let me talk to him. Just let me talk to him."

"I will if you promise to control yourself."

"Okay. Okay, let me go. I'll be good, I promise."

Kohl released my arm as I jerked it away.

I walked over to the car. Dad sat back from the window with tears of frustration wetting his face. I don't ever remember seeing him cry. He turned his face away, ashamed. It ripped my heart out, and I wanted someplace to vent my anger. If Good had still stood close enough to me, I'd have ripped his head right off his shoulders and kicked it down the street.

I opened the car door. Dad turned his head even more and wouldn't look at me.

"It's okay, Dad. I'm here now. Everything's going to be okay. Just tell me what happened."

He started to sputter. All his words cluttered together, caught in his throat, and came out in a jumbled rush.

CHAPTER FORTY

"DAD, IT'S OKAY, I know you didn't do it. Tell me what happened. What did they say you did?"

He composed himself and turned to look me in the eye. Some of his pride returned and he grew stronger by the second. "It's that nice Mrs. Whitaker, over in East Compton. She lives in that old estate off of Atlantic Drive, the one with the big long lot in the front and the long tree-lined driveway. Lots of pink crepe myrtles, absolutely beautiful when they bloom. I deliver mail to her every day. She's on my route."

With all the stress, he threw in a lot of extraneous information. I didn't stop him. I let him tell it in his own way.

He said, "We talk now and again. She invites me in on hot days for iced tea." He shook his head. "She called the sheriffs on me, Son. She told 'em I tried to rape her. You know better than that, Bruno. I don't know what got into that woman. I never so much as touched her. I thought we really got along just fine."

The image of the midnight-blue Eldorado lady horned into my thoughts. I wanted to ask him about her. Was she the nice Mrs. Whitaker? Had to be. Right then wasn't the time. But he'd just said he'd never touched her when I'd seen him hugging and kissing her on our front stoop.

I patted his shoulder. "I know. It's all right. I'll take care of everything. You just sit tight, okay?" I'd calmed down a little listening to him talk and couldn't help but sense the fear that had edged into his voice. It made a lump rise in my throat. No way would he go to jail. Not if I could help it.

I eased the door closed and turned to Kohl, who waited close by—close enough to stop me if I tried to let Dad out of the car.

"You have to believe me," I said to Kohl. "He'd never do anything like this. I don't understand why—"

Wicks' words echoed in the back in my brain. *"Blue and Thibodeaux are going to try and dirty you up. They need to more than ever now."*

What if they thought I couldn't be dirtied? Not in the more obvious ways, like accepting the skim? Would they be low enough to set a frame on my father in order to put me in a box?

What a dumbass question; of course they would. They were contract killers without a conscience, without moral compasses. Rogue cops who killed people for profit.

Kohl read my expression. "What, Bruno? What did you just think of?"

"What? Oh, nothing." As quick as the thought came, so did the admonishment that I could tell no one of my undercover status. I understood the reason why now. We'd need the wiretap to help Dad. But if it ever came down to the job or keeping my dad out of prison, I'd shout it to the world. I said, "What do you have? What kind of case?"

"You know that would be improper for me to tell you."

"It's me, Sarge. This is me, Bruno Johnson. You know me. I won't hang you out. You have my word."

He hesitated and reached into his suit coat.

I sucked in a breath. He actually had physical evidence? Of course they would. No way would Kohl arrest Dad without it.

He pulled out some Polaroid photos and again hesitated. I held my hand out and didn't try to take them until he made up his mind.

He handed them over.

The photos stunned me. They depicted a close-up of an older woman's naked breast, the whole breast, white skin with freckles, along with a few age marks. Ugly purple bruises in the form of fingers from a large hand outlined the breast. Someone had viciously grabbed her and squeezed, squeezed hard enough to leave bruising. How that must've hurt. How the threat of more must've menaced and intimidated. No woman should ever have to go through something like that for any reason.

But there was a worse part. Worse for Dad, anyway.

The woman was white.

The Stops hot-link sandwich and chili fries turned in my stomach. I swallowed hard to keep them down.

Kohl lowered his voice. "We have an independent witness that saw your dad at the victim's house today. The wit puts him on the scene at the time of the incident."

"He was delivering the mail. So, of course, he's going to be there."

"Bruno, the wit says he went into the house. Was in there for a few minutes, maybe as long as twenty."

I handed him back the photos. "He didn't do this."

"I know he's your dad and all—"

"Trust me when I say he didn't do this. I can't tell you right now how I know, but I promise you, I'll get it all straightened out. Can I talk to him one more time, please?"

"If you know something about this mess, you better tell me."

"I can't, not right now."

"You can't get anywhere near this thing, Bruno. I mean it. Let me investigate it. I'll get to the bottom of it, I promise you. But if you stick your nose in it, and I find out, I'll arrest you for obstruction. You understand?"

I nodded. "Now, can I talk to him, please?"

"Okay, make it quick."

"Thanks. I owe you."

I went back to the car and opened the door. Dad looked up with eager eyes, his expectations far too high. And it hurt to have to disappoint him.

"Listen," I said, "they're going to take you to the station and book you in."

"Really, Son? You can't do something? Can't you please do something? I didn't do this."

An hour ago, he'd have been too proud to beg me like that, but handcuffed, sitting in the back of a cop car, looking at an ugly crime like attempted rape would scare the strongest of men. And Dad was the strongest man I knew.

He'd only ever been to jail once, when Mom died, and he'd told me long ago, in a moment of weakness, that he'd never go back. Never.

"I know you didn't. I know who did and I promise you, I will get this all straightened out."

"You know who did this? How do you know? Wait, wait, Bruno."

He rarely called me by my name. He always called me *son*.

"Don't you go after whoever did this. You hear me? Please, let the law handle it."

He saw the rage building inside me. He saw the consequences it would bring, the danger in it.

"I am the law, Dad."

"Bruno, you listen to me. Bruno, promise me that you—"

"Don't say a word to anyone. You understand?"

"Bruno—"

"Do not give any kind of statement. I'll follow you in to bail you out. You won't be in there long."

"What? Wait. I have to bail out? How much?"

"I don't know, maybe twelve or fifteen."

"Fifteen hundred? Oh, we can scrape that much together. I got that much in my savings. Bruno, I don't want you—"

"You sit tight. You won't be in there long, I promise." I didn't want to correct him, tell him not hundreds in bail, but thousands. It'd only serve to scare him more. I reached in and squeezed his shoulder. "You hang in there, Dad."

"Bruno?"

I closed the door.

I tried to control my rage at Thibodeaux and Blue. They'd made it personal and gone after my family. If I wanted to get them, I needed to be smart like they were and not fly off the handle. To meet them head to head with gun or knuckles would get me nowhere. I turned back to Kohl. "What's the bail?"

He shrugged. "Not good."

"What? Why?"

"Bruno, I can't treat him any different than anyone else. You know that. This has to go down by the book."

"What's the bail, damn you?"

"Fifty K."

"Fifty thousand? No way. Why? That's not fair."

"The attempted rape, the sexual battery, and the burglary."

"Burglary?" I said the word, but he didn't have to explain. The elements of burglary are: the unlawful entry with the intent to commit petty theft, grand theft, or any other felony. Attempted rape accounts for the *any other felony* part and fulfilled the last element in burglary. Though the entry with the intent might be a hard pull.

"Yeah, like I said, I can't show any favoritism. As it is, the press is going to eat this up with a spoon."

"Where am I going to get fifty thousand dollars?" That's fifty thousand in collateral. Ten percent of that goes to the bondsman, gone forever. Five thousand of that fifty is going to be a total loss.

Wicks said that Blue and Thibodeaux would try and offer me some of the skim. Wicks didn't say they would give me a desperate reason to accept it. The carrot and the stick. Those assholes.

"I'm sorry, Bruno. I gotta go and get him into the station. The clock's ticking on the arrest." He stuck his hand out to shake. For the briefest of moments, my anger at the system, the one that was now trying to eat my father alive, transferred to Kohl, who was only trying to do his job. I gritted my teeth and shook his hand. "Thank you. I'm sorry for being such an ass."

"I understand. I'm sorry for having to be the one to do this."

"I know you are."

He went around, got in the black-and-white, and drove off down the street with my father handcuffed, his face in the back window watching me.

CHAPTER FORTY-ONE

I WENT INTO the house and phoned Robby Wicks. Barbara answered, said she hadn't seen her husband since the day before.

"What's wrong?" she asked. "What's the matter?"

I didn't know how much she knew, and didn't need the added problem of telling her something she wasn't supposed to know.

She didn't seem concerned that her husband hadn't come home overnight. If you hunted men, I guess it sometimes went that way. I hung up and tried to put aside the emotion of the situation and think clearly. The adrenaline bled off and my hands shook. I paged Wicks.

After running through every option and coming up blank, I didn't have any choice. I'd have to track down The Bing and make peace with him, do whatever it took, up to and including getting down on my knees and groveling.

I checked the phone book and found him in the yellow pages. I really should've remembered the number. The Bing's ugly face smiled at me from every bus bench in the ghetto and even a few of the billboards as well. Not many crooks could forget his stupid slogan: *Bing's Bail Bonds, We'll get you out if it takes twenty years.* He'd stolen the slogan from another bondsman he'd run out of the business with his cutthroat tactics.

I dialed and got his answering service. I left a message that I wanted to see him right away and said my name again at the end just in case he missed it. I didn't let on as to why.

Then I paged Wicks again and waited.

And waited.

How come he didn't call right back? I'd only left him in the parking lot of Stops thirty minutes from the time I paged him the first time.

I paged him again. Waited.

And again.

He said to call him if I needed anything. Well, I needed something right damn now. He'd been the cause of all of this mess and he was going to help me get my dad out of jail or we were going to have a big problem. I paced the living room like an animal in a cage, wringing my hands.

Mrs. Espinoza sat in the rocker, rocking Olivia. She watched my movements going back and forth across the living room floor, the same as if she were watching a tennis match.

I tried to force out the image of Dad sitting in that booking cage with other criminals, real criminals who might have a grudge against me for past arrests, for the nightstick curbside justice I had occasionally meted out. I forgot to tell Dad to keep quiet about his name and that he had a deputy for a son. Dad possessed street smarts like no one else I knew. He wouldn't do a stupid thing like that, right?

The phone rang. I grabbed it up and said, "It's about time you called me back."

The caller said nothing.

"Hello?"

"Take it easy, big man. I only just got the message a few minutes ago."

The Bing.

J. D. Bingham. We called him The Ham in elementary school. He'd never shed his chubby baby fat and carried it over into adulthood. Nowadays he used his surety bond company to let out every criminal I threw in jail. He worked as the hinge on the forever-revolving door of the justice system. He represented the legal side of the bad and didn't mind walking that razor edge, half in the real world, half in the underworld. He made money, lots of money, off the backs of the victims who lived in fear once he wrote the bond to let the violent offenders back out.

"I need a meet."

He gave a raspy cackle. "That right? What happened to the last time when you called me, ah . . . what was it? A slimeball. A piece of lowlife gutter trash. A—"

I cut him off. "Nothing's changed. That last time when I called you those things, you'd just written a bond on Maurice Tubbs. You knew all about Maurice, how violent he was, how he preyed on people. You got him out before I'd even turned in my paperwork. Tubbs assaulted his dad and threatened to kill him. And you let him out, remember? As soon as he got out, he went right back to his parents' house. He took a piece of garden hose with a steel pressure nozzle on the end and beat his eighty-year-old parents near to death. All so you could make that ten percent on the bail. Like I said, nothing's changed."

He stopped laughing. "Bruno, business is business. I told you that, but you just don't seem to get it. If I didn't go the bail, someone else would've. You do what you do, and I do what I do. That's just the name of this dance we do. That's life in the ghetto."

"You can't see the difference? You're a mercenary that preys off—"

"And you're any better than me? Is that what you're saying?"

"Yes, I'd like to think so."

The phone beeped to let me know of a call waiting.

"You're no different than me, big man. You clubbed your brother Noble over the head with your gun and arrested him for murder. Now he's sittin' in the can waiting trial and you're the star witness. So don't talk your shit to me. I'll write your bond for your dad and I won't charge you a dime for it. Your dad was always good to me when we were kids. He always fed all of us kids no matter the time of day. He always had a hot meal for us who didn't have it at home."

I couldn't talk, couldn't reply. I'd berated this man and thought ill of him. What was the matter with me?

"That it?" The Bing asked. "Anything else I can do for you?"

I forced the words out. "You know about my dad getting arrested?"

"That's right, I know everything that happens in this hood. Everything."

"Why are you doing this? Why are you going his bail?"

"I told you."

I said nothing.

He paused, took a breath. "Okay, okay, listen. You're going to find out anyway, and Lord knows I don't wanna be on your bad side. I don't want you to club me over the head and drag me off to the can. A guy named Wicks called. He said he'd personally go the bond. He's putting up his house. He's on his way here now with the five K in cash. I don't know how you have a friend like that. I hope you don't talk to him like you talk to me. Good-bye, Bruno, The 'Bad Boy' Johnson. Don't call me again."

I hung up the phone, stunned.

Wicks did that?

CHAPTER FORTY-TWO

I WALKED TO the door, needing something, anything, to do and looked out the side window to the empty curb, wishing Dad still sat out there in the cop car and at the same time hoping that an obvious solution to the problem would just pop in my head.

The pager went off. I checked the readout. Wicks.

I went to the phone to call, ready to lavish him with many thanks, a little ashamed that I'd ever doubted him. Before I could dial, the phone rang. I picked it up and said, "I can't tell you how much I appreciate what you've done and—"

"Hold on there, cowboy. Don't know who you think this is, but I know you're not gonna be happy about this. I'm calling you back in."

"What? Who is this?"

The strong and confident voice locked in. Blue.

"We've got a job going down. I need all hands on deck."

I immediately shifted from grateful acknowledgment toward Wicks to pure hate for Blue. I really had to fight to keep that hate from permeating my tone. If I didn't play the game and play it well against these people, I'd lose. And they'd already doubled down on the stakes, pulling in Dad and now Olivia by default.

No way did I want to go in and face Blue and Thibodeaux. I didn't think I could keep from ripping their heads off.

And more important, I needed to get Dad out of jail, pick him up at the station, and drive him home. I needed to reassure him that I had everything under control.

When I really didn't.

Right now, Blue controlled everything. I needed to change that balance, and fast. "You sure you need me?"

"Is your daughter still giving you a problem?"

I gritted my teeth, closed my eyes, and put my head against the wall. He knew exactly what kind of problem I had and now he wanted to play word games. "No, I got that all straightened out, thanks."

"Good. See you in twenty."

He didn't wait for an acknowledgment and hung up.

The phone rang, my hand still on it.

I turned around and looked at Mrs. Espinoza sitting in the rocker, rocking Olivia. She smiled, but not the huge one she usually gave me, one more like wilted lettuce.

Yeah, I knew what she was thinking. What kind of son would do something that would risk the health and welfare of his wonderful dad? A dad now sitting in the can, accused of a despicable crime he would never in a million years commit? I wanted to kick the wall in and scream.

The phone rang again.

I'd been burned twice in one day answering like some kind of fool and it wouldn't happen again.

I picked it up and this time just said, "Hello."

"Bruno? I can't tell you how sorry I am about your father."

Wicks.

At the sound of his voice, and without warning, my grateful attitude suddenly shifted. If Wicks had not talked me into going undercover, going up against Blue and Thibodeaux, two men filled with a malignant evil the likes of which I'd never experienced, Dad wouldn't be up to his ass in alligators and fighting a false allegation of rape.

The rape of a white woman was a charge that, true or not, did not bode well for a favorable jury verdict. Those photos of the bruised breast could not be shown to a jury, especially not in conjunction with a witness that put him at the scene. If I couldn't prove the conspiracy against Blue and Thibodeaux, Dad was headed for prison, no two ways about it. The enormity of the situation settled on my shoulders, smothering me.

"What are we going to do about it?" I said through clenched teeth.

"We need to talk. I'm coming to you. No, second thought, make it location number two."

Location number two. Why was he talking in code? Did he think Blue had our lines tapped?

"I just got a call from Blue," I said. "He called me back in for a dope buy or something. He wants me there in twenty minutes."

Long pause.

"You still there?" I asked. "Did you hear me?"

"He didn't say exactly what it is you're going in to do?"

"No, and I'm not going back there at all until we get the charges dropped against my dad."

"I know you don't want to hear this, buddy, but there isn't anything we can do about that until this whole damn thing plays out. I'm sorry."

"Don't you dare call me *buddy*. Is that why you posted his bail, so this thing had more time to play out? So you could play this stupid little game a little longer?"

He paused. When he spoke, his words came out tight. "No, I posted your dad's bail because you're a member of my team, and I take care of my team. I told you. I warned you this could get rough."

"You never said anything about pulling my dad down into the sewer with these animals."

"That is unfortunate and I'm sorry. I wouldn't wish this on anyone. I didn't think they would stoop this low either. The deputy chief is aware and he's ready to talk with the DA, as soon as this thing resolves itself. There's nothing we can do but play along. We cannot, under any circumstances, let them know we're on to them. Bruno, this is a test to see if you're working them. We can't show our hand now. This'll sound crazy to you, but this is a good thing. What's happened with your dad means they're about to let you in. That is, if you don't blow it. You have to rein in that temper and play it smart."

Common sense and logic agreed with him, but the emotions of the situation worked hard on me. No way did I want it to go down the way Wicks wanted it to. I needed Dad out now. The charges dropped, now.

I said nothing and tried to work out a solution. I either didn't have the knowledge or experience or no other option truly existed.

"Bruno?"

"Okay. But I want someone to meet Dad at the jail and give him a ride home."

"That's already taken care of. Did Miller get called in with you?"

"I don't know, probably. Blue said all hands, so I guess that means her, too." I squinted my eyes closed and fought with myself over telling him about Chelsea. To keep it from him would be to play a dangerous game with Dad now in the mix. I asked, "What do you know about her?"

"Miller?"

"Yes."

"Why? You think she's somehow part of all this? Is she working with Blue and Thibodeaux? She just got on the team like you."

"I didn't say that."

"Talk to me, Bruno."

"It was something she said."

"Come on, give."

"She referred . . . I mean, on some other topic, nothing about Blue and this conspiracy, we were just talking. She used the term 'dog heavy.'"

Wicks sounded a little distracted. "That right? I've only ever heard the chief use that term."

"I know. That's what you said. I've never heard it before, either."

He paused, the phone line quiet as he puzzled over this new information. "Well," he said, "there's really only one explanation, and if that's the case, we don't need to worry about her. You stay focused on our two targets, and I'll look into this. I'll ask the chief about this right now. You good?"

"I guess I have to be, don't I?"

"I didn't have time to wait on you to write up that supplemental report on the money taken from the rock house on Peach. I wrote it and signed your name to it. It's exactly what you told me, short and sweet. You good with that?"

"I guess I have to be."

He'd just committed a terminating offense, falsifying an official document. And he'd told me about it. That's how much he trusted me. That also meant he wanted me to know that he had a lot of skin in the game. Not as much as Dad and me, but his admission went a long way to assuage some of my misgivings about being used as a puppet.

"We're coming up on the wire," he said, "in about three hours. You just need to hold on a little longer. We're almost there. I'm bringing in the rest of our team now to help. You keep in touch."

He hung up. He didn't want me to complain anymore or try to throw other options or scenarios out there.

And I *did* have one. When he said there could only be one explanation, he meant Chelsea was working for the deputy chief as a secondary undercover, someone else used as a backup plan in case I couldn't pull it off.

Or someone just to keep an eye on me.

I agreed with that premise and understood it. But there was another side to that coin. If Wicks would just take a step back and look at all the information as a whole, then he'd see that the chief could also be the dog heavy, pulling the strings on Blue as well, using Wicks like a little puppet, having him take out these targets. Like the victim under the stake bed truck at the Mona gas station.

And that maybe the chief put us all in play to manipulate the game, his game, and in some way defer his involvement. If this game all went to shit, the chief could just say, "I have no idea what you're talking about. They did what? My God, what a horrible breech of integrity."

At that point, I, Wicks, Chelsea, and even Blue and Thibodeaux all became scapegoats.

Wicks liked and respected the chief. I'd never met him before the barbecue. With tact and diplomacy, I'd have to find a way to float this option by Wicks.

I kissed little Olivia good-bye, stroked her soft hair a couple of times, and headed back to the office, where I would need an Oscar-level performance to keep Blue and Thibodeaux from reading what I really thought, from reading what I wanted to do to them.

CHAPTER FORTY-THREE

MY FEET THUMPED up the wooden steps outside the narco trailer in back of the station. I hesitated on the stoop, took a deep breath, and passed through the door. Blue and Thibodeaux sat at their desks smiling as if one of them just told a lurid joke at Chelsea's expense. Chelsea sat at her desk not smiling. Her eyes said she needed to tell me something and couldn't. At least that's what I wanted to believe. I started to feel a little ache for her in my chest, just as I used to with Sonja. There wasn't time for any silly high school crush, so I pushed it aside.

Even in distress she looked radiant.

Blue and Thibodeaux were the source of her distress, had to be. I clenched my fists and counted, like Captain Stubbs had the day before, to get my anger under control.

At the same time, that unmistakable aura surrounded the whole trailer, the constant low-level hum of potential violence that at any moment, for no reason at all, could erupt in knuckles, boots, and gun smoke.

"Hey," Blue said. "Sorry I had to call you back in. How's your kid doin'?"

"She's fine." I worked at not grinding my teeth and put up a false smile. Maybe he'd think my stiff demeanor came out of not being able to be with Olivia.

Thibodeaux stood and took the couple of steps over to me and offered up his hand, along with a pasted-on smile, all of us actors today. "Sorry, pal," he said. "I was a horse's ass this morning. I had time to think about it and, well, I had no right to treat you like that. Blue's right, we need to be a team around here and trust each other."

I looked at his extended hand instead of his eyes to keep from ripping that smug smile off his face and making him eat it. "No hard feelings," I said. I took his hand, cold, sandpaper-rough, and strong enough to clamp down on an innocent woman's breast, strong enough to leave ugly purple bruising. I squeezed in return and gave back a small sample of his own smugness, an arrogance that came with the knowledge that, one way or another, Thibodeaux would pay for all of his wickedness. Comfortable in the knowledge that Wicks had the wiretap in his pocket and it wouldn't be long now.

But I wouldn't let Wicks have the satisfaction, not this time. He wouldn't track Thibodeaux down in some back alley like at 123rd and Central. This time I'd be the one to take Thibodeaux down, the hard way with a lot of black baton action, curbside justice with broken teeth, ribs, and arm bones. He'd resist arrest whether he wanted to or not. The thought made me smile for real. For a fleeting moment, I didn't like the sudden and bitter taste of revenge, and I fought it, a battle of right and wrong that didn't last. I slipped that much closer to the other side, to the evil I'd dedicated my life to chasing.

I broke eye contact with Thibodeaux and moved around him to my desk. I needed to sit down to keep my knees from quaking from so much pent-up anger and the need to act. Chelsea watched my expression the entire time, as if she thought I might explode at any moment. But that couldn't be right. How could she know about the frame that locked down Dad, the reason for my anger?

Blue let his smile take a walk and said, "We're waiting on a CI who's coming in to give us a location on one Jaime Reynosa, who can give us

Mo Mo. Folks, that's just one degree of separation. We've never been this close to Mo Mo before."

I nodded. "Cool." And looked straight ahead at the cheap wood-paneled wall. I needed to get out of there so I could breathe again. "Hey, Chelsea, can I talk to you outside?"

Blue and Thibodeaux looked at each other. Thibodeaux said to me, "Man, you work fast."

"It's not like that," I said, the words too sharp.

Chelsea got up. "Sure, Bruno." She walked on past me and out the door.

I hesitated, something my pride required, and then followed along.

Chelsea stopped at the bottom of the steps. "Come on," I said, and moved to the center of the parking area, knowing full well both Thibodeaux and Blue were watching from the trailer windows. I gently took her arm and escorted her farther yet, over by my Ford Ranger. The late afternoon sun now sat far below the roof of the station and gave off more of a subdued yellowish-orange light. The heat remained and hung heavy in the still air.

"Take it easy, Bruno, you're hurting me."

"Oh, jeez, sorry, I didn't mean to. Really, I didn't."

She looked back at the trailer with a nervous glance. "It's not a good idea to be doing this."

"Do what? Why?"

She rubbed her arm. Her big brown eyes gave off an innocence that made me want to hold her in my arms and kiss her. How insane was that? The thing with Dad screwed with me, made me emotionally vulnerable.

"They already have the wrong idea about us," she said. "What is it you want that can't be said in there?"

"You wanted to meet up with me, remember? What was that all about?"

"Nothing. It's nothing."

She broke eye contact and looked down and to the left.

"Hey, hey," I said. I tried to get her to look at me. "Did Blue say something to you in there? Did he do something to you?"

She looked up at me, her eyes fierce. "What are you talking about? I'm perfectly capable of taking care of myself."

For a moment, her act convinced me that maybe she did just roll in from a Public Relations gig and really didn't know the kind of viper's nest she had landed in at the Lynwood narco team. Then I remembered her words, the reference to the "dog heavy."

No, she knew exactly what kind of game she played. Only she played better at it than I gave her credit for.

CHAPTER FORTY-FOUR

"HEY, DON'T BULLSHIT me," I said. "Something's bothering you, something you thought I should know. That's why you wanted to meet me at my dad's house."

"Look, it's none of my business. I decided I don't want to talk out of turn here. It's just not my place."

"Come on, this shit is serious . . . my . . . my dad . . ."

I almost told her about Dad being framed by Thibodeaux, but the little bit of doubt that she might not really be involved up to her pretty little nose kept me from saying the words.

"What about your dad?"

"Never mind, but you and I both know . . . I mean, I know, you know what's going on around here."

"What are you talking about now? *What's* going on around here? Bruno, you're sounding paranoid. I think you need to take a vacation."

Wicks' admonishment to tell no one about working undercover sounded in my head, loud this time, like a gong.

"*I'm* paranoid? Then why don't you really tell me what you wanted to talk about at my place?"

She did it again, looked down and to the left. A tell, like in poker, indicating her next words would be deceptive. "I . . . ah . . . I just thought that I wanted to get to know you better, that's all."

My heart gave a little skip at the thought, but the truth spoke louder and overpowered the idea.

"Bullshit."

Her sheepishness fled, replaced with anger. She poked me in the chest. "Don't you try and tell me you know what I had on my mind." She turned to leave.

I grabbed her by the hand and held on. "Chelsea, I'm sorry. Please, tell me what you were going to tell me." The touch of her warm skin in mine made me wish we'd met under different circumstances.

She looked at my hand on her wrist and then up at my eyes. Hers softened. And I wished like hell I could read her mind for real. She felt something, too; that's the way I read it.

She took a step closer into my space and lowered her voice, her breath warm, with a hint of cinnamon. "I don't know what kind of screwed-up game you and those two hard cases in there think you're playing, but I want no part of it. You understand?"

"What are you talking about?"

"If you're going to play dumb, forget it."

She tried to pull away. I held on. "Please, tell me."

She turned angry when I wouldn't let go. "Okay," she said, "I do know what's going on."

"You do?"

She, too, was undercover and was about to break the cardinal rule and cop out to it.

"That's right, I do. You came from the violent crimes team, an assignment half the detectives in the department would sell their souls for. You were only there on paper for a couple of weeks and then you get transferred over to this street narco team. It doesn't take a rocket scientist to figure it out."

I stuck to the cover story, didn't have a choice. "That's right. Blue asked for me. Called the deputy chief and personally asked for me because he needed someone of color to do street buys."

"Now it's my turn to call bullshit."

"Why? Come on, tell me why you're sayin' that."

"Your boss on the violent crimes team was Robby Wicks."

"That's right. So?"

"You're playing me for a fool here, Bruno, and I don't like it."

She'd either backed away from the edge or she wasn't undercover.

"I don't know what you're talking about. Really, I don't."

She looked into my eyes, searching for the lie that wasn't there. "Okay," she said, "I'll play along with this bullshit game you're playin'. But not for much longer, you understand? And so help me, if you're playing me—"

"I'm not, I promise."

"You remember that story about Blue?"

For a moment, I didn't know what she meant. "Oh, the story from Gale Taylor, the sergeant working the women's jail? The story about how Blue shot and killed his own father?"

"That's right—Gale. I also told you Gale said she was doing Blue, really tearing it up with him, remember? Well, she fell for Blue, fell hard. I didn't put together the part about why you're here, not right away. Not why you suddenly transferred from the violent crimes team. I did put it together, though, once I found out who your boss was over there in violent crimes, Robby Wicks. Then it came together all nice and neat."

"I'm sorry, Chelsea, I'm still not following you."

"Jesus, Bruno, I really hope you're not playing me for a fool. If you're not, you're one big chump. And to tell you the truth, I don't know which would be worse."

I said nothing. I didn't want her to think ill of me. I really didn't know what she was talking about.

"Gale Taylor, the woman in the jail, she went back to using her maiden name. Her married name used to be Wicks."

Her words hung in the dry, heated air, unable to sink in because of the absolute havoc they would cause.

"Ah, son of a bitch." I turned and slowly eased my arms and forehead down on the hot hood of the Ford Ranger. The burning heat on my exposed skin just didn't matter.

My God, what a chump I'd been.

CHAPTER FORTY-FIVE

"BRUNO, ARE YOU all right?" Chelsea put her hand on my back. Even in my emotionally distressed state, I found her familiar touch, the thought that she cared about me, comforting.

"I'm sorry," she said, "I shouldn't have said that thing about you being a chump. I really thought you knew. Wicks is a lot like Blue. They both use people and when they're done with them, they wad them up and throw 'em away. They just don't care about anybody but themselves. Wicks is using you, and I'm sorry I'm the one who had to tell you."

I looked up at her, trying to fight through all the crazy thoughts she'd unleashed and at the same time listen to what she was saying. "What are you really doing here?"

She looked shocked. "What are you talking about?"

"Did you really just transfer in from Public Relations?"

"Yes, what do you think I did?"

"Nothing. You just seem to have too much information, that's all."

She chuckled. "What, you think I came from Internal Affairs, or something like that? I told you, I came here to get some real-time street experience and found myself caught up in a bunch of bullshit games men play when their testosterone levels get out of control. Like that's never happened before."

"Okay, okay. For the moment, let's continue with the premise that I'm a chump. Tell me how you think Wicks is using me and how you came to that conclusion?"

She visibly squirmed and started to pull away. I again took hold of her hand, gently this time, and said, "Please?"

She didn't resist at all and glanced back over her shoulder. I followed her gaze. Thibodeaux came out of the trailer and stood on the stoop, his forearms resting on the railing as he smoked a cigarette and watched us. He was too far away to hear what we said.

I squeezed her hand. She looked back at me, her brown eyes large and innocent. I no longer believed her innocent of anything, not anymore, no matter what she tried to feed me. No one had ever confused me emotionally like this. I could no longer pick out the truth.

She nodded. "It's simple. Just a little simple bit of deductive reasoning. That's all."

"Spell it out for me, please."

"Wicks is given his own team to run, a team with little or no oversight, and what does he do? The first thing he does is insert one of his men into a street narcotics team to try and get something on the man who banged his wife."

"That's it? That's how you arrived at me being a world-class chump?"

"Well, is it true? Were you transferred or were you inserted to rat on Blue? If you're here as a rat, I think you're one dirty dog for doing it. I think Blue likes to walk the line, and may step over into the gray area a little every now and then, but he doesn't deserve to have someone looking over his shoulder. Not the way I see it. Not because Wicks wants to get even with him."

I didn't like the admiration in her eyes over Blue, and recognized this reaction of mine, in part, as a twinge of jealousy. I fought the urge to tell her about how Blue killed people for money. See what she thought about him then.

I didn't want to lie to her, but in that moment, I realized lying was the bulwark of the undercover assignment. "No, I was transferred in. I didn't get along with Wicks. As it turns out, he's a bigot and he gave me my choice of assignment for transfer."

Her mouth dropped open. She pointed to the hood of my truck. "Then what was that display all about just now?"

"I . . . I . . ."

I needed another lie and couldn't think of one close at hand.

"You what?"

"I shouldn't be telling you this, but Wicks called me today and asked for a meet. He wanted to know about Blue."

Now, all of a sudden, the lies came easier and spewed out like poison leaving my body. I'd worked the street busting crooks long enough to know the best lies contained at least a small kernel of the truth. I was walking a dangerous line with this one.

"What'd you tell him?"

"What could I tell him? Nothing. I told him Blue really knew the job. I told him how we took down sixty-seven suspects in one search warrant. What I didn't know at the time was Wicks' motivation. Just now, when you told me about the thing with his ex-wife, the reason for that meeting finally made sense to me. Now if he asks again, I'll tell him to go take a flying leap."

She smiled. "Good. I'm glad we had this conversation. We better get back inside."

Now I knew for sure that she came to the team without any hidden agendas. She'd just landed at the wrong place at the wrong time. Sadly, when the takedown of Blue and Thibodeaux occurred, a little of the ugliness would rub off on her reputation, no matter that she was involved or not.

She'd also know that I lied to her.

Ollie Bell drove up in her van and parked next to the steps of the trailer, just like she knew exactly where to go, like she'd been there before. Chelsea and I headed over as Ollie opened the van door and kind of half-rolled, half-fell out of the van.

Up on the stoop, Thibodeaux flipped his cigarette out into the ten-foot chain-link fence that separated the station from the neighborhood. He went inside.

I walked along with Chelsea. My mind returned to Sunday, the day of the barbecue. I should've asked more questions, a lot more. The biggest question I should've asked was who initiated the black bag wiretap on Blue and Thibodeaux when they worked at SPI. I knew the answer now, though. But did Deputy Chief Rudyard know?

And did it really matter? Blue and Thibodeaux had killed people for money. Killed three people just at the Mona gas station robbery surveillance. If the chief did know about Blue having an affair with Wicks' first wife, then no way could he allow Wicks to investigate Blue. That's why Wicks kept that information under tight wraps.

Still, omission of the information to me was the same as a lie. How did I know if anything Wicks said about Blue was true? Was there really a recording of Blue taking a contract? Had Blue really taken money to kill anyone? Or was all of this some elaborate ruse to take Blue down for stealing Wicks' wife away from him?

The one true piece of evidence that Blue and Dirt were exactly what Wicks said they were was the fact that Dad had been set up for attempted rape.

All of these things and more ran through my brain as I stood by the van and watched Ollie negotiate the three steps up to the stoop, her bulk almost too much for her legs to handle. The purple satin under her arms looked darker from sweat. Chelsea and Ollie disappeared into the trailer.

Blue knocked on his window and waved for me to get inside.

If I had been smart, I'd have turned around and gone to find Wicks, made him tell me the truth before this whole thing blew up in my face.

But I wasn't smart; I *was* a chump. I didn't want to leave Chelsea alone with those two men in the trailer. I climbed the steps and went inside.

CHAPTER FORTY-SIX

OLLIE STOOD IN the only place that would allow for her bulk, close to the open door next to the row of file cabinets. She picked up an empty file folder and fanned herself. The heat hung in the small mobile home, and the stress from climbing the three steps just about did her in. Her breath came loud and fast.

I shuffled past her, made it to my desk, and sat down. Now Ollie was the only one standing.

Blue sat in his desk chair and swiveled to face her from his place four desks over. "Well? Jaime, is he there? Is it a go?"

Ollie held up her hand as she tried to catch her breath. "Dear Lord in heaven . . . if it ain't . . . hotter than the hubs of hell . . . in this place. Don't you all have an air conditioner?"

"Is Jaime there or not?"

"I needs a drink of water." She spotted the water cooler and went over to it. The wooden floor squeaked and whined under the load. She looked all around for a cup. "He's there, but there's a problem."

"What problem? Stop dickin' around and look at me. What problem?"

"I . . . I . . ." Rivulets of sweat striped her face.

"Ollie, tell me, what kind of problem?"

She continued to look around for a cup and spotted the one on the file cabinet by the door, the one with the "*Danger Biohazard*" sticker on it. The one Blue had pissed in and tossed his urine outside toward the fence and into the neighborhood that ratted on him to the captain. She waddled over, grabbed the plastic cup, and turned back with a huge smile.

I turned to look at Blue, waiting for him to stop her. His angry expression over Ollie dodging his questions shifted to a smile that matched Ollie's.

Ollie made it back to the water cooler and started filling the cup. Everyone watched. The water cooler bubbled and glugged.

I again looked back at Blue. He saw me this time and shook his head. He didn't want me to interfere and to let it play out, let her take her drink.

Ollie watched the cup fill like a woman lost in the desert for days. Her tongue snaked out and licked her dry lips at the prospect of wetness. She let off the spigot and stepped back. She started to raise the cup to her lips.

Blue was going to let her do it.

I jumped to my feet and quick-stepped over to Ollie. Just before the cup's rim touched her lips, I grabbed it from her, jostling the cup, which sloshed some water down the front of her ample breasts, turning the purple fabric dark and making it dip down into her cleavage.

"Hey, hey, what the hell? Gimme that back."

I moved around her to the door and tossed cup, water and all, outside. I came back and tried to move past her.

She socked me in the chest. "You dirty rotten bastard. You're no good, you."

I went over to Blue's desk, grabbed his personal plastic cup, and scowled at him. I whispered, "That wasn't funny. That was crude and rude."

Blue shook his head. "I don't think you're going to make it here, Bruno. You don't have a sense of humor. And if there's one thing you need for sure in this job, it's a sense of humor. Ain't that right, Dirt?"

"You know it, boss." He winked at me. "That and the sole desire to make these streets safe for white women and children."

I held his gaze a moment longer.

I moved back to the water cooler. Ollie socked me again. This time, Blue, Thibodeaux, and even Chelsea chuckled at my expense. I filled the cup and gave it to Ollie, who put one hand on the desk to steady herself, tilted her head back, and guzzled down all the water.

When she finished, I filled it for her again and handed it to her. This time she reached up and patted my shoulder. "Sorry about hittin' you, slick, but I was about ready ta DFO."

Ghetto slang for *Done Fell Out.*

She drank half of the second cup and let out a long sigh.

"Okay," Blue said. "Now are you ready to tell us what the problem is?"

"He at the Park View Hotel in Huntington Park jus' like I said he'd be. And trust me, he knows everythin' about Mo Mo's operation. Used to be his right-hand man until he got all caught up in dat heron. You take his heron away, and he'll give up his mama and all his chillrens."

"And?"

She shrugged and gave him a hesitant smile. "I don't know what room."

Blue stood. "That doesn't do us any damn good at all. We can't kick in every door, not without alerting him."

As if we could kick in any of the doors without probable cause and without a search warrant.

Ollie put the cup to her lips, tilted it back, and drank down the rest. She handed me the cup for another refill. I obliged.

The water cooler glugged again. For a fleeting second I had the thought that the five-gallon water cooler might not be enough.

"It ain't that bad," she said. "Ol' Jaime, he either in 103 or 207. Dey in there cuttin' up nine grams of heron, or will be shortly. You all are gonna have to move if you're gonna get him."

CHAPTER FORTY-SEVEN

BLUE REACHED INTO his jeans pocket, took out a small wad of bills, peeled off two twenties, and walked over and handed them to her. "Thanks. You page me in about an hour. We get him, you get the rest. Now get out of here."

Ollie shook her head. "You always did know how to treat a lady like a lady."

Thibodeaux, leaning back in his desk chair, said, "You ain't no lady."

Ollie shot him a scowl but knew better than to banter with a rabid dog.

I wanted to kick a lung outta that dog.

Blue put his hands on Ollie's shoulders, turned her around, and escorted her to the door. They stepped out onto the stoop. He stuck his head back in the office and said, "Suit up, boys and girls. We're going to war."

Outside the door, Ollie turned a little to the side and surreptitiously handed Blue a folded-up piece of paper. Blue took it and unfolded the used piece of cheeseburger wrapper spotted with grease. He looked at it, smiled, folded it back up, and stuck it into his back pants pocket. He looked back to see if anyone had seen the transaction. I quickly glanced away and at Chelsea. She'd missed the quick exchange altogether as she got ready, donning her Second Chance vest.

I pulled my bag from under my desk and started putting on my body armor. Blue came back in and took his bag out from under his desk. Thibodeaux still hadn't moved and leaned back in his desk chair, his feet up on the desk as he watched us. His darkly tanned face was now marked with more lines than the first time I'd met him not so many nights ago. The tuft of white hair amongst all the jet-black on the top of his head stood out like a beacon and reminded me of an eight ball.

I looked at Blue. "Isn't he going with us?"

"Ol' Dirt, he's old school. He believes in fate, not body armor. Ain't that right, Dirt? Go on, tell 'em."

Thibodeaux smiled. "A bullet is life's coupon to the unknown, and since we're redeemed in death, what does it really matter?" He stood and swung his gun belt around his slim hips.

I looked over at Chelsea, who'd paused in putting on her gun belt. She shrugged, as if saying, "What a twit."

I agreed with her, only I hoped he'd get redeemed a lot sooner than later.

I pulled on the green raid jacket with "Sheriff" in bold yellow letters on the back.

Blue put his on. "Okay, here's what we're going to do. Since we don't know which room, we're going to hit them both at the same time. Miller, you're with me. We're going to the room on the first floor. Dirt, you and Bruno take the one upstairs, 207. Questions?"

Chelsea said, "We don't have warrants. What if they won't let us in when we knock?"

Blue looked at me to answer that question, a strange thing for him to do because I didn't know any better than she did. Not for sure, anyway. I thought about it for a moment, tried to think like Blue, and said, “Okay, we have reason to believe a felony is occurring in these two rooms. If we wait to get search warrants, the evidence could be gone or destroyed, so we’re going to secure both locations pending a search warrant.”

This worked in part as a true statement, according to law, but not within department policy. Like the rock house on Peach, this concept sat way out there, just beyond the edge and deep into the law’s gray area.

Blue slapped me on the shoulder and smiled. “Maybe you’ll make it here after all, kid.”

Chelsea said, “Is that exactly legal?”

Thibodeaux picked up his bag and moved past us. “It’s close enough for government work, chicky baby.” He stopped and nodded toward the window where, outside, Ollie mounted her van to leave. The whole left side dipped as she got in. “You know why they wear purple like that?”

Neither of us would answer him. Something we didn’t want to know.

He chuckled. “So the lions won’t chase ’em.”

Another rude slur aimed indirectly at me. He worked overtime trying to get me to fight him. I wouldn’t do it. I wouldn’t play the game his way. Not until the time came. Then he’d better look out.

Blue said, “Knock it off, Dirt.”

Thibodeaux shook his head in disgust. “Like you said earlier, you gotta have a sense of humor. And I think it’s really sad, but I think you lost yours, Blue. Come on,” he said to Chelsea. “If you’re ridin’ with me, let’s roll.”

Blue eased past me then stopped and looked up into my face. “I guess that means you’re ridin’ with me, big man.” He stayed there for an uncomfortable moment. His breath smelled of spearmint that tried hard to mask spicy food.

I broke away first.

I wanted to ride with Chelsea, but Thibodeaux and Blue had different ideas, almost as if Thibodeaux and Blue planned it ahead of time, which didn't bode well for what awaited Chelsea and me.

Out in the parking lot, Chelsea opened the passenger door to the lime-green Ford Thunderbird. She hesitated for a moment, looking back at me. She got in and closed the door. Thibodeaux did the same, only he grinned and gave me a knowing nod before he got in the driver's seat. Again with that Cheshire cat kinda grin.

I got in the passenger seat of the '79 Nova just as a thought hit me. An ugly thought that made me into a chump all over again. This Jaime Reynosa that, according to Blue, we now pursued for the sole purpose of getting at Mo Mo—had Reynosa's name come up on the wiretap? Was Reynosa Blue's next victim? I couldn't call a time-out to contact Wicks to find out or to warn him. Blue made sure of that by having me ride with him. I could only stay close to Blue, and if that was the case, try and keep Reynosa alive. Blue assigned me to go with Thibodeaux to the second-floor room. I could handle Thibodeaux, and that gave Reynosa a fifty-fifty chance to stay alive.

CHAPTER FORTY-EIGHT

Blue steered the Nova north, weaving in and out of side streets as he headed to Huntington Park trying to avoid the last of the go-home-from-work traffic and failing miserably. The normal twenty-five-minute drive would easily take an hour.

I didn't want to speak, afraid he'd read my anger and resentment toward him.

The hot summer wind blew in both open windows and did little to cool down the heated world around us. The Nova had a bench seat, and when sitting behind the wheel, Blue didn't look as intimidating. But that meant about the same as saying the skinny tiger didn't look that hungry.

I didn't like Chelsea with Thibodeaux out of my sight. She'd said she could take care of herself and maybe she could under normal circumstances, but not with the likes of Dirt.

Blue came out of a side street in South Gate and took Atlantic Avenue north. Alameda probably would've been faster. We fell in with all the cars backed up for miles in a long string of changing red and green lights. We caught the red at the first signal.

"With this traffic," I said, "we might not get there in time."

Blue didn't look at me. "He's a heroin hype with nine grams, what do you think he's gonna do once they cut it up?"

"Good point."

Blue said, "So, what did you think of working with Wicks?"

I took a hard look at him for the first time since getting into the car. Here it was: the real reason why he wanted me to ride with him. He wanted to goad me a little to find out if I'd break, find out if I worked for Wicks or if the transfer to his team was legitimate.

"What do you mean?"

"I heard he's really something to work with. Kinda always out there on the edge."

Now look who's calling the kettle black.

When I didn't answer right away, Blue said, "I wish I had the opportunity to work with him. I think we would've made a good team. We could've taken down some real heavies. I put in for that violent crimes team, one of the many hopeful fools, and didn't get it. I gotta tell ya, I was surprised as hell that you wanted to leave that team and come here to work on this one."

Blue never put in for the violent crimes team, he just wanted to bait me, draw me out. Wicks and Blue would never click. They'd be at odds from the moment they met. And the irony that he would comment about how Wicks lived out on the edge, as we headed to kick in some doors in Huntington Park, wasn't lost on me.

"You asked for me."

He looked at me. "I what?"

"You personally called the chief and asked for me."

He smiled. "Someone's yankin' on your dick, my man. Not that I don't want you, but that didn't happen."

"Oh."

My mind spun at the implications. Now who was lying? The most logical answer would be Blue. More misdirection to put me off my game.

"I didn't get along with Wicks," I said, "and I grew up in Willowbrook, so I thought I could make a real impact out here on this team."

The lie even sounded good to me.

Blue nodded. The signal changed to green. We advanced, but not enough to get through the intersection; it'd take another cycle or two.

"So," Blue said, "what do you think of the narco team so far?"

"I like it better than the violent crimes team. That was really something on Peach, the way that whole thing went down. The birdcage, all those arrests."

He nodded. "Yeah, but we missed Mo Mo."

"Sounds like we're gaining on him now."

Blue said nothing. We rode in silence. I looked straight ahead at the traffic, trying to see the lime-green T-Bird, a useless endeavor in the vast river of cars.

Blue broke the silence. "You know, you always act like you got something on your mind, like you're distracted. Like maybe you're dying to ask me something."

He knew exactly why I was distracted. He and Thibodeaux had caused that distraction with the senseless and unwarranted abuse of Mrs. Whitaker. He was playing me like a cat plays with a mouse. Anger rose up and I pushed it down. I didn't look at him.

Play it cool. Play it cool.

The signal changed to green for the second time. We again inched forward. I felt Blue's eyes on me the whole time.

He leaned over on the bench seat and patted my leg. "Hey, we need to trust each other. We're a team here; it's important. Go ahead and ask me anything you want."

I turned to look at him. "And you'll answer it honestly, no bullshit?"

He gave me a huge patronizing smile. "Of course."

"Did you do it?"

His smile tarnished a little. "Heh. Do what?"

"You know what."

He shrugged, the smile gone now. "Don't play games with me. You wanna ask me something, go ahead and do it."

"Okay, did you really shoot and kill your father?"

His expression didn't change, but his eyes did. They hardened. I'd just prodded the skinny tiger with a stick. Now we both wanted the same thing: to tear each other's heads off and kick them down the road. I stood a head taller and at least thirty pounds heavier and he still scared me. I didn't think I could take him with an empty hand.

He looked at me and said nothing. I didn't think he would.

I pushed a little harder. "Like you said, if we're going to be on a team together, I think whether or not you shot your own father to death is something I should know, don't you?"

"I thought we'd have other, more important, issues to discuss besides some ancient history that has no bearing on what we're doing here today."

He wanted to talk about the jam Dad was in and maybe offer some alternatives to get him out of that jam. That's why he'd started the conversation. Only, it wasn't working out for him.

I shrugged. "Okay, sorry, I didn't know that wasn't on the table to discuss or that it was such a sore subject."

"No, no, if you want to . . . no, if you need to know about that horrible event that happened to my family, I'll tell you all about it. I won't be happy about it, but I'll tell you. And fair is fair. After I tell you, you gotta tell me something outta your past." He let that hang a moment and then said, "You still wanna play this silly little game?"

I broke eye contact and looked out the windshield. He knew about how I'd pistol-whipped my brother, Noble, and arrested him for a triple murder. How Noble, at that moment, sat in jail waiting trial and that I'd be one of the star witnesses. Everyone in the department knew. That's the story Blue would ask about. No way did I want to dredge up all that hot emotional soup, something so intimate and painful, especially not with the likes of Blue.

He who lives in glass houses . . .

He'd made me see the two incidents side by side, tried to make them comparable. I swallowed hard. I didn't want to be like Blue. Not the cold-blooded killer part.

"Okay," I said, "let's just let it drop."

"You sure?"

I said nothing more. We rode in silence.

Now I brooded about Noble. Couldn't help it, and realized I'd been wrong to prod Blue about the killing of his father. How spiteful of me.

"Hey," I said, "tell me about Jaime Reynosa."

Blue took his sunglasses off the dash and put them on. "He's the guy who's going to lead us right to Mo Mo. We take Mo Mo down and we take down the second-largest cocaine operation in LA. Papa Dee has the number-one spot. He's next."

That raised the question: Then why weren't we going after Papa Dee first?

Noble had worked for Papa Dee, selling cocaine for him. I wanted to go after Papa Dee to redirect some of the pent-up rage over my brother about to go to prison for life.

"What does Reynosa look like?"

"Your standard, skinny Mexican heroin hype. You'll know him when you see him. He's got these big letters, 'FFL,' tattooed on his neck, right here. They're real obvious and stand for *Fucked For Life*. And that's what he's going to be once I get my hands on him."

"You sure he can lead us to Mo Mo and be able to hang a case on him?"

Blue lowered his chin and pulled his sunglasses down his nose, looking over the top of them at me. "That's what Ollie says, and I've never known her to be wrong about anything."

He hesitated and said, "You don't seem convinced. You still act like you got something stuck in your craw. You better get used to what we do here, the way we do things, because this is how it is on our team. This is what we do—we turn people, make them give up other people." He put his sunglasses back up where they belonged and looked out the windshield. "Sometimes bad people help you do good things."

That last statement struck an odd cord and it shouldn't have. For some reason, I now questioned whether Blue really did walk on the dark side of the law. One thing I knew for sure, though—Blue truly believed he wasn't doing anything wrong.

CHAPTER FORTY-NINE

BLUE PULLED INTO a Church's Chicken fifty minutes later and drove right up to Thibodeaux's T-Bird already waiting there. He stopped, driver's window to driver's window, standard cop positioning. The Church's Chicken rendezvous proved Blue and Thibodeaux had talked about a plan before Ollie even arrived at the narco trailer.

What else did they have planned?

The sunlight faded by the minute, with dusk coming in fast to finish off the day.

In the T-Bird, Thibodeaux smoked a cigarette with his window down. Chelsea looked okay. She fanned the smoke and leaned a little toward her open window for fresher air. I would've really liked to have heard the conversation in their car on the ride up.

Blue said to Thibodeaux, "You know what to do. We roll up hot and go inside. You and Bruno take the stairs. Boot the door and if Jaime's there, you secure him. You wait there. If he's not, you haul ass down to us, because that's where the action will be." Blue turned to look at me. "You got that?"

I nodded.

"Then get out. Get in Dirt's car." He turned back and spoke louder. "Chelsea, you're with me."

I got out and left the door open. I moved around, passing Chelsea. We locked eyes. I said, "Keep your head down." She nodded and went on by. I found it kind of hard to believe she didn't squawk at yet another one of Blue's capers that walked just outside the black-and-white line of the law, a place where an error of any kind could ruin a career, her career being the sole motivation for transferring to Lynwood narcotics.

I hesitated before getting into Thibodeaux's car. I didn't like Blue for what he stood for, the laws he broke, the killings, but with those things excluded, in another place and another time, we might've been able to be friends. With Thibodeaux, I couldn't stand him as a person, as a human. I got in and slammed his door.

Blue took off, chirping his tires. Thibodeaux followed. We pulled back out onto the street.

The T-Bird smelled of soured nicotine and pine scent. Thibodeaux, his sleek sunglasses covering his eyes, said, "This one really has the potential to make your asshole pucker, so be sure you got your Kotex firmly in place, huh, Nancy?"

I said nothing and tried to keep the Polaroid photos of Mrs. Whitaker's bruised breast out of my mind. But that was like trying not to think about pink elephants when someone tells you not to think about them.

In three long blocks, both cars bounced into the lot of the rundown hotel, The Park View, at the corner of Slauson and Seville in Huntington Park.

Hypes, hookers, and street urchins scattered.

We bailed out of the cars and ran for the front door, Blue in the lead with Chelsea right behind him. Blue held Wicks' Smith and Wesson 9 mm down by his leg. He pulled on the double glass door.

Locked.

Blue moved to the large window, tapped, and pointed the automatic at the hotel clerk who controlled the button for the solenoid release.

The door buzzed.

Chelsea yanked it open. We flooded in. Blue put his hand on her chest, stopped her, moved her aside.

"Go, go," he said to us. "We'll give you a short count of five."

With Thibodeaux close at my heels, we ran up the shabby stairs, the carpet worn through to wood. I ran down the wide hall to room 207, stutter-stepped to get my stride correct, and booted the door on the run.

The door flew open.

A woman screamed.

A hooker sat on the edge of a dirty swayback bed, half-naked, her tattooed breasts sagging down between her legs, the john standing in front of her with his pants at his ankles.

Dirt shoved me in the back. "Come on, the action's on the first floor."

Now I followed him back the way we came. He ran slower than I wanted to go. I fought the need to shove him out of the way as we descended the steps, taking them two at a time. I couldn't remember the room number Ollie said for the first floor. No way would I ask Dirt.

We hit the bottom of the stairs and ran into six Hispanic gang members who'd just come in and clogged the hallway. Dirt didn't hesitate; he plowed into them yelling, "Sheriff's Department. Get down, get down." He clubbed the closest one and shoved into the others. The gang members, in a daze, slowly started to comply, easing to the floor.

Dirt yelled, "I got these guys. Go, go." He swung his gun and hit another one across the jaw who didn't comply fast enough. He'd been right to take control of them, as we didn't know if they were related to Jaime Reynosa, and they outnumbered us.

I didn't want to leave him with six against one, but he seemed to have them in hand, and I pitied those guys if they decided to try and take him on. No doubt Dirt would smoke them all and never lose any sleep over it.

I needed to get to Chelsea and followed Dirt's orders. I ran full speed down the hall until I came to the only open door.

Inside the small 10'x15' room, five suspects fought with two deputies, Blue and Chelsea, a clusterfuck of the first order. Elbows and fists and legs worked hard to injure and overcome. Yelps and grunts and fists connecting to muscle and bone.

I almost didn't slow down in time. I crossed the threshold to jump into the fight.

A gunshot went off.

In the small confines, the explosion stunned me. The concussion slapped me in the face. All the combatants in the room hit the floor, the same as if someone flipped off their power switch.

Blue, like a startled cat, leapt into the air, turning as he did, aiming the automatic for any kind of target. He fell backward onto the bed, his eyes locked on me.

"No, no," I shouted. "It's me—Bruno. Don't shoot."

For one long second, one that didn't want to click over to the next, Blue's wild-eyed look said that he'd come far too close to gunning me. His eyes shifted back to normal and he lowered his gun.

Chelsea stood alone, over by the corner, her gun in her hand. Gun smoke rose all around her in a strange aura. "It's okay. It was an AD. It was an accidental discharge. It was me. It's okay."

Blue got up off the nasty bed, chuckling. "Good thinking, Miller. Shooting your gun like that took the fight right outta these assholes. Let's get 'em all cuffed and sorted out."

I put my gun in my holster.

Thibodeaux ran into the room with his gun drawn.

"Ho," Blue said. "We're code four; it was just an AD."

I bent over and started cuffing the Hispanic male closest to me. Chelsea and Blue did the same. I went to cuff the second one when Blue turned his next one over. "Hey, this guy's shot."

I stepped over another one, still facedown on the floor, to see where Blue pointed. The guy close to Chelsea's feet, a Hispanic gang member wearing a white strap t-shirt, had a through-and-through bullet wound to his right shoulder. Blood soaked his shirt and pooled on the floor under him. The gang member didn't display any symptoms of pain or discomfort. That's what heroin did for you. He said, "I'm suin' all your asses. You wait and see. I'll own all your asses. Fuckin' Five-O just kickin' in our door. You assholes are done."

Blue looked up at Chelsea. "Looks like you got one, kid. This one your first?"

Chelsea turned pale and swayed on her feet. "I didn't mean to. We were fighting. I had my gun in my hand. I hit that guy. He was trying to grab for my gun. He . . ." She looked at the gun in her hand as if it were an alien piece of metal. "I hit him with my gun. And it just went off."

"*Shh,*" I said. "Don't say anything else."

Blue said, "That's right, listen to Bruno. Bruno, get her outta here. Go to the desk and call for medical aid. Dirt, let's get the rest of these guys secured."

I gently took Chelsea by the shoulders and guided her over and around the human obstacles on the floor. Out in the hall, I took her hand that held her gun and stuck her gun back in her holster on her hip and snapped it.

"Hey, you got socked in the face pretty good. I think you're gonna have a black eye."

"Bruno, he was trying to get my gun from me. You believe me, don't you?"

"Of course I do. We need to get some ice for that eye. You're fine, trust me; it's a clean shoot. Don't you worry about it. You going to be okay? I need to go to the desk . . . never mind, you're coming with me." I guided her down the now-empty hall. All the gang members had fled with the sound of the gunshot.

"Bruno, we didn't have a warrant to go in that room, and I shot someone inside that room where we didn't have a legal right to be. I'm in deep shit, aren't I?"

"I told you, everything's going to be fine."

But I didn't see how it could be. Wicks had warned me that Blue and Thibodeaux would try and dirty me up. They'd missed me and just dirtied up Chelsea.

CHAPTER FIFTY

CHELSEA EASED DOWN and sat cross-legged on the floor by the front desk. The top edge of her body armor pushed up under her chin. I stood close by and called dispatch and asked for paramedics and a black-and-white. I also asked dispatch to make all the other notifications: to the headquarters narcotics desk, to Stubbs, the Lynwood captain, and to Homicide so the OIS—the officer-involved-shooting team—could respond. I got a clean towel from the hotel desk clerk and some ice. I helped Chelsea to her feet, put the ice pack on her eye, and we went back to the room.

All the suspects, except the gunshot victim from in the room, sat on their butts with their backs to the wall in the hallway. Thibodeaux and Blue stood watch, lording over them. Blue smiled when we came back. "We got him. He's sittin' right there. We got him." He pointed at a skinny punk with glassy eyes and the "FFL" tattoo on his neck. One of the first ones I'd handcuffed right after the round went off in the room.

Chelsea raised her voice. "Yeah, we got him. But at what cost, huh? At what cost?"

Thibodeaux snorted. "Take it easy, chicky baby. This is all good."

"No, it's not, Dirt. How could it be?"

Thibodeaux tried to take her arm to escort her down the hall away from the ears sitting on the floor. She jerked her arm away.

Blue stepped in between them before Chelsea could slug Thibodeaux in the face. "Come on down this way. Let's talk this out before everyone gets here."

As a group, we moved ten feet away and lowered our voices.

Thibodeaux said, "Okay, this is what we're going to say."

I raised my voice. "We're not going to say anything that didn't happen. We are going to tell the truth."

Thibodeaux glared at me. "That right, cowboy? That really the way you want to play this one?"

Chelsea held her arms across her chest, the towel with the ice in her hand not doing her eye any good. "Bruno, that's real easy for you to say. Let Dirt talk. Let's at least see what he has to say."

"Everybody just take it easy," Blue said. "This is a clean one. Listen, this is exactly how it went down. We came to the door and knocked. Someone inside said, '*Quien es?*' I said, 'It's me, man. Open up.' The guy opens the door. I look in the crack in between the door and the jamb and see four or five assholes sitting on the floor with a plate of Mexican tar heroin.

"Plain view doctrine says I have every right to force entry and secure the evidence. That's what we did. Once inside, everyone resists arrest and we have to fight them. I see the guy, who's later gunshot, grab onto Miller's gun. In my book, that's attempted murder of a police officer. Miller jerks the gun away and clubs him with the gun. The gun discharges into the guy's shoulder. He's lucky Chelsea didn't give him all six in the gut, because she was absolutely justified."

Chelsea's grim expression turned into a half-smile that got bigger and bigger as Blue spoke. She slowly moved the ice pack back up to her injury. Her eyes spoke of a deep admiration for this new savior. I got mad at Blue all over again and shouldn't have—not for that reason.

Chelsea hugged Blue. He wrapped his arms around her, his eyes still on me, his smile saying it all.

He'd won over the girl and I'd lost big-time.

I turned and walked back to the room. On the floor, right in the center of the room, sat the plate of Mexican tar just as Blue described. The black sticky heroin was cut up into individual doses, making the plate look freckled with little clumps of grease. Multicolored toy balloons sat in a small pile next to the plate, ready to be loaded.

Sirens from outside reached through the walls to us as they drew closer. There wasn't much time before the whole world rolled in.

The problem with Blue's fairy tale was that when I came in the room, the main body of the fighting happened right where the plate sat. No way could the plate and the empty toy balloons still be sitting there undisturbed. The coolheaded Blue thought far enough in advance to get Chelsea and me out of the room while he set up the props to his little staged play. The way he designed it, no one would question what happened.

He'd saved Chelsea's career; I had to give him that much. He really knew how to cover everyone's ass.

Chelsea moved up beside me in the doorway of the room. She clandestinely touched her fingers to mine, which hung down at my side. Her voice was barely a whisper. "You good with this, Bruno?"

She knew she needed the whole team's buy-in.

I shook my head as the little angel on my right shoulder fought with the devil on the left. "Sure, Chels, I'm good. You don't ever have to worry about me."

She squeezed my fingers and whispered, "Thank you, Bruno. I owe you."

I turned to face her. "Why would you owe me anything? Like the man said, that's exactly the way it went down."

She nodded, and from the doorway of the room, her eyes furtively looked down the hall to where Blue and Thibodeaux quietly talked.

With her other hand, she reached over and stuck something in my front pants pocket. It felt like a piece of paper.

She wanted me to have her phone number or her address, or she'd written something personal on a note. My heart glowed warm. Maybe Blue hadn't won over the girl after all.

She smiled and shook her head, whispered, "Not here."

She didn't want me to look at the paper where Blue and Thibodeaux could see me. My heart sank. Maybe it wasn't something personal. Maybe this note simply said that she did work for IAB after all and that she wasn't transferred in from Public Affairs.

Now I really needed to know. I needed to look at that piece of paper.

No time now.

Down the hall at the front door, paramedics came in carrying all their gear. Blue escorted the two paramedics over to the room. Chelsea and I moved out of the doorway so they could enter. They set their gear down next to the wounded suspect, the one who'd grabbed on to Chelsea's gun. The one who committed attempted murder, this according to Blue.

Blue said, "Be careful of that plate of dope. It's important evidence."

Wicks' 9 mm stuck out of the front of Blue's waistband and made him look like some kind of ghetto gunfighter. Back in the day he would've fit right in with Pancho Villa's brutal crowd.

If he'd shot me with that 9 mm when I came through the hotel room door, as he almost did, how would he have justified that? How would he have arranged the props to that crooked little play?

Blue looked all around the dirty bed where he'd leaped in the air and landed when the gunshot went off. He patted his pants pockets and jacket.

"You lose something?" I asked.

"What? No, no. Just makin' sure *I didn't*. Last time I dropped my badge and didn't realize it until I got back to the station. No, I'm good here. Go on, wait outside. This is a crime scene."

I guess I liked him a little more, covering Chelsea the way he did, though not enough to keep from taking him down when the time came.

And that time continued to draw closer by the minute.

CHAPTER FIFTY-ONE

"BRUNO? BRUNO?"

I sat up straight in bed, rubbed my eyes, and shook myself. "Yeah, Dad, what's going on? Is Olivia okay? What's the matter?"

I glanced at the clock on my old nightstand in my room on Nord. Nine o'clock.

Nine o'clock!

"Dad, why'd you let me sleep? I was supposed to be at work thirty minutes ago."

"Bruno?"

I jumped up, looking around, frantic to be on my way, not knowing what to do first. I found my pants I'd worn the day before and hopped around getting into them.

The shooting team didn't get done with us until close to midnight. Blue wanted to go out and get a few beers to celebrate "Chelsea popping her cherry," her first shooting. Neither Chelsea nor I wanted any part of that mess. I offered to drive Chelsea home, but she said she preferred to be alone. I told her that wasn't a good idea. She insisted.

Maybe I had read her all wrong. And that's all I thought about or could think about.

Too pent up to sleep, I tossed and turned in bed until at least three. The emotion in Chelsea's eyes, her expression, the way she looked at Blue when Blue told us the scenario that really happened in that motel room, continued to play in my head and kept sleep at bay. If Blue had been a good guy, I'm sure I wouldn't have been as upset at losing Chelsea to him.

"Bruno, someone's here."

This time I caught Dad's tone, froze, and looked at him. He stood in the doorway to my bedroom wringing his hands, a confused—no, a scared, expression—on his normally calm and congenial face.

"What is it, Dad? What's going on?"

"CPS is here. They say I have to leave. They say I can't live here right now."

"CPS? What are you talking about?" The sleep clouding my thoughts cleared. Child Protective Services?

I moved over to him and took hold of his shoulders. What he'd said sank in. "That son of a bitch," I said. "I'm gonna kill that son of a bitch Thibodeaux." I ground my teeth and gently moved Dad aside.

"Don't, Son. Wait. Wait."

I walked down the short hall to the living room wearing just my jeans, no shoes or shirt. A black woman who hadn't missed a lot of meals and wore a blue dress that went down to the floor stood by the open front door holding a clipboard. "Are you the father of Olivia Johnson? Are you Mr. Bruno Johnson?"

I caught her eyes moving up and down my naked torso.

"That's right. What's this all about?" But I knew. Thibodeaux had stiffed in an anonymous call to CPS, for no other reason than to be vindictive and nasty, to rub our noses in the ugliness he'd perpetrated upon us. I didn't think I'd be able to keep from hurting him this time. Hurting him real bad.

The woman stepped over, offering a piece of paper. "I'm sorry, this is an order by the court that says until your father's case is adjudicated he cannot be in the presence of your infant child."

Even though I'd figured the play, her words socked me in the stomach. I couldn't imagine what they did to Dad. I took the paper and I looked over at Dad, who sat on the couch, pale and crestfallen, ashamed beyond belief. I crumpled the paper into my fist and silently swore.

Mrs. Espinoza sat on the couch at the opposite end from Dad, holding little Olivia. What the hell kind of world had we brought her into? A world where a man like Dad gets treated this way.

I turned back to the woman, a strange calm settling over me. "Yes, thank you. This has all been a huge mistake, and my father did nothing wrong, but we will be happy to comply with this order."

"Again, I'm sorry," said the woman. "I have been assigned this case and just so you know, I will be making periodic calls on the child to see that the court order is followed."

"I understand. I'm a Los Angeles County sheriff's deputy and you won't have to worry about us complying."

"I'm aware of your employment, Mr. Johnson."

I waited for her to turn and leave. No one said anything.

She finally said, "I have to wait until your father vacates this residence."

Dad said, "Oh, dear Lord."

I went over and got down on one knee in front of Dad, put my hand on his leg. "Listen, I will handle this thing today. I promise you, I will make it go away, today."

Tears welled in his eyes and it ripped my guts out, made tears blur my vision and my chin quiver. I wanted to crush and stomp Thibodeaux into the ground, grind him into an unrecognizable pulpy mess.

Dad put his hand on mine. "No, Son. Let your sergeant, that nice Mr. Kohl, handle it. I'm scared for you."

"Nothing's going to happen to me, Dad. I can take care of myself."

"That's not what I'm worried about." He lowered his voice, glanced up at the woman still standing in our family's home over by the door, then looked back at me and said, “I know your temper, Son. I can see it in your eyes. Don’t do this, Bruno. It’s not worth it. Nothing’s worth that kind of heartache. Please, I’m asking you to leave it alone.”

“I understand what you’re saying, but it’s not like that. I promise you I will handle this professionally and get it taken care of today. Now come on, let’s get you off to work. Hey, why aren’t you at work? It’s—”

Dad reached out and gripped my hand.

I nodded, letting him know that I understood and that those words didn’t have to be aired in front of the CPS worker or Mrs. Espinoza.

The postal inspector would be doing an investigation into the allegation Mrs. Whitaker made about the attempted rape while Dad delivered her mail. They’d have placed Dad on administrative leave pending the outcome.

And now, with no work to keep his mind busy, the county was kicking him out of his own home.

No way could this situation get any worse.

Oh, but I was wrong.

CHAPTER FIFTY-TWO

I GRABBED MY shoes and socks, my shirt and my gun, and followed Dad out into the front yard. We sat on the curb while I dressed, the bright summer morning already warming up the day. Cars drove by, some of them neighbors, the last of them on their way to work or going to the grocery. They slowed to look at us and at the beige American Motors Ambassador sedan with the red-and-white county seal on the doors, sitting in front of our house. What they must think about Dad not going to work, and at the same time, question the county car. The county car always meant something bad. The awful embarrassment for Dad.

Dad never took a sick day; his strong work ethic wouldn't allow it. And now I'd brought this mess literally right to his door.

I finished dressing, put the gun in my holster, my sheriff's star clipped to the front of my belt. "Dad, where are you gonna go? You can use my place if you want."

"That's okay, I'm going to head over to Tommy Tomkins'. I already called him. He's off sick again, but I think he took off today to go fishing. We'll get a late start, but it doesn't really matter for bonita."

Dad worked with Tommy at the post office. Dad liked him well enough and would never say an unkind word about him. But based on what I'd seen in the past, Dad could only take Tommy in small doses. Dad would never admit to it. According to him, Tommy qualified for the best-friend-in-the-world category. Anyone who made it into Dad's sphere of friendship qualified that way.

"That's good. You two should go fishing."

He nodded. "Listen, Bruno, I meant it when I said you needed to let your department investigate this thing. It'll get all straightened out without you getting involved. The truth will come out all on its own."

For someone so knowledgeable about life, he knew little about the law, its hidden prejudices and sometimes its ignorance of the truth.

I reached over and put my arm around him just as the dedicated woman from CPS came out of our house, walked across the short yard, and got in her car. She sat in the car and waited. She wanted Dad not only out of the house but out of the area as well.

We'd already complied with the order and didn't need to leave right then. Let her wait a little. I still needed to talk with Dad. I needed to assure myself that he was okay emotionally with what had happened. And maybe I also needed to assure myself he didn't blame me, even though he should have.

"Dad, what is it you've always told me?"

"I've told you a lot of things."

"Don't play coy. You know what I'm talking about."

He nodded but wouldn't say it.

"You always told me," I said, "that 'all evil needs to succeed is for good men to do nothing.' Are you saying that I'm not a good man? Is that it?"

"Don't be ridiculous, Son. You know better. You have no idea how proud I am of you."

"I know, Dad. And this . . . this thing I got you involved in isn't going to resolve itself on its own. Trust me on this. I don't think you understand what's going on here. I know more of the key components than anyone else. I have to get involved now. It's what these men want.

That's why they're doing it. I can't explain it all right now, but when it's over, we'll sit down and have a long talk, okay?"

"You know what's best. Just be careful. When you get angry and see red, that real dangerous shade of red, you know what happens. You start burning the world down. Remember what I'm telling you right here, this minute: you now have a far greater responsibility, more so than you've ever had before, with that little girl in there."

The way he said it and put the emphasis on the key words really hit home. "I will, I promise. Now I need to ask you a very personal question. And I wouldn't ask it if I didn't think I needed to."

He turned to look me square in the eye, and for the first time I noticed little wrinkles at the corners of his eyes, along with the first errant gray flecks in his black hair, cut short to his scalp. Had the added stress of the last few days caused him to age ten years, or had I been too busy in life to notice it before?

"Go on then, ask it. I have nothing to hide, especially from you."

I took a breath and nodded, dreading this.

He said, "Is it really that bad? Go on, Son, you can ask anything."

"The woman in the midnight-blue Eldorado, the one you kissed good-bye yesterday on our porch, was that Mrs. Whitaker?"

His mouth sagged open more with each word, his eyes turning from fear to sadness, to shame. I couldn't have read emotions that clearly on anyone else but my own father.

His lips quivered a little. "Son . . . I . . . I . . ."

"Ah, Dad, was that Mrs. Whitaker?"

He shook his head.

"No? Ah . . . well, if it wasn't her, don't worry about it. Then it's none of my business."

Again, I realized that I truly didn't know my father like I thought I did. This revelation about Dad being a lady's man, coupled with the way he had just reacted, changed my entire historical view of him and shook the foundations of everything I held dear.

"No, no, you have a right to know." He looked away, ashamed.

I wanted to say that I didn't want to know but couldn't get the words to come out fast enough.

"I guess, like you said, you must've seen her yesterday."

I said nothing, and couldn't now.

"It was Mrs. Bingham."

"Mrs. Bingham?"

That didn't make sense at all. The Bing's mother? She was black. "J. D. Bingham, the Ham, the guy I went to school with? That Bingham?"

"No, no, you know who I'm talking about."

"No, I don't. I—"

Then I did know. An old memory came bubbling up. Mrs. Bingham, the wife of the owner of Bingham's grocery store chain. Oh, my God. The first woman I'd ever seen naked way back when I was only a kid. And Dad was now dating her?

The memory came flooding in, making the air turn thick.

Christmas morning, years ago, I awoke to the smell of smoke. Noble, at that time my neighbor and best friend, had spent the night at our house over the protests of his father, Eli. Dad had talked Noble's father into it, kind of strong-armed him into it, and probably saved Noble's life.

Noble wasn't my brother yet.

With the smell of the smoke I got up and ran outside to find Noble's house fully engulfed in flames. Noble's father and Mrs. Bingham sat on the outcropping on the second story. Both of them buck naked.

Mrs. Bingham's skin was white and overly freckled, her naked breasts, her long, long legs, her—

Noble's dad yelled, "Xander, get the children, save the children."

But Noble's brother and sister perished in the fire that Christmas morning. Days after, Noble's dad just disappeared. Noble came to live with us, and Dad adopted him.

"Do you know who I'm talking about, now?" Dad asked.

"Yes. Ah . . . is she . . ."

"No, no, she's long divorced now. I would never do that. You know me better than that. I never told you because of . . . well, you can understand. I didn't know how Noble would take it."

How would Noble find out? He was sitting in jail awaiting a prison term, the longest kind.

"It's okay. Of course, I understand."

Dad now dated the woman who broke up Noble's family. Dad had his reasons; the biggest one had to be loneliness. I'd been too busy with my life to recognize it.

I wanted to ask him one more question: How long had it been going on? But since it didn't pertain to the Mrs. Whitaker incident, it was none of my business.

We stood. I hugged him, looking over his shoulder at the woman in the beige AMC Ambassador. I hugged him a little harder, and a little longer.

I didn't hold any animosity toward the CPS woman. She was only doing her job—the most important job in the county, by my book. She watched over the children. It was a duty often overlooked by society. And when we do finally pay attention, the regular rules don't protect the children well enough and come too little, too late.

I walked Dad over to his car, closed the door for him, and stood in the street and watched him drive off. I turned and waved to the CPS worker. She nodded, started up, and left.

I got in my truck and started it up. I headed out to violate a direct order from two supervisors, Lieutenant Wicks and Sergeant Kohl. A policy violation I could lose my job over.

I went to find Mrs. Whitaker.

CHAPTER FIFTY-THREE

I DIDN'T KNOW where Mrs. Whitaker lived, not exactly, and found my way based on Dad's description. Long lines of pink crepe myrtle trees in bloom and the deep driveway set the house apart from all the others.

I drove the Ford Ranger down the driveway and tried to imagine Dad delivering the mail day after day. I couldn't do a job with that sort of routine. I'd go stir-crazy. I needed the constant threat of the unknown, going from call to call, interjecting myself into problems people couldn't handle themselves, people who'd called for help.

But I didn't work the street anymore and had chosen a different path where I chased the worst of the worst. Only at that moment, those worst now chased after my family and me.

I parked under a tired old porte cochère that needed paint ten years ago, turned off the truck, and stepped out. On occasion, Dad had parked his mail truck in this same spot to visit with Mrs. Whitaker. From pure nervousness, I stuck my hand in my left pants pocket. My fingers touched a folded-up piece of paper I didn't remember putting there. I pulled it out.

A yellow, grease-spotted piece of cheeseburger wrapper. What the—?

I'd seen it before, only my mind couldn't put together where. How did this get in my pocket?

Ah, Chelsea.

She'd put it in my pocket yesterday evening while standing on the threshold of the hotel room, right after the shooting. The note I'd forgotten about. I hadn't seen her do it, only felt her put it in my pocket. But a cheeseburger wrapper? Not what I'd expected at all. Somehow my mind imagined white scented paper, with little hearts drawn over the i's, nothing more than sappy high-schooler thinking.

Once the paramedics arrived at the Park View, along with the homicide shooting team, coupled with the admonition from Chelsea not to let Blue or Thibodeaux see me look at it, the note just stayed in my pocket and eventually slipped my mind.

Then the other memory kicked in. Before we'd left for the hotel, Blue stepped onto the stoop outside the office mobile home and Ollie slipped him the paper, the cheeseburger wrapper.

I fell back against my truck, leaned into it. That meant that when Chelsea hugged Blue, the time when I'd thought Blue had won over the girl, at that moment Chelsea had the presence of mind to pick Blue's pocket. After she took the paper from Blue, she slipped the paper into my pocket when Blue and Thibodeaux weren't looking.

What the hell?

Right after the shooting, I thought Chelsea had been too distraught to think straight. She'd gone and really pulled off something amazing.

That's what Blue had been looking for in the hotel room when he made up that bullshit story about losing his badge on an earlier caper.

"Hello? Can I help you?"

A Caucasian woman with a pleasant face and black hair going gray stuck her head out the huge front door, ready to slam it closed at the first sign of trouble. Her expression was that of someone afraid to come outside even during daylight hours.

"Yes, I'm Deputy Sheriff Bruno—"

Dad had the same last name. I didn't want to spook her.

"I'm a deputy sheriff from Lynwood Station and I just have a few more questions for you if you don't mind."

She steeled herself and stuck her head out a little farther to look each way. "Where's your police car? Sheriffs don't drive trucks."

I held up my hands. "It's okay, here's my badge." I stuck my hip out so she could see the sheriff's star clipped to my belt. "You're Mrs. Whitaker, right?"

"That's right." She opened the door a little more.

"Would you mind if I came in to talk with you? Or we could talk out here if that would make you more comfortable."

She hesitated while she tried to decide.

"I can wait right here while you go in and call Lynwood Station to check on me." A bluff. If she made that call, I'd be in the grease for sure.

I stuck the paper back in my pocket still folded, the relationship with Mrs. Whitaker too tenuous to risk the slightest unnecessary movement.

She still said nothing.

"If you're busy," I said, "I can come back later."

"No, no, please. I'm acting like a stupid little scaredy cat. Please come in." She stood back and opened the door the rest of the way.

I pasted on my biggest smile and went in. "Thank you for seeing me." She closed the door.

The inside looked better cared for than the outside. In days of yore, a house of that size would have required at least one full-time servant to keep it up. Mrs. Whitaker obviously lived alone and did the best she could.

I followed her off to the right into a huge dining room with dark-brown hardwood floors that would be difficult to maintain, all the buffing, the waxing. She pulled a chair out at the head of a long wood table, one with twelve chairs. "Please, have a seat. Can I get you some sweet tea?"

"No, thank you."

Dad said he'd come in and sit with her to drink tea and talk. Thibodeaux must've set up on Dad, followed him on his mail route and seen that he went inside this house to talk with this gracious lady. Thibodeaux saw this as his opportunity to create havoc in our lives. This poor woman became a random victim of violence for no other reason than to forward a treacherous agenda.

I took a seat to put her more at ease. She sat two chairs over with her hands in her lap. She wore a pleasant and trim off-the-shoulder floral dress that made her breasts appear large and prominent. I tried not to look at them, tried not to call up the image of the Polaroid photo Sergeant Kohl showed me in our front yard moments before he hauled Dad off for the crime of attempted rape. The photo of Mrs. Whitaker's naked breast that Thibodeaux, with malice and forethought, had crimped down on like a vise with his strong hand, causing pain and fear and tyranny.

The ugly, purple, finger-sized bruises.

She must've read my mind, as she brought her arms up to cover her breasts.

"I know this is a delicate matter," I said. "And I won't take up very much of your time."

I was stalling. I really didn't know how to get at the information without spooking her, without embarrassing her or myself.

We both sat there quietly waiting. For what, I had no idea.

She said, "I grew up in this house. My parents both died here."

I nodded.

"This used to be a grand neighborhood, with great people," she said. "I have pictures that show nothing around this house except acres and acres of orange groves. Before my time, of course. Then Los Angeles just continued to expand and expand until it ate up everything and then these little cities incorporated until, pretty soon, this wonderful place turned into . . . turned into this horrid little corner of the world."

One tear filled her eye and rolled down her cheek.

"Yes, ma'am," I said. "I grew up in Willowbrook, over in the area called The Corner Pocket."

She nodded, as if acknowledging that I knew what she meant.

"I know you went through an awful experience and I don't in any way want to make it worse. I just—"

Her mouth dropped open. "You're Xander's son. He told me his son was a sheriff."

I said nothing.

"Oh, my God, I can see him in your eyes." Now tears rolled down her cheeks in earnest. She shook her head and said, "I am so terribly sorry. Please tell Xander I'm so terribly sorry."

I got up and moved to the chair closest to her. "That's right, my name is Bruno, and I came here to try and get to the truth."

She shook her head. "No, I'm sorry, I can't talk about this. I can't."

"I understand, I do. I know what really happened. I know the man who did this awful thing to you and—"

"Then if you know him . . . then you know, I cannot, will not, tell you anything." She stood, hugging herself even tighter. "Please leave." She raised her arm and pointed toward the door.

I got up but hesitated.

"Please go."

I turned to leave. I walked with heavy feet and in possession of confirmation that Thibodeaux had done this awful thing.

At the door, I turned. She'd followed and stopped a few steps back in the hallway next to the entrance to the dining room, half her face in shadow. "Please tell your father that I am so sorry and that if there was anything that . . . well, just tell him I'm sorry."

I slowly raised my open hand. "Please, it's not your fault, and my dad understands. He really does."

She nodded. "Thank you for that."

I moved my hand to my hair. "Did the man have a tuft of white hair, right here?"

Her hand flew to her mouth. She shook her head. "I won't answer any of your questions. Now it's time for you to leave. Please leave."

I nodded. "Just so you know, his name is Claude Thibodeaux, and I'm sorry it happened to you. I'm going right now to make sure he never hurts anyone again. You'll never have to be afraid of him, not ever again. You understand? I'll make it right."

She reached out with one hand for support of the wall, her eyes hopeful.

I turned and left.

CHAPTER FIFTY-FOUR

OUTSIDE AT MY truck, I watched the door to Mrs. Whitaker's house, hoping she'd change her mind and come running out ready to recant her accusation about Dad. That wouldn't happen, not until Thibodeaux came off the balance sheet and I had paid him in full what I owed him.

I reached into my pocket and took out the folded piece of cheeseburger wrapper Ollie had given to Blue and Chelsea then stole from Blue. I no longer had any illusions about the note being romantic prose, though I still didn't know what I'd find when I opened it.

I unfolded the paper to find an address written in an uneven hand and difficult to decipher at first glance. I had to turn the paper this way and that to read it in and around the grease spots:

Bof

DoubleD

Aqua Glasshouse

Downey

An address. Well, a location anyway. Oddly, I knew what Ollie meant by her shorthand. I tried to visualize the place, an exclusive neighborhood of condos and new custom homes on the other side of the river, in Downey.

Mo Mo.

Ollie had slipped Blue what Blue wanted all along: how to find Mo Mo. The misadventure in Huntington Park at the Park View Hotel didn't need to happen. He'd only taken us there as a cover, as a misdirection. He didn't want anyone else to know that he knew where to find Mo Mo. The way it all went down, the way Ollie gave Blue the paper out on the stoop, the way he'd tried to conceal it, the way he frantically looked for it in the hotel room and then made up the lame excuse, all of that convinced me that Blue intended to go after Mo Mo himself and kill him. That's why Blue had been so hot after Mo Mo. That's why he'd targeted Mo Mo, the number-two dealer in LA, and not Papa Dee.

And Chelsea had given me the paper from Blue's pocket. Did she know what the note contained? I didn't think she did. How could she? I stood too close to her from the time the shot went off to the time she slipped me the note. She never had the opportunity to read it. Still, I needed to talk with her and ask her why she gave it to me.

I folded the note up and put it back in my pocket. I got in my truck and drove back to the station.

I parked in the back lot two rows over from the narco trailer, got out, and headed that way. Something didn't feel right . . . the door to the narco trailer was closed. Anytime someone worked in the hot trailer, they left the door open for ventilation.

Sergeant Kohl, in a dark brown western-cut suit, came out of the patrol unit service area, walking with deliberation right at me. I stopped and girded myself for a verbal thrashing, the one I more than deserved.

He stopped in front of me and spoke in a calm and controlled voice that made it even more painful. I respected the man too much and I'd gone and put him in an untenable situation. I wanted him to yell and scream. He said, "I just got off the phone with Mrs. Whitaker. I told you, Bruno, not to stick your nose into this thing. I warned you."

I said nothing.

"Now you've forced me to do something I didn't want to do. I'm obligated to turn it over to IAB. You're gonna get racked up on this one. If you're lucky, you'll keep your job, but you'll be sent back to the jail where you'll never get out. You'll work there the rest of your career."

Working the jail again? What an awful prospect. I couldn't do it, wouldn't do it.

I said nothing. To have said I was sorry would only patronize him and make it worse.

"I also came back here to tell you to call Lieutenant Wicks ASAP." Kohl turned and left.

I slapped my left hip where I normally kept the pager. Not there. In my rush this morning, when Dad woke me, I'd gone off and left it on the nightstand. Wicks must've been going crazy when I didn't answer. And Blue might've been trying to get a hold of me as well.

I turned back to the trailer. Blue was peeking through the blinds by his desk and had seen the entire exchange with Kohl. The blinds went back to normal. I headed for the trailer door that for some unknown reason was closed.

"Bruno?"

I stopped.

Kohl headed back toward me.

I waited.

He came up and stopped, closer this time. He said, "We're friends, aren't we?"

"Yes, I'd like to think so . . . yes, we are."

"Then man to man, not sergeant to deputy. Just man to man. Tell me what's really going on. I want to understand it. I can help. You can trust me."

I opened my mouth to spill it, to tell him all of it. He'd be able to stop this mess right then and there. He wouldn't let it go any further.

Based on what happened to Mrs. Whitaker, he'd be able to hang a conspiracy case on Thibodeaux and Blue, shut down their little game without any further risk and without anyone else getting hurt.

I opened my mouth to say the words, but Blue opened the door to the trailer and yelled, "Bruno, you're late. Get your ass in here."

I looked at Kohl and then back at Blue. For what Blue and Thibodeaux had done, a simple little conspiracy charge wasn't good enough. Besides, conspiracy was one of the hardest charges to prove in court. And no way would Mrs. Whitaker testify against Thibodeaux. Blue and Thibodeaux knew that.

I shook my head at Kohl and headed toward the open door to the trailer where Blue stood.

Kohl said, "Wrong choice, Bruno. You're not making the right choice here."

I didn't turn around. I just waved my hand over my head as if I really didn't care what Kohl had to say. But I did. I just couldn't look at him anymore for fear of giving in to the easiest path and asking him for help. Stepping away from the fire I was playing with and letting him handle everything.

I made it to the bottom of the steps and looked up at Blue.

Blue grinned. "Where you been, big man? You were about to miss out on all the fun."

He stepped back out of the doorway so I could see in from where I stood on the ground. Jaime Reynosa sat in a chair by the filing cabinets, just inside the door, handcuffed behind his back. Sweat ran down his face, and he blinked rapidly to keep it out of his eyes. He looked scared, real scared, and he had a right to be. I went up the steps and inside.

Blue closed the door and locked it.

CHAPTER FIFTY-FIVE

INSIDE THE TRAILER, Thibodeaux sat at his desk with his usual shit-eating smile. Blue wore a green-and-gold tank top with LASD in big yellow letters on the front. He acted as if he loved the sheriff's department. He looked calm, in control, as if he always had a wild-eyed, handcuffed crook in his office.

I recognized Jaime Reynosa from the day before at The Park View. Only then he'd been smacked-back, under the influence of heroin, sedate, without a care in the world. Now he bounced his legs as he sat in the chair. His whole body hummed. His nose and eyes and sweat glands worked overtime secreting, all symptoms of opiate withdrawal. He smacked his lips a lot from his overactive saliva glands.

"What's going on?" I asked.

Blue, stoic, serious, all business now, said, "What's it look like? We're about to interrogate a major player in Mo Mo's organization. Jaime doesn't want to tell us where his boss is laying his head, and we were just about to convince him otherwise. You want a piece of this?"

"I tolt ya," Jaime screeched. "I don't know anything anymore. I haven't been up in there with Mo Mo for months now. I'm tellin' it straight. Tell 'em, would you, Deputy Johnson? Please tell 'em."

"I know you?"

"Ah, man, come on. You let me walk about two months ago on a possession beef. I gave you Maurice, remember? After he beat his ma and pa, tolt ya he was layin' his head over off Alabama and a hunert and seventeenth. Southa there, in that old two story. You caught him and beat the livin' shit outta him. He's still in the jail ward. You did him in good, Deputy Johnson. He deserved it, though. Everyone on the street says you did the right thing."

"That right?" Blue asked. "Jaime's good for his word?"

I moved past Jaime and tried to remember. I sat at my desk across from Thibodeaux. I remembered Maurice, no way I could forget. "You lost some weight," I said.

"That's right. I was healthy back then. That's right."

"Yeah," I said, "now I remember. He's good. He'll tell it to you straight."

"Thank you, Deputy Johnson, thank you." He still sat forward, his legs bouncing.

With the door closed, the place reeked of sour body odor and an uncomfortable humidity that radiated off his body. Having Jaime in the office for the purpose of finding Mo Mo's location was my fault. I had the piece of paper Blue wanted in my back pocket. Blue must not have seen or remembered what the note said when he opened the cheeseburger wrapper and only glanced at it the day before when he stood on the stoop with Ollie. Or since Blue wasn't from this area, hadn't worked there that long, he didn't understand what it meant.

Blue could always call Ollie and ask her again. Maybe he'd already tried that and she'd gone to ground after she fulfilled her obligation to us. That's what I'd do with the likes of Blue and Thibodeaux and Mo Mo all wrapped up into one big ugly mess.

I could take the paper out of my pocket and end Jaime's bumpy interview, but I didn't want to give anything to Blue, and especially not to Thibodeaux.

Blue said, "Ol' Jaime here says he doesn't know where to find Mo Mo."

"I'd believe him then."

Thibodeaux leaned back in his chair and flicked open his switchblade, closed it, and flicked it open again. He pointed it at me. "Homeboy, you fucked the dog yesterday."

"Let it go, Dirt," Blue said.

"No, no." He pointed the switchblade at Jaime. "Yesterday, you handcuffed and searched this little turd and you missed this." He picked up a plastic evidence bag off his desk that contained a small automatic pistol.

"What?"

I'd been handcuffing Jaime when Blue found the guy gunshot by Chelsea. "I did search him." I tried to think back how thorough a job I'd done and couldn't remember clearly enough.

"The hell you did." He tossed the gun on the desk across from him. It clattered. "I found that little cop killer in his crotch. You missed his crotch. You a homophobe, Bruno?"

Under the circumstances, I guess I could've missed the gun. A cardinal rule in law enforcement is you always searched the crook to the best of your ability no matter what circumstances. "I'm sorry."

"You're sorry? He says he's sorry, boss. What good does that do us now, huh? This little prick here could've killed us all with that little popgun."

Thibodeaux was an asshole of the first order, but he was right about this. I'd screwed up on a grand scale. The worst part, I'd done it in front of these two master criminals. I'd shown them that I was a screwup of the first order and that they didn't have to worry too much about me if I couldn't do a simple pat-down.

Blue didn't seem to care about my screwup. He only wanted one thing: information from Jaime. Blue picked up the plastic bag with the gun. I got a better look at it, a model 84 Berretta .380. He carried it over to Jaime, waved it around in his face. "You're an ex-con. An ex-con in possession of a handgun is some heavy time."

"I'd tell ya, Blue, if I knew. I swear on my baby's eyes I don't know where Mo Mo's layin' his head."

I swiveled in my chair and picked up the phone. I needed to call Wicks. I dialed. Wicks picked up on the first ring. "It's me," I said.

Thibodeaux stared at me.

In the phone, Wicks said, "What the hell's the matter with you? You stuck your nose into that thing I told you not to. I told you that it would be taken care of after this whole thing blew over."

He spoke in code about going over to Mrs. Whitaker's. He didn't want to wait to meet. He was mad enough to risk someone on my end overhearing.

I needed to meet, though. I had too many questions I needed to ask him. Like, did he initiate the black bag wiretap on Blue, the man who'd cuckolded him? Did the deputy chief know? I needed to ask for proof that Blue asked for me to come to this team, which Blue denied.

Just to name a few of the pressing issues on my mind.

I said to Wicks into the phone, "How's Olivia? She getting any sleep?"

Wicks said, "You really screwed the pooch on this one, Bruno. They're starting an IA. Kohl called IAB. We now have about twelve hours before this whole op gets shut down. Maybe a lot less."

"Try giving her another bottle."

Blue turned his back on Jaime and ejected the magazine from the Berretta and shoved it in his pocket. He turned back and pointed the gun at Jaime. "You're going to tell me here and now what I want to know or I'm going to blow your head off."

I'd become desensitized to Blue's lawless methods. Threatening a crook with death not only violated his Miranda rights but was a felony as well.

Wicks said, "Did your friends make that offer you've been expecting?"

He wanted to know if Blue and Thibodeaux had brought me into their confidence, asked me to help with a contract, or offered me any of the missing skim.

"Last chance, asshole," Blue said. "You're going to tell me or I swear to you, this will be your last day on this planet."

I watched Blue point the small automatic at Jaime's head from less than three feet away and couldn't believe how calmly I accepted this illegal act.

I held the phone away. "Come on, Blue, quit messin' around. That thing can go off."

"You bet it can because I'm gonna drop the hammer on this little puke."

I said to Wicks, "About that other thing, I think I've figured out . . . the ah . . ."

"The next target?" Wicks said. "Yeah, if you'd answer your pages you'd already know that. We intercepted a phone call. We don't have it clearly stated, they talked in that jumbled code bullshit, but we think it's—"

Bang!

The explosion in the confined space echoed in my head.

The Berretta leaped out of Blue's hand and thumped to the floor. He stutter-stepped backward. "Oh, shit. Holy shit."

Jaime fell over in the chair. He tumbled to the floor, messed and pissed his pants.

Wicks' small voice in the phone said, "Bruno? Bruno? What's happened?"

My hand fumbled as I hung up on him.

I muttered to no one, "Blue just killed Jaime Reynosa."

CHAPTER FIFTY-SIX

THIBODEAUX BOLTED OUT of his chair, clapped his hands like an excited kid, and yelled, "Hot damn, Blue, that's some shit right there." He threw his head back and cackled, "*Woo-wee!*"

I slowly stood from my chair as the gun smoke rose in an even bank and clung to the ceiling like a fog. The acrid odor bit at my nose and masked the reek of excrement and urine in Reynosa's pants.

Seeing Thibodeaux act the way he did made me realize that white tuft in the sea of black hair on his head might've been caused by severe head trauma and because of it he no longer accepted or followed regular social norms or social values, and made him more dangerous than I first believed.

Thibodeaux stopped laughing, lost his grin, and squinted. I followed his gaze to the row of filing cabinets.

"Ah, shit, Blue." Thibodeaux pointed. "You missed the little peckerwood and hit the filing cabinet. Damn."

In direct line with where Jaime had been sitting, the top file drawer now sported a bullet hole, a blemish difficult to explain in the best of circumstances. I went over and carefully picked Jaime up, still in his faint, and put him back in the chair. Thibodeaux squeezed by, chuckling to himself. He pulled open the file drawer. "Hey, Blue boy. You hit the B's solid in the informant file. Blew a hole right through Ollie Bell's informant file. Is that some kinda omen or what?"

I stepped over and slammed the file drawer. I whispered, "What kind of idiot are you? You don't talk about an informant in front of other crooks."

Thibodeaux stared at me for a moment. I tensed, ready for the violent confrontation, one that I wanted, one that I needed.

It didn't materialize.

"You're absolutely right, old son." He patted my shoulder, turned, and went back to his desk.

What the hell was going on? Why'd he back down?

The phone on my desk rang. I went over and picked it up. "You okay in there?" Wicks asked.

"Yeah, sure."

"Meet me, location two, one hour." He hung up.

Blue came out of his trance. He picked up the gun from the floor. He extended it out to me. "What the hell happened?" He took the magazine from his back pocket and showed it to me. He said, "I pulled the magazine. You said it wouldn't fire with the magazine out."

I took the gun and magazine. I shoved the mag in, released the slide, and let the hammer down easy. "This is a Berretta. It doesn't have a mag safety like the Smith and Wesson. It'll fire the one round in the chamber without the magazine seated." I pulled the mag out, ejected the round, and handed him the gun back.

"Oh." Blue thought about it a moment more and said, "Oh."

Thibodeaux said, "It's okay, Blue. Your piss-poor aim saved all our asses today, no doubt."

Blue sat down at his desk. His reaction didn't mirror what I'd seen of him the night of the Imperial and Mona gas station shooting. That night he displayed a devil-may-care, stone killer look in his expression, especially in his eyes.

Maybe because Jaime, in Blue's mind, didn't deserve to die like the others he'd killed. But that theory didn't work either, not if he truly possessed a cold-blooded killer mentality.

Jaime started to come around. His eyes rolled and stabilized. "What happened?"

I said, "You're going through severe heroin withdrawal and you're hallucinating. You passed out and fell off the chair."

He looked at all three of us one at a time, nodded, and said, "Really?"

Thibodeaux said, "You gonna tell us where Mo Mo is now or are we gonna give you another hallucination?"

"No, no. Don't do that. I told you I don't know. But I can find out for you, you let me go."

Thibodeaux looked at Blue. Blue nodded.

"Nah, man," Thibodeaux said, "that ain't the right move here, Blue. We got him on the ropes. We just need to squeeze him a little more."

Blue glared at Dirt.

Thibodeaux took the cuffs off. "Come on, I'll 849b-1 you out of the jail. Give you a citation."

Thibodeaux helped Jaime to his feet, supported him under one arm so he wouldn't fall on his face, and walked him out the door and down the steps.

I sat back down at my desk and looked over at Blue.

Blue stared back. He finally said, "You going to report what just happened here?"

"Hell no, not with the way you got my nuts in a vise."

"What are you talking about?" he asked, his expression neutral.

"You know exactly what I'm talking about. You and your butt-boy hung a case on my dad. What do you want from me? What do you want me to do to get that case taken off him? I'm ready to do anything."

"I really don't know what you're talking about."

"Mrs. Whitaker, down in East Compton?"

"Nope."

"Come on, don't bullshit me. That's why I'm late this morning. I went down there. I found a witness that saw Thibodeaux with his white tuft of hair and his puke-green T-Bird. In the future you might have him wear a cap and drive a less memorable car." I was lying, trying to bluff.

Blue stood and stepped over to me. "Stand up."

I did, and I towered over him, hands at my side, fists clenched, ready for anything he could throw at me.

"Lift your arms."

I did.

He patted me down, the thorough kind of search, not missing a thing, looking for a wire.

He went back and sat down at his desk. He grinned. "I told Dirt too many times, that hair of his would get him in trouble."

CHAPTER FIFTY-SEVEN

I GRITTED MY teeth. The casual way Blue spoke about the crime, admitting what they'd done to Mrs. Whitaker—to Dad—made me want to yank him out of his chair and beat that smile out of him.

"What do you want from me?" I asked. "What do I have to do to get Thibodeaux to back off Mrs. Whitaker so she can recant her accusation?"

Blue lost his smile and stared at me for a moment.

"I want you to—" He looked to see if anyone stood in the doorway and lowered his voice. "I want you to take out Mo Mo."

My heart raced. This had been what I'd been waiting for, the whole purpose of my assignment. "What are you talking about? You want me to whack Mo Mo? No way. You're kiddin', right? This is some kind of test, right?"

I'd never put a case together for a murder for hire. I didn't know what I needed as far as the elements of the crime. I did know for sure that at that moment it was Blue's word against mine. No district attorney would file any kind of charges with that kind of evidence. I needed more, a lot more.

And Blue knew it, too.

Blue watched me close, as if trying to read me. "That's the cost to pull your dad back from the edge."

I looked at him. "Murder? I don't know about that. I—"

"Mo Mo's a dirtbag sellin' drugs. He's got a huge operation. Do you know how many people he's killed with those drugs? Probably hundreds if you add up the overdoses, the killings over drug turf. And that doesn't even take into account all the families ruined by the addicts. Do you know how many more people he's going to hurt and kill with those drugs?"

"But murder?" I said.

"It's not murder if he resists arrest when you go to take him down."

That's what Blue had done at the Mona and Imperial gas station shooting, covered it in the name of the law.

"Why me? Why in the world would you think I'd do something like this?"

"I asked around about you. When you caught up with Maurice Tubbs, you put the boot to him for what he did to his parents with that hose nozzle. I'd have done the same thing. You also tracked that car for five miles in the summer heat, pulled a guy through the screen door, and put the boot to him for what he did. He killed a little girl, ran her down in the crosswalk, and took off. And Mo Mo, he's ten times worse, the worst of the worst."

Mo Mo wasn't the worst of the worst. I was looking at the worst of the worst now: Blue.

"I take out Mo Mo, you'll drop the charges against my dad?"

"That's right. You have my word."

"What, the word of a contract killer?"

"You want to call me names, that's fine, get the hell out. Let your father rot in prison."

"No, wait, I didn't say no. I just don't want to get taken for a ride, that's all. Set up like a chump and left blowin' in the wind."

"What are you talking about?"

"On Peach, Ollie said the bag was supposed to have sixty-two thousand five hundred in it. Thibodeaux checked in forty at narco headquarters. I checked."

Blue smiled. "You know, I thought you might be a hard sell on this. Dirt thought . . . well let's just say, I'm pleasantly surprised. So, you're saying, for a sign of good faith, you want that skim, the twenty-two five?"

"That's right. I know you have to be getting a nice chunk from whoever it is asking to have this done. Who is it?"

"Who do you think it is? You won't ever know for sure. It could just be me wanting to rid the streets of scum like Mo Mo."

"Nah, you wouldn't do it without compensation. So, if I had to guess, it's Papa Dee. He probably wants to take out his competition, and he's willing to pay good money to have it done."

I didn't want to get anywhere near the information about the EME, the prison, and the information the black bag wiretap gave us. That would tip off Blue for sure.

"You really got it goin' on, big man. The whole twenty-two is too much, though. Let's not quibble about the price. What's your bottom-dollar offer to do this thing? And keep in mind we're also throwing in your father."

Had I even taken a half step into his morally bankrupt world, I'd probably have done it just to get my dad off. He didn't know that because he didn't feel the same way about his father. He'd shot and killed *his* father.

I stood. "Right now, I got somewhere I have to be. I don't think you know how to find Mo Mo, so twenty-two five is my number. Let me know if it's good for you."

"You know how to find Mo Mo?"

"That's right, I do. I grew up on these streets."

He smiled. "All right, big man, you can have the whole thing, but you have to get to Mo Mo first if you want the money. I just unchained Dirt, told him he could have his original split for the job and the whole skim if he takes Mo Mo down fast. This needs to be done in a hurry. Don't underestimate Dirt; he's very resourceful."

"I want the money up front."

"Not gonna happen. And . . . and for that kind of money, I want Mo Mo to disappear, no resisting arrest bullshit. I want him the kinda gone that's like, poof, into thin air. I want proof, too—photos of him dismembered if you want that kinda money."

"All right, you got a deal."

CHAPTER FIFTY-EIGHT

I DROVE IN and out of side streets for forty-five minutes. In and out of the housing projects, the Nickerson, and Imperial Courts to check for a tail. Then I pulled into Stops, the hot-link place across from Nickerson Gardens. The sweet barbecue aroma wafted on the warm summer air and made my stomach contract. I hadn't eaten breakfast, and now it was almost lunchtime.

Wicks waited for me around back of the restaurant and stood by the trunk of his car with his arms crossed, angry enough to chew nails. Johnny Gibbs sat in the passenger seat watching me in the side mirror. Wicks had brought the team in on the investigation—just not the whole investigation. What must Johnny think of me? Bruno the rat. Maybe Johnny didn't want to get out of the car and eat lunch with the likes of me.

I parked away from them, got out, and walked to the front of the restaurant. Wicks hurried to catch up. "Hey, hey. Where do you think you're going, mister? Get your black ass back here."

I got in the long line of people waiting to be served lunch at the counter. Wicks came in and stood right beside me.

"You think this is a good idea?" I asked. "Being seen together like this in public?"

The black man and woman in line ahead of us turned a little to see who'd said it. The woman looked me up and down. Her eyes lingered on the gun on my hip and the badge clipped to my belt before she ruled me safe and turned back around.

Wicks took a twenty from his wallet. "Get me the usual." He left.

I made it up to the counter in another ten minutes and said hi to Nancy, who gave me a huge smile. I gave back the same smile, only a little tarnished. I couldn't get Chelsea out of my head, and needed to. I needed to focus.

I paid, left the rest of Wicks' money as a big tip for Nancy, picked up the tray with the food, and headed out.

"Thanks, Bruno," Nancy yelled.

I set the tray down on the picnic table around back where we stood and ate.

"I picked up an extra sandwich for Johnny."

Wicks calmed some, nodded, and took a long drink from his Coke.

"I told him to stay in the car and listen to the radio for me. We're still up on the trailer in back of the station."

I nodded and chewed.

"What happened back there? Was that a gunshot?"

I nodded again and didn't want to talk with a mouth full of chili fries and hot-link sandwich.

"Wait, it *was* a gunshot?"

I waved a hand and spoke around the food. "It was nothing. An AD, that's all."

"An AD with a handcuffed suspect in there? I can only imagine."

Wicks really hated Blue.

He said, "We saw Thibodeaux bring Jaime Reynosa from the jail back to the trailer. Did Reynosa tell you where to find Mo Mo?"

I shook my head and continued to eat.

"Come on. Knock it off, Bruno. Talk to me."

I swallowed. "Did you find out about Chelsea, where she transferred in from?"

"No, and I'm the lieutenant here, and you're going to answer *my* questions."

I took another bite of sandwich and shook my head "no."

"What do you mean 'no'? You're—"

"What did you find out about Chelsea?"

He gave me the stink eye and let the moment hang. "I'm hitting a roadblock with that. Human Resources says they lost her file."

"That's convenient."

"It happens."

"What did the chief say about her?"

"I'm not going to ask the chief a question like that, question his integrity. He's a chief, for crying out loud."

I nodded again as if I understood, but I didn't, not when so much was at stake. Wicks probably wanted to make captain and didn't want to confront someone as powerful as a deputy chief, force him into a corner. Then again, captains no longer got to go out in the field and hunt dangerous men.

"We got until tomorrow morning to kick this thing in the ass and get it moving, then IAB will stick their oversized noses in it, and we'll lose the whole thing. We won't get squat on these guys."

"On the phone, you said you figured out the next target."

"That's right, but it came out in their usual word play, all jumbled, and we can only make an educated guess."

I said, "It's Lucas Knight—it's Mo Mo, right?"

Wicks had started to put his hot-link sandwich to his mouth for a bite but now let it sag. "That's right. Hey, did Blue and Thibodeaux bring you in?"

I chewed and nodded.

Wicks slapped me on the back, his smile huge. "Excellent. Excellent. What happened? Give it to me word for word. Wait, let me get my notebook out."

I nodded and spoke around the food in my mouth. "First I need to know something."

He froze. "Bruno, you don't get to call the plays here."

"You were the one who initiated the black bag wire on Blue. You're the one who started this whole mess, right?"

He took a step back and threw his sandwich on the table. "Goddamn you, Bruno. You're not running this op, I am. And when I tell you to do something, I damn well expect you to do it. Now tell me what happened. Tell me right now what that son-of-a-bitch Blue told you."

I continued to chew and watched him. "It *was* you, wasn't it? You're too close to this thing and you should conflict out. You should hand over the lead to someone who doesn't have a vested interest."

His face bloated with rage. "What difference does it make? It doesn't, not in the whole scheme of things. So, leave it alone."

I dropped my sandwich and took a step closer to him. "It makes all the difference."

He brought his hand up and poked me in the chest. "You will tell me what I want to know right now or—"

I grabbed his finger and inverted it in a pain-compliance hold. I moved my face right up next to his as he grimaced and tried to pull away. "I know about Gale Taylor, your ex-wife, the woman Blue took from you. Now, *was* it you who came up on the black bag wire?"

CHAPTER FIFTY-NINE

HIS EXPRESSION SHIFTED from pain and confusion to fear. I had yet to see fear in Wicks and had come to believe he didn't own any part of that emotion. "Let go."

I shoved him away. "You played me right from the beginning," I said, "and I'm not happy about it."

He rubbed his hand and stared at me. His expression transformed back, right before my eyes. His pride and hubris returned stronger than before. "So what? It doesn't matter now. I was right: Blue and Thibodeaux are the worst kind of criminals and that wire only proved it. I'm going to take them down with or without you. Now tell me what happened."

"You're really something."

"Spill it."

"We take them down according to policy and procedure. What we're not going to do is take them down the Robby Wicks way. You understand? They get the same benefit of the law just like everyone else."

"What you must think of me. Of course, we give them every chance. But you have to understand these guys aren't like your regular desperate criminals who don't want to go to prison. These guys are trained the same way we are. They think just like we do. You give them one blink of a chance and they will take your own gun from you and stick it up your ass. So we'll give them every chance, but you just keep that in mind when you're backing me up on the takedown. Now, tell me."

What he said made a lot of sense and also made me realize how far out of my depth I'd ventured.

"Blue turned Thibodeaux loose to find and take out Mo Mo. Blue said that if I got to Mo Mo before Thibodeaux, he'd not only take care of the case against my dad, he'd also give me the skim. Blue doesn't want Mo Mo taken out in some kinda mocked-up, justified officer-involved shooting. He wants him to disappear. He wants photos of his dismembered body as proof. He wants a finesse job, something he knows is beyond Thibodeaux's capability."

Wicks nodded, his eyes off somewhere else. "Yeah, all that backs up what we got off the wire. Now it all makes sense. You didn't tape this conversation with Blue, did you?"

"What do you think?"

"I liked you better when you were respectful."

"Then give me something to respect. You broke the law with that black bag wiretap and—"

"Grow up. And if you want a piece of me for that great self-initiated piece of police work, go ahead and try and prove it. Until then, we need to work together to take these two off the board."

Couldn't he hear his own words? He broke the law with his illegal wiretap to chase someone else who broke the law. What gave him the right?

Moreover, as Blue had shoved in my face, how the hell could I accuse him of violating the law when I was no better? I'd meted out curbside justice on those two prior occasions: the hit-and-run driver with the cowboy hat who'd run down the little girl, and Maurice Tubbs, who'd beat his parents near to death. I had no right to sit in judgment of Wicks. I didn't want to believe it, but maybe we were built more alike than I wanted to accept.

"I'm sorry," I said. "I was out of line."

"That's okay." He offered his hand.

I took it and shook.

He said, "None of this gets us any closer to the dog heavy. And there is a dog heavy. I confirmed it with that last phone intercept. There is a third person. We just don't know his name."

"Don't get mad, but I have an idea about the dog heavy."

"Who?"

"It's kinda way out there."

"Don't yank my dick, Bruno. Give."

"What if, like you said, the chief inserted Chelsea into this game as a backup to oversee what's happening?"

Wicks didn't show the slightest bit of anger. "What do you mean? Talk me through it."

"The chief could've put Chelsea in to keep an eye on Blue, Thibodeaux, me, and even you, through me." As I talked, my mind spun out ahead, checking known information against everything that had happened so far in conjunction with the chief's role.

"Okay, and what would the chief's motive be?"

"Ah, shit," I said.

"What?"

"I just thought of something."

"What?"

"Something you said the first day the violent crimes team met."

"I said a lot of things. At times, I can be a real gas bag."

"You said that the team had full autonomy to go after any target of our choice."

"That's right."

"We were all set to go after Damien Frakes Jr., the Holly Street Crip wanted for the jewelry store robbery."

"Yes, and I did go after him."

"But you said the chief pulled the team off him and gave us Pedro Armendez."

"Ah, son of a bitch." Wicks eased down and sat on the picnic table bench as he thought it through. "But how could he know that you'd put Armendez down? That was just a lucky fluke—the way Armendez cut his own throat like that. You said yourself you weren't going to shoot him."

"Not if the chief thought you'd be there like you were supposed to be. You'd have dropped the hammer on him, right? Remember that little conversation you had with me after everyone left? You wanted to make sure I'd do the right thing and pull the trigger."

"Damn it, Bruno. No way do I think this is right, but I'll look into it. I have to now. We got some time, still. You can't do anything until we get a line on Mo Mo."

"I know where to find Mo Mo."

"You do?"

"Yeah, but I need to talk to someone first." I started to walk off.

Wicks said, "All this is coming to a head. Be sure to answer your pager. That's an order."

"I forgot it at home."

"Bruno?"

I lifted an arm over my head, waved, and kept walking to my truck.

CHAPTER SIXTY

I DIDN'T GO back to the house to get my pager. And "short on time" was the first excuse that bubbled up to act as a smoke screen for the real reason that I didn't want to go home. In reality, I didn't want to see Mrs. Espinoza or the woman from CPS at the house, a reminder of the painful issue with Dad.

So instead, I sat in my truck on Old School Road in Downey, watching the location described on the greasy cheeseburger wrapper:

Bof

DoubleD

Aqua Glasshouse

Downey

Blue had just transferred to Lynwood. I didn't think he could've translated the note even if he still had it in his back pocket where Chelsea had lifted it. I'm not sure I could've had I not been friends with Patrick Hickox, a guy I'd worked the street with who now worked at headquarters narcotics. On several occasions I met him halfway between Lynwood and HQ at a donut shop called The Donut Dolly. Pat was sweet on the owner, Eva. A real looker. The kind of woman who had the power to make a guy do anything she wanted. And I worried about Pat. I now saw that *do anything she wanted* look in Pat's expression every time I met with him. Not a big deal, if she loved him and didn't screw him over. Only I didn't know Eva well enough. Pat said Eva was on parole.

Not good.

She was an ex-con that owned a donut shop that lots of cops frequented. The odds for a favorable outcome for Pat didn't bode well.

As soon as I left Wicks at Stops, I'd driven over to Chelsea's apartment in Torrance to talk to her. When she didn't answer her door, I waited outside for a while. I stood there staring at the door, wishing it to open, or I paced back and forth like some kind of lovesick puppy.

In one of the passes, I caught my reflection in her window and froze. I didn't like what I saw. The same as Pat Hickox, I, too, carried the *do anything Chelsea wanted* look. Carried it like some kind of virus.

And it scared me.

So I left and headed to Downey.

In Ollie's note, *DoubleD* stood for *The Donut Dolly*. *Bof* stood for *back of*. And *Aqua Glasshouse*? Well, I wasn't sure what that meant, but figured it out as soon as I drove down the street directly behind The Donut Dolly. A '73 Buick Riviera, painted metallic aqua, sat in front of an upscale condo. The '73 Buick was called a glass house on the street because of the long and wide back window.

Out in front of the condo, just down from the '73 glass house, I sat in my truck and checked my watch every few minutes as the hours eased on past. I continually reached for where my pager should've been clipped on my belt, and found it missing.

Dad referred to my pager as an electronic leash. With the pager, the Sheriff's Department could yank my chain, make me roll over and sit anytime they wanted. At that moment, without it, though, I felt disconnected from the world.

I'd come to depend on the pager to keep me informed not only for work but with my personal life as well. I worried about how Dad was doing. How Olivia was doing.

I sat scrunched down in my seat with sunglasses and a ball cap, surprised with every passing minute that one of the neighbors hadn't called in the black man sitting in his truck in a predominantly white section of town.

I didn't take action and only watched. I didn't know if Mo Mo was in the condo. If I knocked or forced entry, and he wasn't there, that was it. The place would be burned just like the rock house on Peach. So there I sat, incommunicado, with anxiety continuing to build and darkening my soul with each passing minute.

Who knew what could be going on? What Blue or Thibodeaux were doing? If Blue had been trying to page me, or if Wicks found out something important and couldn't tell me? Hell, for all I knew, the whole thing could be busted wide open and nobody knew where to find me.

I waited and waited, and that left plenty of time to go over every last detail of what had happened since I accepted the undercover assignment from Wicks: the briefing the first day at Lennox station, Wicks assigning me as the team leader while he went after Damien Frakes Jr.; the foot pursuit and capture of Pedro Armendez, his blood all over me, that horrible taste of copper; the long debriefing by homicide afterward; Wicks showing up at the crime scene on Holt that next morning and—

I bolted upright in the seat, my heart racing. Wicks showed up at the crime scene on Holt, the place where Pedro Armendez bled out and died.

Wicks had been paged again and again the night before and never answered. He'd been busy, tied up in his own officer-involved shooting debriefing over the killing of Damien Frakes Jr. But then he just showed up on Holt, right out of the blue, said he wanted to back his team. Said that he wanted to help me out.

And he'd been the one to find the bloodied X-Acto knife blade.

How did he do that? When did he do that?

He wasn't there when I pulled up and parked in front of the Armendez crime scene. Sure, I'd sat there in my truck in an emotional and fatigue-induced funk, but I would've seen him searching the ice plant looking for that small blade that he found too fast. When the forensics team, in their meticulous ways, couldn't.

Why didn't I see the continuity error at the time? How could he have found that knife blade when he'd only just pulled up?

At the time, I wanted to believe he'd found it. That's why. Pedro Armendez cut his own throat, and I had an overwhelming need to see that blade. So, I easily accepted the find of the blade, no matter how unlikely. For me, there was no doubt that Armendez had done the deed.

But, besides my statement, there just wasn't any other explanation or physical evidence. That night, we never found the blade and never would have, not in all that ice plant.

Wicks found the blade after only a couple of minutes at the scene. That's all the time he could've been there.

Wicks told me Blue called the deputy chief and asked for me to work on his team.

Blue said that never happened. Of course, Blue could be lying.

I gripped the truck's steering wheel as hard as I could and twisted.

Wicks hunted down Damien Frakes Jr., shot and killed him. Could Frakes have been marked as a contract hit? No one would've looked at it too closely, not after Frakes killed those poor folks in the jewelry store and then shot a cop. At the time, every cop in the western states was looking for Frakes. And Wicks had been the one to find him.

Wicks never said how he accomplished that minor feat. Was Wicks the dog heavy calling the shots, even telling Blue what to do?

But that didn't make sense either, not with Blue stealing Wicks' first wife away from him. Unless Wicks really didn't care about Gale Taylor and already had his eye on the lovely Barbara.

My mind spun round and round trying to make it all fit. The end result: I couldn't trust anyone involved. No one.

I couldn't give in to my paranoia. Thibodeaux and Blue had made me that way. Never in my life would I have believed two cops could get away with what they had. Murder for hire, of all the crimes.

I got out and walked across the street to the sidewalk, where I followed it to the door of the condo, the one I'd been watching. I couldn't sit in the truck any longer and wanted to roll the dice.

Needed to roll the dice.

The unit, unlike the others in the area, sported an exterior metal frame with a wrought-iron door in front of the wood one. I knocked, stood off to the side, drew my gun, and held it down by my leg.

The inside door opened.

Chocolate stood in the open door, the beautiful young girl from the rock house on Peach. Mo Mo's rock house. That made Chocolate Mo Mo's girl.

She opened the wrought-iron door, standing off to the side just out of public view, and smiled hugely. "Well, hello, Deputy Johnson. I didn't know you were coming over. You should've called first. I would've dressed for the occasion." She slipped her dress off her shoulders and let it drop to the floor.

No panties, no bra. She cocked her naked hip. She wore only shiny black spiked heels. And of course that huge smile.

CHAPTER SIXTY-ONE

I STEPPED IN. Close.

She didn't move back. I put my hand high on her chest to move her back so I could close the door.

She took my hand and moved it down to her breast. "You don't need that gun, cowboy. You can have anything you want."

"I want Mo Mo."

She lost her smile. "Why do you think Mo Mo would be here?"

I took my hand off her warm, soft breast. I raised my gun and moved deeper into the condo. "Mo Mo," I called. "LA County Sheriff's Department. Come out with your hands raised."

Chocolate followed along. "Hey, hey. You can't just come in here without a warrant."

I checked the bathroom and master bedroom first, under the bed and in the closet. I made sure he wasn't out the sliding-glass doors on the small patio. I checked the other rooms next, but no Mo Mo. I went back into the master bath, took a white satin robe hanging off the door, and tossed it to Chocolate. She shrugged into it. The white satin made her look even more appetizing, smooth milk chocolate wrapped in whipped cream. She reminded me of Eva at The Donut Dolly, the one my buddy Pat had fallen for, that kind of beauty.

I had to focus to keep from getting aroused.

I holstered my gun and took her by the hand. "Come on, let's sit down." I guided her back into the living room with its plush wall-to-wall, white fur-like carpet.

I sat on the black leather couch. She sat next to me, too close, her thigh touching mine. I put my hand on her hip and shifted away from her. "Listen," I said, "this is serious business. I need to find Mo Mo, and I need to find him right now."

"I don't know what you're talking about, sugar."

"Are you someone who keeps her word?"

"You know I am." She reached to put her hand on my leg.

I gently took hold of it and held on. "The other day, in front of that rock house on Peach, Mo Mo's rock house, you said you owed me one, remember?"

She again lost her smile. "Yes, but that's not what I meant. You know what I meant. You're the best-looking deputy I—"

"Listen to me, some very bad men are after Mo Mo. They want to kill him."

Her expression turned to panic, which she tried to conceal. She loved Mo Mo and would do anything to protect him. That's why she'd come on to me. If she'd gotten me to cave to her beauty, to her gorgeous body, she and Mo Mo would own me. She'd love to give me to Mo Mo as a gift.

"What are you talking about?" she asked.

"Do you trust me? Have I ever lied to you?"

"You're starting to scare me, Bruno. Who are these men who are after my Mo Mo?"

"The worst kind of men. Cops. It's Blue and Thibodeaux."

She jumped to her feet. "No, no, I don't believe that. Not those two. They wouldn't."

"Wait, why don't you believe that it's those two?"

She turned back around and took a step closer, her one leg forward, which made the robe part to expose the joining of her two slender legs, the dark and wondrous triangle, inches from my face, beckoning.

The hidden dog within me let out a little groan before I could stop it. "Chocolate, this is not going to happen, so stop it. Tell me why 'not those two.'" I took hold of her hand and pulled her back down. She sat on the couch. "Tell me."

She jerked her hand away and rubbed her wrist, her mouth in a pout. She hadn't been turned down too often, if ever, and didn't like it.

"If you don't tell me, I don't know how you're going to live with yourself if those two get to him before I do."

That got her attention.

"You really think they're gonna kill Mo Mo? How do you know?"

"They told me so. They hired me to do it."

She let out a yelp and again tried to jump up.

I held on to her arm and leaned into her. "I'm not going to kill Mo Mo. I want to get him into protective custody until we get this whole thing straightened out."

She shifted from trying to pull away and leaned into me, her hands going to my face. She took hold and pulled my face close to hers. "Are you telling me the truth?"

"Do you honestly think I would pass up an offer like you just made me if I wasn't here doing my job?"

She broke away. "Oh, my God, you *are* telling the truth. They're tryin' to kill my Mo Mo. What are we going to do?"

"Can you get Mo Mo to come here?"

"Yes, of course I can."

"Then call him. You can be here when I explain all of this to him. Then you'll see I'm telling the truth."

"He'll kill me if he shows up here and finds out I set him up."

"Don't tell him I'm here. Let me worry about convincing him. We'll just tell him I showed up after you'd already made the call. I promise you, I am not going to arrest him. I am not going to hurt him in any way. I only want to protect him."

She got up and went over to the phone. She picked it up and dialed, her other hand on a hip canted to the side. The robe fell open, displaying everything important.

I groaned again and muttered, "You're killing me here."

She suddenly turned her back to me and said into the phone, "Hi, sugar. It's me."

She didn't want me to see her lie to her lover. She could lie to anyone else but not him. This came hard for her.

"I need to see you right away. Yes, babe, it's an emergency."

CHAPTER SIXTY-TWO

CHOCOLATE HUNG UP the phone and pulled her robe in tight, clutching it between her breasts. "He'll be here as soon as he can." She looked scared to death.

"When will that be?"

"I would think within the hour, maybe twenty minutes. I don't know for sure. I've never called him and said things like that. Told him it was an emergency. He's really gonna skin me; I just know it."

"No, he won't. Not once I explain the—"

"I was a fool to listen to you. I know better. You don't know him. You don't know what he's capable of. I do. I've seen him—"

Her words faded off as I tried to think of what to do once Mo Mo arrived. He wouldn't cooperate, not in the least. I'd have to make him. Then what? Where would I take him? I needed help. But who would I call?

I went to the phone. The good little angel on my right shoulder said "don't do it," and recited the cardinal rule Wicks told me about working undercover: *tell no one—not under any circumstances.* The bad little devil on the left shoulder said, "Show some balls; take the leap. No one in the history of undercover work ever encountered circumstances like these."

Oddly, the devil's voice resembled Blue's. I didn't like Blue talking in my ear.

I didn't want her to hear what I said on the phone. "You better get dressed."

She looked down at her thin robe, her near-nakedness. "Oh, my God, yes." She rushed from the living room and down the hall. Her white satin robe flowed and blew up in the back, revealing long and lithe athletic legs.

I turned back and dialed the phone. When the operator at Lynwood Station answered, I said, "This is Deputy Johnson. Please let me talk to Sergeant Kohl." I continued to fight the urge not to tell him, but I needed someone I could trust. "No, I'm sorry, tell him this is the Bad Johnson."

Two minutes later: "Kohl."

"Sergeant Kohl, this is Bruno Johnson."

Silence.

I said, "You know that talk we had, the one in the parking lot where you said we could talk man to man?"

"Yes, I do. I also remember that you just turned and walked away from me without so much as a 'fuck you.'"

"I know, and I'm sorry. Really, I am. Is that offer to talk still on the table?"

"Of course it is."

"Can you come to 17632 Old School Road in Downey?"

"I'll be right there."

"Sergeant Kohl?"

"Yes."

"Don't come in a black-and-white."

"I understand."

He hung up.

"Who was that?"

I turned. Chocolate stood in the living room looking over at me from the dining area, totally dressed with her shoes in one hand.

I said, "It was a friend. And I really need one right now."

She wore expensive slacks and a matching blouse, her feet bare. She still hugged herself as if cold, her arms across her chest. "This is a bad idea. I'm telling you this is a real bad idea. Mo Mo is going to be mad as hell that I did this. I can't even imagine."

I didn't need her getting me all jacked up over what may or may not happen. I had complete confidence that I could handle Mo Mo alone. But if he brought along some of his people, his thug nasties, the situation could get out of hand as soon as they walked through the door.

Now the question was, would Kohl arrive first? With Sergeant Kohl on scene, nothing could go wrong. He'd know exactly how to handle the situation. He had the time and experience. "Come on," I said. "Come over here and sit down on the couch. Everything's going to be okay." I gently took hold of her elbow.

She jerked away. "Don't touch me. I think I just really screwed up a good thing. Mo Mo takes good care of me and look what I just did. You made me do it. I hate you, Bruno Johnson."

A sliver of something silver glinted in her hand under her arm. "What do you have?" I grabbed onto her wrist. She tried to jerk away. I held on and wrapped my arms around her from behind. She relented. I pulled her hand from under her arm. She gripped a Raven Arms .25 automatic, a Saturday night special with no stopping power, but it could kill you just the same. She didn't want to give up the gun. I pried it out of her hand and let her go. I checked the magazine.

Loaded.

I press-checked the chamber.

Loaded.

"What were you going to do with this, shoot me?"

"I thought about it. It would really put me in good with Mo Mo if, when he gets here, he finds you gunshot on the floor."

"Shame on you. And I thought we were friends."

"Not friends enough that I'll let you get me killed over all this mess. I mean, I like you and all, Deputy Bruno, but friends only takes it so far. I got a lot more skin in the game than you do."

"You just said that you hated me. You're going to be fine. Trust me, okay? Go on over there, sit down on the couch, and relax."

She stuck her lip out in a pout. I bet that got her most anything she wanted from Mo Mo.

She moved over to the couch and plopped down. "How can I trust some dude who doesn't take any sugar from me when it's offered to him? You aren't playing for the other team, are you, Bruno?"

I looked around for someplace to put the gun, reached up and set it out of view, and out of her reach, on top of the chrome entertainment center, next to a silk plant. "No, I'm not like that, and if I wasn't working, you better believe I'd take you up on your offer." I only said it to assuage her ego. I didn't think I could ever have any sort of relationship with Chocolate, casual or otherwise. It wouldn't be healthy for either one of us.

I went over and sat on the couch close to her. The long black second hand on the clock on the wall ticked and ticked.

And ticked.

I figured fifteen minutes max from Lynwood Station to Old School Road in Downey. Much faster if Kohl put his foot on the accelerator. Sergeant Kohl wouldn't do that though, too straitlaced, too much by the book.

Now I could also tell him about what happened in East Compton at Mrs. Whitaker's, explain how Dad wasn't involved and that Blue and Thibodeaux framed him.

Five minutes went by. With each one that passed, the chances increased that Mo Mo would arrive first. He'd have at least one thug with him, probably three. I resisted the urge to pull my .38 and hold it by my leg.

I wished Wicks were here; he'd be cool and calm, ready for anything. Ready to pull the trigger when I wasn't at all sure I could. I'd never fired my gun on the job except at the range.

I wished I had the gun Wicks gave me to carry, the one Blue never let out of his sight, the one with fifteen rounds in the magazine instead of the six in the gun at my side.

I'd forgotten to tell Wicks about that part, that Blue carried his gun.

Someone knocked at the door. Loud. We both jumped.

I got up. "You stay right there." I went to the door. I stepped to the side and peeked out the window blind.

Sergeant Kohl.

I turned the dead-bolt lock on the steel-framed door, opened it, and let him in. I took a look outside and then closed the door.

"What the hell's going on, Bruno?"

"I need your help."

"You got it, buddy. No problem. Whatever you need, I'm here for you."

CHAPTER SIXTY-THREE

KOHL CAME DEEPER into the room, his eyes scanning everything, looking for any kind of threat, a true deputy on full alert. He wore the same brown western-cut suit, his sheriff's star clipped to his belt in front. His brown hair was parted but mussed a little, like Opie Taylor on *The Andy Griffith Show*. It made him look innocent and unassuming and younger than his years.

"Sergeant Kohl, this is Chocolate."

I had known her so long as Chocolate, I couldn't remember her real name.

Kohl moved quickly over to her with his hand extended and shook hers. "Nice to meet you."

He turned to me. "What's going on, Bruno? Why am I here?"

The admonishment from Wicks not to tell anyone about my undercover status caused the words to clog on the tip of my tongue. Did I trust Wicks or did I trust Kohl? I'd only known Wicks a short time, but his reputation continued to echo around the county. I'd worked with Kohl for two years at Lynwood Station, and he'd always been a solid supervisor, who, to the man, everyone liked.

"Bruno?" Kohl nudged.

"Yeah, yeah, I just need a minute. Just give me a minute."

Chocolate sat down and immediately stood back up, wringing her hands. "We don't have a minute," she blurted out. "Any second now, Mo Mo's going to walk through that door."

"What? Lucas Knight's coming here? Talk to me, Bruno. Is that right? If that's the case, we need to call in some backup, like right now."

"Too late."

The deep voice came from the hallway that led to the master bedroom. The owner of the voice must've come in through the slider in the master bedroom. Chocolate must've unlocked the steel and wrought-iron-reinforced slider when she went to get dressed.

Mo Mo stood at the threshold of the living room holding a deadly looking Colt Python .357 Magnum. "What the hell's going on, Chocolate?" He pointed the gun in the general direction of both Kohl and me. "You two don't move or I swear I'll bust a cap in both your asses."

Chocolate moved around the coffee table and headed for Mo Mo. "Baby, am I glad you're here. I—"

Mo Mo held up his hand. "Hold it right there, woman. Don't you cross in front of this weapon. Sit your ass down. Right there, sit. Is this why you said it was an emergency, 'cause you got two asshole cops all up in your crib?"

Mo Mo had dark skin that made his crooked teeth look even whiter. He stood about six feet with broad shoulders and weighed about 200. He wore a gray velour warm-up top that matched the bottoms. On his feet he wore British Knight basketball shoes with blue laces. The zipper, half-down on his shirt, displayed his muscled chest and a thick gold chain with a big "M" that dangled down about midway. The "M" was encrusted with small diamonds.

"I made her call you," I said. "I needed to talk with you."

"Talk? Or take me to jail?"

"We don't have a case on you. You're clean right now, except for that gun you're holding on two law enforcement officers. Put it down now, and we'll overlook that felony."

"I don't believe you. You two, go on, toss your gats on the floor. Do it with two fingers. Go on, take those guns out and drop 'em."

I looked over at Kohl.

His expression didn't change. He looked indifferent to the gun pointed at him.

Number-one rule they drilled into us at the academy: never, under any circumstances, give up your gun.

"That's not going to happen," I said. "You might as well shoot us and get it over with. We're not gonna give up our weapons. We came here to talk. That's all."

Mo Mo pulled the hammer back on the Python, the click loud and disturbing in the room, which just grew a lot smaller. "Cops make me nervous, so if you even twitch the wrong way, I'm not gonna hesitate. You understand? Start talkin.' You got thirty seconds."

I again looked at Kohl, who still seemed unfazed by the sudden change of events. I said, "There are two cops out there on the street right now who want to take you out."

Mo Mo smiled. "Just two?"

"I'm not kidding. There's a contract out on you and two cops—"

Kohl's head whipped around, his eyes moved from Mo Mo over to me. "A contract? What are you talking about, Bruno?"

Mo Mo said, "Man, how come *he* doesn't know what the hell you're talkin' about?"

"What's going on, Bruno?"

"I'm sorry, I was going to tell you, but Mo Mo got here a little sooner than I expected."

Kohl said, "What two cops? What's this about a contract? How do you know this?"

I sucked in a deep breath. "I'm working undercover in narcotics. I'm still on the violent crimes team and I was put on the Lynwood narco team to ferret out the two cops."

There, I'd said it.

Mo Mo turned the Python onto me exclusively and spoke to Kohl. "That what you wanted to hear? That he's still a Boy Scout jus' like you thought? Now give me my money back."

My knees went weak and I wavered on my feet.

Please, God, not Sergeant Kohl.

Kohl pulled his gun and pointed it at my gut. "What's the matter, Bruno? You look a little pale. Maybe you better sit down before you fall down." He reached over and pulled my gun from my holster.

I stood my ground, unable to move.

Mo Mo said to Kohl, "Where's my sixty-two thousand and my two keys of rock you promised? I did what you asked."

Chocolate said, "Mo Mo, what's going on?"

"Shut up, bitch. Can't you see the men are talking here?"

In my mind, all the recent contacts with Kohl flew by: He'd been the one to run the robbery surveillance of the gas station at Mona and Imperial Highway; he'd been the one to bring in the narco team with Blue and Thibodeaux to supplement the surveillance; he'd been the one that didn't move Blue back to his original position; he'd been the one to investigate Dad's attempted rape case; he'd been the one who'd contacted me in the parking lot right in front of the narco trailer with Blue watching; and he'd been the one to tell me we could talk man to man, all along wanting me to rat on myself, wanting me to violate the cardinal rule of the undercover.

All of it a setup.

I muttered, "You're the dog heavy."

"I don't know what that is," Kohl said, "but we thought you might've been a plant, and if so, we also needed to find out how much the other side knew about us."

I slowly brought my hand up to rub my face. "That meant Blue made sure I saw Ollie pass him the note. Jesus, what a fool I've been."

From down the hall, Thibodeaux walked up behind Mo Mo, stuck a gun to his head, and said, "Don't move, nigger." He reached around and took the Python out of his hands. He shoved Mo Mo deeper into the room, closer to Chocolate, and looked at me. "That's right, you made it easy for us. Blue started planning the whole thing the moment you walked into our narco trailer. That's how good he is. That's how fast Blue thinks on his feet. You people never had a chance against the way he can think."

I shook my head in wonder and muttered, "Number-one rule, tell no one you're undercover. Jesus, why didn't I listen?"

Nobody knew where I was or whom I was with. In all my life I never felt so alone and helpless.

What was Olivia going to do without a father?

I swallowed hard, took in a long breath. "How does Chelsea figure into all of this?" I had to know, and their answer scared me more than their guns or what they intended to do to me.

Thibodeaux opened his ugly mouth to reply, but Kohl said, "Shut your trap, Dirt. Don't say another damn word. You said too much already."

I let out a long sigh. "She's working with you, isn't she? She's a part of this whole thing, isn't she?"

CHAPTER SIXTY-FOUR

"MO MO," CHOCOLATE said, "what's going on?"

"Baby, looks like I jus' got double-crossed by these two asshole cops."

"Shut up, the both of you," Kohl said. He looked over at Thibodeaux. "Is Blue coming out?"

"No, he said he needed to go for a long run to clear his head. He kinda liked this smoke here. Don't know why." He pointed the gun my way. "Blue just didn't believe he could be a rat. I told him I could handle this. No reason at all Blue should have all the fun."

Kohl didn't look happy. "What'd he say to—"

Mo Mo roared and lunged at Thibodeaux, his arms outstretched, fingers splayed.

Thibodeaux let out a chuckle, took a step back, and shot Mo Mo in the face. White smoke billowed in the living room. Chocolate screamed and went for Mo Mo.

Kohl took his gun off of me and took aim at Chocolate. I dropped my shoulder and drove with my legs, caught him low in the gut, and rammed him right into the wall. The plasterboard caved in. He grunted and dropped his gun.

Rage roiled up and out of me. I bellowed like a bull and slugged Kohl in the face again and again. I slugged him for Dad. I slugged him for Mrs. Whitaker. I slugged him for all the men he'd been a part of killing.

Thibodeaux stepped over and pistol-whipped me across the back of the head. I went to my knees. The world wobbled and the lights flickered. I fought to stay conscious. If I went out, I'd never wake again.

Strange words entered my head. "FBI! Open the door. FBI! Demand entry."

Thibodeaux, about to hit me again, said, "What the—?"

The wobble in the world cleared a little more. Someone pounded on the wrought-iron security door to the condo and couldn't get in.

Thibodeaux shuffle-stepped back over to Chocolate, who, with tears streaking down her face, picked up a lamp and threw it at him. He cackled, dodged the lamp, and swung the Python again, catching her on the side of the face. Chocolate dropped straight to the floor the same as if someone turned off all her power.

I got my feet under me and came in low. Thibodeaux spun, bringing the gun around. The Python spit flame again. This time the sound came out muted in my ringing ears. The bullet furrowed down my back like a farmer's plow that laid open skin and muscle, instantly turning my shirt wet. I no longer felt pain, or heard, or sensed anything at all. With every part of my being I wanted nothing more than to crush Claude Thibodeaux out of his miserable existence. End his ugly, pathetic life.

We collided and flew back. We slammed into the chrome entertainment center and went to the floor. Glass shattered. The TV tumbled to the floor. The tube exploded and crackled.

Thibodeaux's fingers clawed at my eyes while he tried to push me away with his knee, the Python pinned between our bodies. He couldn't bring it to bear. He gave up, let the gun go, pulled his arm free, and slugged me in the face. I struggled, got up on top of him, and went to work on his face with my fists.

He kicked me off. I rolled and came up on my feet.

Thibodeaux came up, too, with that grin of his, his hands empty. His right hand went down to his leg and came up with the switch-blade. He flicked it open.

The entire structure of the condo shook from a loud bomb-like explosion. Dust filled the air. Behind me, the front door and wall bulged in.

Kohl yelled, "What the hell?"

Chocolate came to and keened over her dead Mo Mo.

Thibodeaux didn't care about the car that was trying to ram into the condo. He lunged at me, the knife held low.

I came at him hard and tried to block the knife with my right arm. The blade slid down the top of my forearm, cutting the muscle down to bone. I butted his face with the top of my head. The blow shook him. He stumbled backward. I stayed with him, grabbed onto his knife hand, and pummeled his face with my fist, my broken knuckles.

The condo shook again. Wood and metal shrieked. The front end of a car appeared and shoved deep into the living room, shoving furniture out of the way.

I spun Thibodeaux around and got him in a choke hold. One I didn't intend to let up. Ever. I would choke the last bit of his sorry life right out of him.

Kohl rose up out of the white dust and clutter of overturned furniture, holding his .38. He shouted, "Let him go, Bruno."

I shook my head and held onto the choke hold as hard as I could.

Kohl said, "Dirt, get down. Gimme a shot and I'll take him out. Drop."

"Freeze! FBI!"

Chelsea stood on the hood of her demolished car, pointing a gun at Kohl.

Kohl ignored her and fired. His bullet thumped into Thibodeaux, caught him in the center of the chest.

My arm choked off a grunt in Thibodeaux's throat. His body went limp.

Chelsea fired three times.

Kohl's body jerked. He flew back against the wall and slid down.

I let Thibodeaux's body drop. I rushed over to Chocolate and hugged her. I tried to pull her away from Mo Mo.

"Bruno?" Chelsea slid off the hood of the car. "Bruno, are you all right?" She coughed and fanned the fine dust that floated in the air. She went right over and kicked the gun from Kohl's dead hand. She holstered and came over and put her hands on my shoulders. "Bruno?"

Chocolate struggled to her feet. "You bastard. You dirty son of a bitch. You did this. You killed my Mo Mo."

A huge lump rose in my throat. She was right. All this carnage, all the mayhem, was because of me, because of my ignorance.

"Oh, my God, Bruno. You're bleeding. Bruno, come over here and sit down."

I shrugged Chelsea off as I held onto Chocolate's arms and hugged her as tight as I could to keep her from hitting me. I didn't know what else to do.

Chocolate's body shook as she wept. Tears burned my eyes.

All that was happening finally slowed down and started to make sense. I looked at Chelsea. "You're FBI?"

She nodded.

"How did you find me?"

"I followed Kohl here. We've been on to him for a while now."

"Son of a bitch," I muttered. "Maybe this wasn't *all* my fault." I owned the largest piece of it, but this could've been handled differently if the feds had cooperated with the sheriff's department.

I held onto Chocolate with one arm, let go with the other, and took hold of Chelsea's wrist. "You mentioned the dog heavy. Was Kohl the dog heavy?"

"Bruno, what are you talking about? You must be delirious from blood loss and the blow to your head. You have a huge goose egg."

"In my truck, out in front of the rock house on Peach, you mentioned the dog heavy."

The excitement in her eyes lost some of the sheen as my words sank in. She knew exactly what I was talking about. "I need to find a phone to call an ambulance for you."

The sound of far-off sirens outside entered the condo through the large hole Chelsea had put there with the car to save my life.

"Tell me," I demanded.

She nodded. "We made a mistake. We caught wind of the murder-for-hire scheme from an informant in federal prison who wanted to make a deal to reduce his sentence."

"And? And?"

"Take it easy, Bruno."

"Tell me what mistake you made."

"We—"

"The FBI."

"That's right, the FBI. When we wanted to infiltrate your department to find out how deep this thing went, we went right to the top . . . almost the top. We didn't know how many or who was involved, so we went to the chief. We talked only to the chief."

"You contacted Deputy Chief Rudyard."

She nodded.

"And he's the dog heavy?"

She nodded again. "We just confirmed it last night on a wiretap intercept. But we don't have anything on him, Bruno. Not enough.

That's why we wanted to let this thing run a little longer. Only you jumped the gun and started this whole mess here today."

I eased the calm and weeping Chocolate over to Chelsea. "Here, take her."

"What? Why? What are you going to do?" She took hold of Chocolate. "Rudyard jumped a plane to Costa Rica. He's out of our reach. We don't have an extradition treaty with Costa Rica."

"I didn't start this mess today. It was orchestrated by Blue."

I got to my feet. My whole body ached and threatened to shut down. I cast about in all the debris until I found my gun.

"Bruno, no. Don't. Let us handle the rest of this. Bruno?"

I picked my way out of the breeched wall and into the sunlight of the dying day. I hobbled over to my truck, blood dripping from my hand onto my gun, making it look like something out of a horror movie. I stuck it back in the holster on my hip. My shirt stuck to my back. I got in and started up.

CHAPTER SIXTY-FIVE

I DROVE TO Lynwood Station in a hazy funk. Like an old horse, the truck seemed to know the way better than I did. Day shift at the station had already left to go home; few cars littered the back parking lot. I parked almost in the same spot as the first day I worked narco, not all that long ago. Maybe a century ago. I got out and stood by my truck, a bloody hand on the fender for support.

The narco trailer door was shut, the lights off. Blue wasn't there. I didn't have anywhere else to go. Logical thought evaded me. Of course I had places to go. I'd always have places to go.

I had a daughter.

Wicks zoomed up in a blue Grand Marquis. He jumped out. "Jesus H., Bruno. What the hell happened?" He took my arm and tried to ease me to the ground. I shrugged him off and almost fell. Johnny Gibbs ran up on the other side of the fence from his car in the neighborhood where he'd been surveilling the narco trailer. Wicks yelled at him, "Call paramedics. Get an ambulance. Get an ambulance, damn it."

I looked at him and focused on his eyes. "Chief Rudyard has fled."

"What are you talking about? What happened?"

"I made a big mistake, a huge mistake."

"Okay, we all do once in a while."

"I told them . . . told the wrong person I was working undercover."

"Ah, shit, Bruno. Was it Blue? Did he do this to you? Where is he?"

"Chelsea's with the FBI. They came to the chief. They didn't know he was the dog heavy. He put Chelsea in the mix so he could control it. He couldn't do anything else, I guess. Not once the FBI came to him. He's gone now. We'll never get him."

"Come on, Bruno. Sit down."

"Thibodeaux's dead. So's Mo Mo."

Wicks took a step back, his mouth sagged open. "And Blue? Did you take out Blue?"

That's all he cared about, his little vendetta.

"That's what I came back here to do, but he's gone. He's probably gone just like the chief."

Two aisles over in the main driveway, Blue came running in from the street, looking over at us as he ran on by.

Wicks stiffened. "Bruno, you wait right here." He took off his suit coat and let it drop to the ground. He walked with deliberation toward the trailer, his gun hand now free to draw his Colt .45.

Blue turned, running backward, slowed, and then stopped. He faced Wicks.

I followed along behind. "Wait. Wait." I didn't want Wicks to gun Blue. I got to within a half a step behind him when he stopped about thirty feet from Blue. I still wasn't thinking too clearly.

Wicks said, "Blue, I need to take you in now."

"I don't think so. You okay, Bruno? You look like hell. You're bleeding. What happened?"

Wicks said, "Thibodeaux's dead."

The light in Blue's eyes shifted to that same look I saw that night in the alley behind the gas station on Mona, shifted to pure predator. "That's too bad. He was a good friend, a good man to have in a pinch. He'll be missed. You have something to do with that, Wicks?"

"Of course I did. But if you're asking if I dropped the hammer, no, I didn't."

"You, Bruno?"

I shook my head. "Thibodeaux put Mo Mo down."

"Like I said, Dirt was a damn good man." Blue started walking closer.

"You don't seem too broke up over it," Wicks said.

Blue shrugged. "Such is life in the ghetto."

That's when I saw it, the sock over Blue's hand. Adrenaline dumped into my system, clearing my head and making every muscle in my body hum with tension, ready to act.

"Wicks?"

"Not now, Bruno."

"Wicks?"

"Bruno, I said—"

Blue raised his hand, the one with the sock. The one with the small .38 hidden inside.

In one motion, I shoved Wicks to the side and drew my gun, the stock slick and at the same time sticky in my hand.

Blue fired.

The bullet zipped by my ear, inches away from being a fatal shot.

I fired one time. The bullet caught Blue in the stomach. He went down hard.

Wicks fired from the ground and hit the trailer behind where Blue stood not a moment before.

"He's down," I yelled. "He's down." I moved into the line of fire so Wicks wouldn't have another shot. All the energy drained out of me.

The first time I ever shot my gun on duty and I shot a cop to the rear of the sheriff's station.

Wicks scrambled to his feet and over to us. "Jesus H. I didn't know he had a gun in his hand. I thought it was just a sock."

On my knees, I took the smoking sock and gun away from Blue, who said, "You shouldn't have stuck your nose into it. Wicks needs killin.' You'll regret it; believe me, you'll regret it."

"Yeah, yeah," Wicks said. "Look who's on the ground gut shot, pal."

Blue got what he had coming, but I still felt sorry for him. And at the same time guilty as hell.

"You saved my life, Bruno. I won't forget that. Jesus H., that was close." Wicks took in a couple of long breaths. "But next time, remember, if he's good for one, he's good for all six. You give him all six next time. You understand?"

"Shut up, Wicks. Would you please just shut up?"

Uniformed deputies and half-dressed deputies from the station ran around the corner, guns drawn, looking for the threat, ready to engage. They came right over to us.

"What happened to Blue? Who shot Blue? Bruno, are you okay? Someone get paramedics."

My God, what had I done? What had I done?

CHAPTER SIXTY-SIX

I SAT ON the couch holding Olivia. For three weeks, while my injuries healed, I stayed home and enjoyed my beautiful baby girl. I didn't want to go back to work. I did and I didn't. The draw to return and chase down dangerous and violent felons grew stronger by the day. Grew stronger as I grew stronger. That urge would eventually win out. Olivia had grown so much in such a short time. She made cute little noises and held on to my finger with her tiny ones. She had the greatest smile. The way she looked at me made me want to give her everything in the world.

Dad came in the front door carrying grocery bags. He set them on the counter and came out of the kitchen. He pointed to the suitcase sitting by the front door. "Son, you going someplace?"

Before I could answer, Chelsea came from the back of the house, barefoot, wearing worn denim pants and a white strap t-shirt. "Hey, Xander."

"Hello, Chelsea. You two were still in bed, so I ran out and got something for breakfast. Is Bruno going someplace?"

She looked at me, waiting for me to field that uncomfortable question. She said, "Bruno, can I talk with you outside?"

I didn't like her tone. Something had happened; something had changed.

"What?" Dad said. "No one's going to answer my question?"

"Sure," I said to Chelsea. I got up and handed off Olivia to Dad, scared now of what Chelsea wanted to tell me. "I'll be back in a minute, Dad, and explain what's happening."

She followed me out to the front stoop. I stood one step lower. That put us closer to the same height, but not quite.

I held her hand and looked into her eyes. "What? Is it my trip? We discussed this. It's something I have to do. I know you don't want me to but—"

Tears welled in her eyes. "Bruno . . . I . . ."

"Ah, man, they transferred you, didn't they?"

Her chin quivered. She nodded.

"Where to?"

She looked away and didn't answer.

She'd been a rising star in the Bureau until the "Dog Heavy Caper." The Bureau didn't like the shooting at the Park View Hotel in Huntington Park. Even though justified and cleared by the DA's office, it didn't matter. FBI agents just didn't have ADs, accidental discharges. And then there was ramming her car into the wall of the condo. She'd saved my life, and Chocolate's, but that didn't matter. FBI agents didn't cowboy like that. When she did ram the car into the condo, she'd also made the choice to end the investigation without prior approval.

"How long have you known?"

She looked back at me. "A week."

I fought the tears welling in my eyes. I kissed her like it was the last time. We broke and I held her close.

She whispered, "I'll be gone when you get back. I didn't want to ruin our last week together. Bruno, I'll never forget this time we had."

"Stop it. You talk like we're not going to see each other anymore."

She held on tighter.

"Where? Where are you going? It's not over. We can commute until you can get reassigned back to LA."

She shook her head.

Now I held her tighter and didn't want to let go.

Wicks pulled up in his car on the street and honked.

"Tell me, where are you going to be assigned?"

She whispered, "Bismarck, North Dakota."

We'd discussed what could happen and she'd told me that transfer assignments reflected just how far down the hole the Bureau tossed you. Bismarck. Well, she'd never dig her way out from there. Her career was finished.

"Then quit and stay here," I said. "You can be a deputy sheriff."

She shook her head again.

She didn't say it, but I knew. She didn't want me taking this trip, and it hurt her that she couldn't stop me no matter what she said.

Wicks honked again.

Dad opened the door. "What's going on out here? Who's honking?"

"Okay," I whispered in Chelsea's ear, "will you call me when you get settled? Please?"

"You know I will."

She wouldn't though.

Wicks honked again.

"Dad, hand me my bag, please."

He did, with a scowl. "You going to tell me where you're going?"

I hugged Chelsea one more time, took the bag from Dad, and said, "Costa Rica, Dad. It's just a quick turnaround trip to Costa Rica."

AUTHOR'S NOTE

When I first started in law enforcement more than three decades ago, I entered into this new world with wide-eyed romantic expectations about the men and women in blue, their honor, their integrity, their cut above in moral standing.

Gradually, over the years, those expectations slowly eroded, and I realized that some cops didn't possess all those stalwart qualities—that they could be people with dangerous flaws and built-in criminality.

I came into work one day and found the station all abuzz. When I asked what was going on, I was told a deputy was accused of raping a woman while on duty. I remember clearly saying, "That's an accusation without merit; that didn't happen." Cops just didn't do that. A few minutes later, the lieutenant came out of the interview with the deputy, stopped in front of me, and said the deputy just admitted to the rape. I was stunned. This was my first experience with the slow decline of that high moral expectation I'd assigned to my brethren, my fellow law enforcement officers.

Then, over the years, three more law enforcement officers whom I worked with became murderers. Two of whom I considered friends. Out of the three, two went to prison, and the third took his own life rather than pay for his grave error in judgment—a premeditated killing.

In the early eighties, two police officers in the largest police department in Southern California were arrested and convicted of murder for hire—contract killings.

In *The Innocents*—originally titled *Dog Heavy*—I fictionalized the characters and the places of these events, which, although only similar in nature, did occur, and I was there to witness most of them. For one—the incident depicting the foot pursuit of Pedro Armendez—he did cut his own throat.

And that was the first time, as a young street cop, that I tasted blood.

Someone else's.